"There's so much I don't know."

Kayleigh's eyes searched Niall's, and suddenly she wasn't talking about the business, but about them, their kiss.

"Kayleigh," he murmured, and he seemed to be holding himself back, his arms rigid at his sides.

"Nothing makes sense anymore."

"Life isn't always logical." Niall looked away, his eyes darker than she'd ever seen them. "And neither is love."

A long moment of silence stretched between them. It hung dangerously in the air, like the calm before a summer storm. This was exactly what she'd been obsessing over since their kiss. If only Niall was a stranger and not her closest friend, someone she couldn't afford to lose if things didn't work out....

Dear Reader,

Romance is a tricky thing to find. It can lurk in the most unexpected places, like right beneath your nose! Such was the case for me and my husband of twenty years, Greg. We were friends for a long time, and I often wished I could meet someone like him to have as a boyfriend. Then one day it dawned on me. I'd already met that person. Greg! It's funny how once you've put someone in a category like "friend" it's hard to take them out of it. There's fear that maybe they won't fit as well in the new category "partner," so many of us wait, reluctant to risk ruining the relationship and losing that person altogether.

It takes a big leap of faith and bravery to move your relationship out of the "friend zone." But when it pays off, you have both your best friend and the love of your life. I recently asked, "What are your tips for lasting love?" in our Wholesome Romance: Harlequin Heartwarming Goodreads group. I was amazed at how many of our fantastic group members (and it's an open group, so please join us!) responded by saying that friendship was a key ingredient to long-term happiness.

When I wrote *Someone Like You,* I drew on the idea that although there is fear and trepidation in moving beyond friendship, it is the best predictor of lifelong joy. My main characters, Kayleigh and Niall, have been best friends since childhood. They have a special bond neither wants to put at risk by following their hearts. Yet finding true love takes real courage, which is, ultimately, the heart of this novel.

I would love to hear from you. To contact me, please email karenrock@live.com. Thanks!

Karen

HEARTWARMING

Someone Like You

Karen Rock

ISBN-13: 978-0-373-36691-0

Someone Like You

This edition published by arrangement with Harlequin Books S.A.

For questions and comments about the quality of this book, please contact us at CustomerService@Harlequin.com.

HARLEQUIN®
www.Harlequin.com

Printed in U.S.A.

KAREN ROCK

is an award-winning young-adult and adult contemporary author. She holds a master's of fine arts in English and worked as an English Language Arts instructor before becoming a full-time author. When she's not writing, Karen loves scouring estate sales for vintage books, cooking her grandmother's family recipes, hiking and redesigning her gardens. She lives in the Adirondack Mountain region with her husband, daughter and two Cavalier King cocker spaniels who have yet to understand the concept of "fetch," though they know a lot about love.

www.KarenRock.com

HARLEQUIN HEARTWARMING

13—WISH ME TOMORROW
37—HIS HOMETOWN GIRL

To Greg, my best friend and the love of my life.
I'm so glad I met someone like you.

CHAPTER ONE

KAYLEIGH RENSHAW'S PEN wavered as she crossed out the last two items on her to-do list: return engagement ring; quit job.

She dropped the pen and shivered, pulling her cardigan tight. These were the first steps toward her new life. She should feel good. Confident. Certain.

Her head dropped to her desk blotter. Oh, who was she kidding? She didn't know how to go forward, and she couldn't go back. Or wouldn't. Not after what she'd seen. Her fingertips pressed against her eyelids as if to blot out last night's image. How could Brett deceive her that way?

Was she doing the right thing? She peered up at a family picture taken the summer before her parents divorced. Her older brother, Chris, smiled back at her from the photo, and tears blurred her vision. She straightened trembling shoulders. He wouldn't have wanted her to be weak, even if last night had shattered her.

While Chris had cannonballed into the deep

end of life, she'd always stuck to the shallow end, where her feet touched solid ground. Now she'd been tossed into untested waters, and she floundered off balance, expecting to sink at any moment.

A light knock sounded on her office door, and she pushed a snarled curl behind her ear before dabbing at last night's mascara. "Come in!"

The door swung open, and her coworker and roommate, Gianna, peered around the edge. Her concerned face brought a stinging rush to Kayleigh's eyes, and her nose burned. She waved Gianna inside and uncapped her water bottle. The long swallow did little to banish the dryness in her tight throat.

"Is it true?" Gianna threw her long coltish shape into a desk chair and leaned forward, her brown eyes searching Kayleigh's. "About you and Brett?"

"How did you hear?" Despair swept through her. Kayleigh had just left her boss and fiancé's vacant office. How could word have gotten out so quickly? She touched the empty space on her left ring finger, her stomach knotting.

"Pam. She found your resignation letter and ring." Gianna nudged the tissue box closer. "The whole department is talking about it."

A groan escaped her that Brett's assistant

had found the envelope. Now everyone would pity the woman whose life had imploded. "I marked the envelope *private.*"

Gianna squeezed Kayleigh's hand. "Sweetie, in Pam-speak, *private* means *open.* You know that."

Kayleigh kicked off her heels and hugged a knee to her chest, cursing herself for not thinking about that. But then, she hadn't been thinking clearly. "I should have put it inside his desk…and padlocked it." Gianna's bark of laughter bolstered her. "Guess twenty-four hours without sleep plus jet lag makes you forgetful."

Gianna's razor-edged bob swung as she leaned closer and rested her elbows on top of Kayleigh's desk—former desk, as her resignation was effective immediately. She gazed across the tastefully decorated room at the framed print of an Impressionist painting, its blurred strokes no longer coming into focus. None of this belonged to her anymore. It was the ghost of her former existence.

"Weren't you supposed to fly back today?" Gianna glanced at Kayleigh's desk calendar. "I wasn't expecting you last night, or I would have guessed something was wrong when you didn't show up at the apartment."

Kayleigh nodded and cleared her throat. "I

left the conference early. Thought I'd surprise Brett on our anniversary. Except I—I spent the night at an uptown coffee shop instead." She'd sat beside a window crying as she'd downed five mocha lattes and a bag of chocolate espresso beans, vacillating among disbelief, hurt and fury. Now her insides were a scalding blend of all three.

"You should have come home to Brooklyn." Gianna's eyebrows came together. "We could have talked."

"I didn't want to wake you, and I needed time to think." She had the rushing feeling of a rapidly descending elevator. How could she have been wrong about Brett? It made her question everything, including herself and her judgment. After a childhood full of hurtful secrets, she should have suspected her "perfect" relationship was too good to be true.

"I would have wanted you to get me up." Gianna's hand tightened around hers. "What happened?"

Kayleigh nodded. "I went to Brett's when I got in last night. Only—" Her voice broke, and Gianna's thumb rubbed across her knuckles.

She'd heard the romantic music and the squealing feminine laughter even before he'd opened the door shirtless.

"I found him with someone else." Saying it

out loud made it real, the words piercing her like shrapnel.

Gianna's olive-toned skin paled. "Who?"

"Melinda Johnson." Kayleigh willed the moisture in her eyes to dry up. Brett didn't deserve any more of her tears.

"He put her in charge of developing your new software app while you were away," Gianna breathed. "You're sure they weren't working?"

"She was snuggled under a blanket on his sectional. No, it was pretty obvious they hadn't been working." The leftover catered dinner on the table, the lipstick on Brett's cheek, the nearly finished wine bottle and empty glasses on the coffee table and the guilt on Brett's face when he'd looked from her to Melinda...all details that she'd absorbed in the moment it took her life to disintegrate before her eyes.

Kayleigh sagged against her chair while Gianna cursed.

"I'm so sorry, Kay. No wonder he gave her your title as team manager."

The double betrayal was an arrow shot point-blank at her heart. Once again, she'd been sidelined and overlooked, trusting Brett that her time would come if she was patient.

Gianna's long nails drummed. "You should say something, Kay. Complain to his boss,

Mr. Green." Her face fell. "Oh, wait. That's his uncle, isn't it?"

"Yes. Plus, Brett will just claim that I'm a woman scorned." A paperweight from Niagara Falls caught Kayleigh's eye, and she clenched her hands to keep from throwing it. Brett had proposed to her there. Had he wanted a spouse or a guaranteed business minion? She dropped the trinket in the trash and it landed with a satisfying thud.

"None of it matters anymore anyway," Kayleigh muttered as she carefully placed her family picture in her briefcase. Brett had broken her heart and his word. She wouldn't keep working at Genesis Software Innovations, regardless. "I'll contact a headhunter. Get another job." She thought of the financial help she'd been giving Chris's wife, Beth, and their two sons since his death in Afghanistan. For their sakes, as well as hers, she needed to find another position. Quickly.

Gianna strode around the desk, pulled Kayleigh to her feet and hugged her. "We'll work this out. I want the best for you."

"Exactly," said a deep voice from her doorway, making them both jump. "Maybe Gianna will talk some sense into you, Kayleigh. Stop you from making a rash decision." Brett filled the doorway in a tailored gray suit with tiny pinstripes, his green satin tie and matching pocket handkerchief making him look slick. Kayleigh gave herself a mental kick for not seeing through his phony charm before.

He crossed the space to her desk and slid her engagement ring across the surface, the Tiffany's diamond creating a prism of light on her ceiling.

Gianna caught Kayleigh's eye and, at her reassuring nod, backed toward the door. "I'll see you later, Kayleigh. Goodbye, Mr. Graham."

Brett ignored Gianna and leaned on the desk, his musky cologne assailing Kayleigh, his thick gold watch flashing when his sleeves rode up. She breathed deep, the familiar scent making her want to burrow into his arms until this storm had passed. Only he'd caused the tempest and would never be her safe harbor again.

He glanced at a picture of them in her garbage bin. "Kayleigh, please. I'm sorry. I screwed up. Big-time. But it will never happen again." He handed her the ring, and her palm itched as temptation battled within to put it on and to take it all back. "We're meant to be together. Besides, you know you won't last a week on your own."

She dropped the ring on her desk. How dare he? She peered up at him, anger warring with fear that he might be right. Was he arguing to save a deal or a relationship? "Don't say that," she whispered, her confidence ebbing.

He came around the desk and clasped her cold hands. "You're a dreamer, not a doer, Kay. An ideas person. It's what makes you brilliant at concepts, but not at execution. Leave that for others. Let me take you out to dinner so that I can make it up to you. What happened last night won't be repeated. Promise. You believe me, don't you?"

But she didn't. In fact, she didn't know what she trusted in anymore except that she had to act, whether she was a *doer* or not. She'd worked with GSI since leaving college seven years ago. Starting over was a risk, but it was better than staying with a liar like Brett. A liar who apparently had zero faith in her. She needed to be strong and make her big brother, and herself, proud.

From now on, she wouldn't be pushed aside, controlled or misled. And if she ever wanted romance again—a concept impossible to imagine right now—it'd be on her terms. No hidden secrets to blow up in her face.

"It's over." She handed him the ring, slipped on her heels and headed for the door, her briefcase in hand.

"I won't accept that," he said, his voice losing its smooth tone. "You'll regret giving up on us."

She stopped in the doorway and stood as tall as her five-foot-three frame allowed. "I'd be sorry if I didn't go. By the end of the week, I'll be developing apps for another company. GSI is about to get some competition."

Brett's surprised exclamation made her whirl. "You don't honestly expect me to recommend you to competitors?"

She stared him straight in the eye. "Don't need it. My qualifications will speak for themselves."

"I give you a month before you come back," he said softly as she strode through the door, her head high. "Think, Kay. No one will hire you without references. This is career suicide, and you're too smart and talented to make that kind of mistake."

She fought to control her face, though her knees wobbled at that cruel truth. Brett had cheated on her. Why would she expect him to play fair professionally?

Heads came together as she passed her coworkers. Their department occupied the entire floor of the ten-story central office, and the tight-knit group behaved more like a dysfunctional family than a set of associates.

Brett followed her to the elevator and waved

his phone. "Call me when you've come to your senses, okay?"

She pulled out her cell and punched in a contact number. He gazed at her, puzzled, when his phone rang.

The elevator chimed, and she stepped inside. When he'd brought his cell to his ear, she spoke into her own.

"I already have," she said as the doors slid closed.

A COUPLE OF weeks later, Kayleigh trudged down the main hall of her grandfather's assisted-living center and halted at the front desk. After making cold-call stops at software companies to check for potential openings, her back ached, her toes hurt and the waistband of her business skirt dug into her skin. Time to rethink the extra ice cream she'd been eating to chase away the blues.

If only she'd found a job by now. When she'd heard the rumor from Gianna that Brett was blackballing her in the software community, she'd been skeptical. But after receiving her tenth rejection this morning, she was worried. What if Brett was right and she had committed career suicide? With limited savings, her options were running out fast.

She must have made a noise because a familiar redheaded woman stopped scribbling on a chart and glanced up. A warm smile transformed her stern face.

"Hi, Kayleigh. Here to see your grandfather?"

"I was, but he's not in his room. It's good to see you, MaryAnne." Kayleigh grabbed the counter's edge to keep from swaying on her feet. It'd been a long day full of dead ends. She really needed one of Gramps's pep talks.

MaryAnne shoved back her bangs and studied Kayleigh. "You don't look so well. Are you okay?"

Kayleigh contemplated the nurse's dark brown eyes. They were so like those of MaryAnne's younger brother, Niall, Kayleigh's former best friend. A familiar emptiness rose within. She could have used his solid strength right now. Most of all, she missed him. How long since he'd stopped returning her calls? Two years? It was hard to believe since, prior to his tour in Afghanistan, they'd spoken at least once a week. Now only radio silence filled his end of their former relationship.

"It's a long story."

MaryAnne closed her chart and stood. "I have time. Let's grab some coffee in the break room."

A minute later they were seated in the small,

sterile space, black brew percolating in a machine on the counter.

"So how's the wedding planning going?" Kayleigh asked. It was a common conversation topic for them since they were both getting married the following summer. Well… one of them was. Kayleigh's heart absorbed the thought without breaking. Good. Progress. Maybe she'd have only one bowl of ice cream tonight.

MaryAnne contemplated Kayleigh's left hand and her eyes widened. "Where's your ring? Did you lose it?"

"I gave it back." Kayleigh's chair scraped when she shoved it back and strode to the counter. "How many sugars do you want?"

"Two." MaryAnne joined her and grabbed a couple of mugs from a cabinet. "I'm so sorry. What happened?"

Kayleigh hesitated before filling the cups. "He cheated on me." The sting of it was still there, but it'd faded, like the shadow of a stain after a hundred scrubbings.

MaryAnne handed her a wooden stir stick as they returned to the table. "Isn't he also your boss?"

"Was." Kayleigh's gulp of hot coffee set her tongue ablaze. She waved her hand in front of her mouth and MaryAnne grabbed some ice from the dispenser.

"Thanks," Kayleigh mumbled around the melting cube.

MaryAnne set her elbows on the table and dropped her round, freckled face into her palms. "No wonder you look worn-out."

Kayleigh nodded glumly. "I've been on ten interviews and haven't gotten a job offer. Even my headhunter has started avoiding my calls. I was hoping to speak to Gramps. Get some cheering up."

MaryAnne's mouth turned down at the corners. "He's in physical therapy and—"

"He'll want a nap after that," Kayleigh finished for her, her spirits plummeting. "I'll come back another time for the chat." Despite her best efforts, her voice quivered.

"MaryAnne Walsh to the front desk," announced a voice on the overhead PA system. "MaryAnne Walsh to the front desk, please."

MaryAnne stood. "I wish I could help." She put a hand on Kayleigh's shoulder. "What about Niall? You two used to be so close. Maybe he's ready to come out of that cave he put himself in since the war. He might know about some jobs. He's been doing independent programming work for software companies."

"I don't think he'll talk to me. He hasn't returned my calls since he got back."

MaryAnne blew out a breath and strode to the door. "There's more to it than that, though he won't tell me. And he avoids everyone, even his family. I hardly recognize the bitter recluse he's become. Seeing each other would be good for both of you.... If I can arrange it, will you meet him?"

Kayleigh's brain fumbled for the right words to say. Niall. A reunion with an old friend would mean so much. He couldn't have changed that much...could he?

"That would be—I mean—thank you, MaryAnne," she said inadequately. "I'd appreciate that."

MaryAnne came back and gave her a quick hug. "I know he always thought the sun rose and set on you, sweetie. When I tell him that you need him, he'll be there. Promise."

But as the door clicked shut behind her, Kayleigh was left alone to wonder.

If he did care, why had he shut her out? They'd supported each other through everything: her parents' divorce and move, his father's death and mother's worsening Alzheimer's. Yet when he'd been honorably discharged after losing his lower leg in an ambush, he'd rebuffed her. His rejection still hurt.

She'd needed to tell him about Chris's death and had wanted to comfort him because of his injury. Sometimes it felt as if she'd lost them both to the war.

They could have helped each other as they had in the past. A team. Inseparable since their summer-camp days.

His withdrawal had left an empty space inside her that no one, not even Brett, had been able to fill.

CHAPTER TWO

"I KNOW YOU'RE there, so pick up!"

Niall Walsh punched another line of HTML code into his computer, then glared at the answering machine vying for position with the modem, external hard drive, printer and fax machine cluttering his two desks. He pictured his determined older sister, MaryAnne, marching through his Bed-Stuy neighborhood, calling on her cell. Had she forgotten yesterday's vow not to check in on him so often?

His phone rang again, followed by the beep. For a low-tech device, it was effective. He should have unplugged it when he'd powered off his cell. "I made your favorite, lasagna," her voice sounded through the speaker.

His stomach grumbled. It'd been a while since he'd eaten. An empty pizza box balanced on his brownstone apartment's radiator. It was the last thing he recalled ordering, and that'd been yesterday. Still, she'd given her word. Hunger or no, he was staying strong and not letting her in. It was better for both of them.

"Come on, little brother," he heard her say after he let the phone ring a third time. "I've got to get back to The White Horse and help Aiden before my night shift. Buzz me in when I get to your building."

He imagined the busy SoHo pub his older brother had managed since their father's fatal heart attack. Aiden had taken charge of the six other children in the Walsh brood, and their Alzheimer's-afflicted mother. At least he wouldn't add to Aiden's responsibilities. If MaryAnne would stop pestering him, he'd never bother a soul again.

He glanced down at his prosthetic lower leg. The last person who'd come to his rescue had paid the ultimate price; the guilt that he lived and his savior did not was a bitter dose he swallowed every day. If not for his actions during the classified mission, that soldier might have been home now visiting with his own sister.

"I promise not to clean your apartment." Her voice turned pleading as she left her fourth message.

He glanced around his small, dim apartment, noticing things as MaryAnne would. Laundry spilled out of an overflowing hamper beside his bathroom door. His galley kitchen counters were covered in empty take-out containers, and his sink was full of dishes. Dust coated his coffee table, but at least he'd put his empty soda cans in the recycle bin.

Beside his shrouded windows hung a lone spider plant, its fronds green despite being watered rarely. He should just let it die, yet once in a while something about its droop made him lumber to the kitchen for a glass.

A loud buzzing sounded. She was here, not fooled at all by his phone screening. He swore under his breath and limped to the door. Some things never quit…like MaryAnne. Plus, she was his sister, and he wouldn't ignore her. Not really. Just teach her a lesson…as in…*keep your word about not coming over.*

"Fine," he called into the intercom, and then pressed the button to open the automatic front entrance. "But no cleaning," he added as he unbolted his locks and slid back the chain.

MaryAnne brushed by him a moment later and marched into his kitchen. "This place is a pigsty!"

He inhaled the aroma of tomatoes, cheese and sausage left in her wake. His stomach grumbled again, grateful to her even if the rest of him wasn't. When would she get the message that he didn't want people going out of their way for him?

"What are you doing?" he asked when she shook out an apron she'd pulled from her purse and tied it around her waist. "I said no cleaning."

His sister slid her eyes his way as she flicked on the faucet. She squeezed his dish soap bottle, got only a faint mist, then uncapped it and smacked the bottom until a dribble of clear gel oozed out.

"This isn't cleaning. It's excavating a toxic waste site."

"I was getting to it as soon as I finished writing a program. I'm sending the prototype to my client this afternoon."

She shot him a skeptical look, then shoved a clean, wet plate at him. He shouldn't have relented, but there was no denying his demanding sister. He grabbed a cloth and began drying.

"You're always working." She passed him another dish. The crystal necklace he'd given her for Christmas winked under the single working bulb in his light fixture. "When are you going to leave the virtual world and start living in the real one? You've been home for almost two years."

Her freckles stood out against her pale, round face, making him wonder how much she got out. She worked in the family pub, at an assisted-living facility and now, at her third job, taking care of him. He ground his teeth. He wouldn't be a burden to her or anyone.

"It's my life, MaryAnne, and that's the way I want it."

She handed him a mug, disapproval twisting her mouth.

"Staying inside all the time. Never seeing anyone. That's not living. It's hibernating."

He shoved the towel inside a glass. "I'm fine."

She arched an eyebrow. "But you're not happy."

He opened his mouth to protest, but the denial stuck in his throat. "Have you picked out your wedding dress yet?"

She shook the sponge at him, then got to work on his counters. "You're not getting me off track, Niall."

"Did you go with the princess or mermaid style?" He recalled her talking about it when she'd visited over the weekend. If lasagna was his weakness, then wedding details were hers. Two could play at this game. He sent out a silent prayer that she wouldn't quiz him on what those various styles meant. He wouldn't have been able to tell the difference between a mermaid style or a princess style if an insurgent rebel had a semiautomatic pistol up to his head.

"Oh, it's got a gorgeous train that's a full five

feet of lace cutouts with—" Her voice rose then trailed off. She swept boxes into a garbage bag and laughed. "You almost got me."

When she struggled to lift the bulging sack, he grabbed it from her. "Can't blame me for trying."

Out in the hallway, he waved to his startled-looking neighbor—Mrs. Robertson…or was it Robinson?—and pushed the trash down the chute. She blinked at him as if he were a ghost, and he supposed, to her, he was. When was the last time they'd run into each other? Six months ago?

Back inside, MaryAnne shoved his laundry into his military bag.

"Leave it, MaryAnne. Aiden needs you."

When she looked up, perspiration glistened on her forehead. She gestured around the room. "Not as much as you do."

He ground his teeth. MaryAnne should be picking out wedding flowers, not wasting her time on him. He coughed at the cloud of lemon-scented furniture polish she sprayed on his coffee table, and gathered up the newspapers tossed beside his couch. When his prosthetic caught on the table's edge, he went down hard.

MaryAnne knelt by his side, but he shook off her arm and stood. "I've got this. Go." He instantly regretted his harsh tone when her mouth puckered. "Sorry. Look. Pick out china patterns and stop worrying about me. I want you to be happy."

Her eyes glistened. "I am. Do you know how lucky we are to have you home in one piece?"

He flinched at her phrase, and she turned bright scarlet. "I just mean I'll never take you for granted. After almost losing you..." She cleared her throat and hurried to the kitchen. "I'm not giving up on you," she added over her shoulder.

The tap turned on then off, and she returned with a glass of water for the spider plant. Light flooded the room when she raised the shades, and he blinked until his eyes adjusted. It was a beautiful day, the kind of day you'd least expect an ambush. His mind returned to the day of his accident, and he whirled from the windows. "Close the shades, MaryAnne."

"This plant's never going to thrive without sun."

"Don't you get it? Nothing *thrives* in here."

She pressed her cheek against his back, her arms slipping around his waist. "Then it's time I got you outside."

"I'll see you next week on the Fourth of July."

"Uh-uh. Not soon enough. You're going out tomorrow."

"Why? I had groceries delivered this week."

A familiar smile played on MaryAnne's face as she ducked under his arm and faced him. It was the kind of expression she wore whenever she'd sneaked medicine into a spoonful of jelly for him. Whatever she had up her sleeve, it wasn't going to be good.

"A friend needs you, Niall. I spoke with her when she visited the assisted-living facility yesterday."

"I don't have any friends," he said drily. Did she think he had some secret social life? His closest relationships these days were with the pizza delivery people.

Her smile widened, and unease twisted through him. He was in real danger when she looked this disarming.

"Kayleigh Renshaw."

The name hit him like a punch to the solar plexus. Kayleigh. His rescuer's younger sister and the best friend he'd ever had.

They'd once been as close as family. Guilt rolled through him at the loss he'd cost her. Worse, he was under orders not to speak about the classified mission, the reason he'd avoided her since Afghanistan. How could he see her and not tell her what had happened? If she knew the truth, she wouldn't want to see him anyway—she'd hate him.

"Tell her I'm too busy."

"She just lost her fiancé and her job." MaryAnne smoothed back his overgrown bangs like a mother fussing over a child. "Kayleigh needs you to cheer her up, Niall. Remember how tight you two were?"

He couldn't forget if he tried. And he'd given it his best shot these past two years. But putting Kayleigh out of his mind was impossible. Then again, what if she really did need help? He'd already stolen so much from her.

He pictured Kayleigh's flashbulb of a smile, her bright eyes and the giggle that'd bubbled up even at the worst of his jokes. Only, he couldn't remember the last time he'd said, or heard, something funny. He'd come to her rescue when her parents had split and she'd needed comfort, distracting her and keeping her spirits up. But he wasn't the hero in anyone's story. Not anymore.

"I'm sorry. The answer's no." He pulled down the shade, plunging his apartment, and life, back into comforting gloom.

MaryAnne planted fists on her hips. "I promised her that you'd see her. Maybe give her some tips on jobs in the software market."

He swept a duster over his end tables, then

plugged in the vacuum cleaner. “I do contracting work from home. I don’t have those kinds of connections.”

“She looks miserable, Niall. Please. Help me keep my word to her, and I’ll promise to keep mine with you.”

He sighed.

“Which one? That you won’t call every day? Bring food twice a week, clean my apartment when it’s fine the way it is?”

MaryAnne snorted. “This is also your office, not a barn. I made a reservation for lunch tomorrow at Five Leaves.”

He rubbed his jaw stubble. “I’m not the right guy for this. Better cancel it.” A restless feeling overtook him, and he wondered, despite himself, if he wouldn’t like to see Kayleigh. Even if it was just to reassure himself that she was all right.

MaryAnne’s eyes crinkled. “What’s the harm in a meal with an old friend?”

He held in a bitter laugh. If she knew the truth… But it was a secret he had to bear alone, the weight of it dragging him to dark places. And that was without the added guilt of a woman’s friendship that he didn’t deserve.

“Out of the question.” He flicked on the vacuum, hoping its hum would convince MaryAnne to leave. He didn’t want to be rude. She meant well. But she needed to focus on herself instead of him—and now Kayleigh.

The vacuum shuddered to a stop, and he glanced up at MaryAnne. She twirled the end of the cord. "She was your friend. Meet with her. Plus, I promise I won't come by for a week except to drop off your laundry."

He drummed his fingers on the handle. Save him from pushy women. Fine. He'd see Kayleigh. He owed her that much. More, really, but it was all he could give.

"Two weeks and no laundry," he countered.

MaryAnne lightly whipped his arm with the cord. "A week and a half, and that's my final offer before I bring her here myself."

He glanced around the cramped space, pulse thudding, and threw his hands up in defeat. "I'll go. But I won't be able to help her. If you see her tonight, tell her that."

"Tell her yourself," MaryAnne called, lugging his laundry out the door before he could stop her. "Twelve o'clock tomorrow!"

Niall stared at the spider plant. What would he say to Kayleigh after shutting her out for two years? How could he face her, knowing her brother's death was his fault?

He didn't have a clue.

CHAPTER THREE

SLIGHTLY OUT OF breath, Kayleigh rounded the corner onto Bedford Avenue the next day and sidestepped a man wheeling a box-laden dolly. When the humid air blew her frizzing hair in her face, she shoved it back behind her ears. She'd been too excited to see Niall to waste time straightening it, and now she wished she had. At least she'd worn her favorite sundress and lipstick. Appearances had never mattered to them before, yet somehow, today, she cared about how she looked.

"What's the hold up? Move it, buddy!" a cab driver shouted at a truck blocking traffic. He laid on his horn, and several beeps behind him filled the air. When she passed the road-rage scene, the moist, fresh scent of laundry exploded from a dry-cleaning business as a well-dressed man exited with bagged garments.

Ah, Brooklyn. She would have missed this dynamic borough if she'd married Brett and moved to his condo. Her neighborhood might not have the Upper East Side's ease of access to Manhattan, but it vibrated with life, with the rumbling of overhead trains, the rattle of store owners opening security gates around the corner from gentrified streets and the ever-present noise of screeching tires, car horns and booming speakers.

Something about Brooklyn's clamoring fervor made her more conscious of the thud of her heart, the rasp of her breath and the heat of her skin. It made her feel alive, vibrant and brimming with possibilities…such as reconnecting with Niall Walsh.

When MaryAnne had called her with the lunch date, she'd had to hear it twice. It seemed unreal, but here she was, moments away from seeing her friend again, and she couldn't be more elated…or nervous. Did he really want to see her, or had MaryAnne twisted his arm? If he'd called her, she'd feel more certain.

Too anxious to sleep, she'd spent most of last night imagining how their lunch would go—what she would say, what he would do…. Would their old friendship rekindle or would they sit awkwardly like strangers? He'd always been her rock, strong and considerate when her world had fallen apart. Her mind flashed back to the summer she'd turned thirteen, when her parents had divorced.

"You're taking me out of camp and making

us move upstate on parents' weekend?" she'd demanded when her mother had called the day before she and Kayleigh's father were supposed to visit her at Otter Creek.

"Well…I…ah—" Her mother had cleared her throat, then seemed to take a long gulp of something before finally saying in a rush, "Your father and I are getting a divorce."

"A what? Why? You and Daddy are happy." Her heart had taken flight in her chest and beat against her ribs trying to escape. How could this be? They'd never fought like her friends' parents. It didn't make sense.

"We're just not compatible," her mother had said with a breathy sigh.

Kayleigh had turned her back on her inquisitive camp director and cupped her hand around the phone and her mouth. "What does that mean?"

"Your father and I don't get along. I'm sorry, but we're getting divorced."

"And why didn't you figure this out before you got married?" Her voice had risen, anger and fear lancing through her. Her artist mother and stockbroker father had always seemed like a mismatch, but they'd made it this far. Why break up? And why call now instead of waiting to tell her when camp ended? When Kayleigh was home, in familiar surroundings, better able to process the devastating news?

It had felt as though the world had reversed its spin, and everything she'd assumed about her life and family was wrong, her faith in both broken.

"We rushed into it. Please understand." Her mother's voice had turned pleading. "If we'd taken more time, maybe this could have been prevented."

"What about Chris and me? Don't you care about us? How we feel?"

"Of course we do. We've waited to tell you until now so that you'd enjoy the first part of the summer with your camp friends and have the second half to get used to your new home. It's what's best for you. You trust me, don't you?"

Speechless, Kayleigh couldn't imagine what to say. How could she trust her mother after this? Dropping the phone, she'd raced outside to discover Niall waiting beneath a pine tree. His eyes had searched hers, and he'd taken off after her as she'd dashed down to the beach, needing to be near water. Its undulating surface and calm blue depths had always soothed her restless spirit.

His shoulder had brushed hers as they'd sat on the dock, their feet swinging. Although he hadn't spoken, his quiet, steady presence had reassured her in a disintegrating world.

"They're divorcing, and they didn't give us any warning. Not even a hint," she'd said at last, her harsh voice startling a mallard that took flight, squawking.

"I'm sorry, Kay. That really sucks." Niall had unclenched her hands and held one in his own. Despite her anguish, she'd felt a shimmer of pleasure at his touch.

"I hate them." She'd chucked one of the rocks she'd scooped up on her run to the navy water, glad at the loud splash it'd made. "They only care about themselves. Not me and Chris. Mom's moving us upstate tomorrow, and I don't even get to say goodbye to my friends." She looked into his large brown eyes. "Except you."

"I don't want to say goodbye," he said, his voice cracking at the end.

Kayleigh chucked another rock, farther than the last. "We don't have a choice, because my parents made it for us. According to them—" she'd made air quotes "—they 'know best' and need to separate because they don't get along."

He'd used the bottom of his shirt to wipe away the angry tears flowing down her face, his touch gentle, his soulful eyes full of concern.

"You said they didn't spend a lot of time together."

She'd swallowed hard, recalling that her mother had often disappeared into her studio behind their brownstone. "If they didn't want to be together, then they shouldn't have gotten married. I'm never going to be like them. Never getting divorced."

He'd pulled her head to his shoulder and rested his cheek atop it. "Lots of people do."

"Not me." Determination had gripped her. "And I know how to make sure of it. Can I borrow your notepad and pen?"

Niall had reached into his shirt pocket and pulled them out. No matter how much he was teased, he'd always carried them around to jot down ideas.

"Are you writing them a letter?" he'd asked. The bright afternoon sun brought out the lighter brown strands in his dark hair and a fleck of gold in his eyes. Funny that she'd never noticed it before. A fluttery feeling took her by surprise. This was Niall, she'd reminded herself. A good friend. Practically a brother. Nothing more. Yet suddenly it'd been hard to look him in the eye.

She'd pulled the pen from between her teeth. "I'm making a list for myself. Traits for the perfect man. That way, if I follow the list, I'll marry someone I'm compatible with. Guaranteed happiness. No surprises. You should make one, too."

Niall's eyes widened. "No. It's not necessary. I—"

Her hand had fallen on his tensing biceps. "Please, Niall. I need to get my mind off my parents. Plus, you should find the right person someday, too. We can share our lists after, okay?"

Yet somehow they'd only gotten around to hearing her list—all fifty traits and her rationale for each. They'd talked until curfew, not wanting to waste a minute before her mother and brother, who'd been away at football camp, arrived the next day and separated them. It hadn't been until he'd stood beside her car, her bags in the trunk, that a thought had struck her.

"You never shared what was on your list." Her flip-flops had traced a figure eight in the sandy soil. For some reason, she'd felt self-conscious. When she'd peered up at him, his eyes had slid from hers.

"There wasn't much to read." He'd rubbed the back of his neck and shifted his weight from one foot to another.

"I'm going to miss you," she'd blurted, then dropped her eyes when his startled gaze had met hers.

"Me, too. But we'll call and see each other when you visit your dad in Brooklyn. I—" But whatever he'd been about to say had been lost when her mother had laid on the horn and Chris had given them a wolf whistle out the window, making her blush. They were just friends, yet somehow it'd felt as if they'd outgrown that term the night before, sitting by the lake.

"I'd better go. Goodbye." Too embarrassed to hug him in front of her family, she'd simply waved and dashed to the car. As they'd backed out of the drive, she'd noticed Niall swiping his eye, as though he'd gotten something in it.

It was one of her most vivid memories, along with holding his hand during his father's funeral the following year. They'd gone through so much together. Maybe now, at last, they'd talk about what'd happened in the war and comfort each other.

And that'd happen in minutes. Her nerves jittered. Would he be the way she remembered or different, the distant loner MaryAnne had described? It was hard to imagine.

She peered down the row of bagel shops, pizzerias and hair salons. Beyond them, she spotted Five Leaves's glass-and-dark-wood exterior and blew out a nervous breath as she quickened her pace.

The old-fashioned gilt letters *Oyster Bar* caught the noonday sun, gleaming above Five Leaves's oversize door. She stepped inside the air-conditioned space, the briny scent of seafood transporting her to Coney Island, where she and Niall had gone on so many adventures as kids. In a moment she'd see Niall again, and the thought made her shiver in nervous anticipation.

"May I help you?" A young woman wearing all black, her hair in a slick ponytail, stepped from behind a small podium.

Kayleigh's eyes followed the hostess's down to the run in her nylon, and she tucked one leg behind the other. "I'm here to meet a man."

The woman's eyes widened, and her nose piercing twitched. "Anyone in particular? There are quite a few at the bar."

Kayleigh felt her forehead bead and started again. "His name's Niall Walsh. He's got dark hair…" Her voice trailed off. Did he look the same after his time in the army? She imagined his tall, wiry form and boyish handsomeness.

"She's with me," a husky voice interrupted her. She whirled, shocked into silence at the powerfully built man looming beside her. He'd definitely filled out from his military days. Her eyes flicked to his left leg, but not so fast that he didn't catch her glance, his lips firming in a straight line. Warmth crept into her cheeks. She hadn't wanted to make him feel self-conscious, but she'd gone and done it anyway. Not the best start to their reunion.

"It's good to see you, Niall." She searched his eyes, a jolt of familiarity zipping through her veins. The deep brown depths held the gold flecks she could count by heart, his lashes so thick they'd look girlish if not for his angular, masculine features. He'd always had high cheekbones, but now there was sharpness in his face, as if someone had chiseled out his firm, square jaw and the prominent brow that gave proportion to his strong nose and full lips.

His chestnut-colored hair was no longer clipped short, but layered lightly across his forehead and ears. He'd transformed from the young, earnest man she'd known to a handsome stranger. She flushed despite the steady stream of cool air blowing from an overhead vent. MaryAnne should have warned her about this change. It was doing something funny to her stomach.

"Shall we?" He held out his arm, and she took it, feeling awkward. Once she would have flown into his arms, and he would have swung her, laughing. But those days seemed distant, out of reach. Hopefully, they'd loosen up over lunch. She'd lost so much since she'd last seen

Niall—Chris, her job, Brett. She wondered about Niall's losses and knew the past few years must have been very difficult for him.

They ambled through the nautically decorated restaurant, navigating a maze of dark wood tables. Kayleigh forced her racing thoughts from the man beside her and surveyed the scene. The room resembled the inside of a ship with a wood-slatted ceiling, a brass railing along the oak bar and fishing nets and lures dangling from the walls.

Locals dressed in shorts, tank tops and flip-flops jabbered around them, their voices competing with a Jimmy Buffet tune. She hoped they wouldn't have to shout to hear each other. There was so much she wanted to say.

She peeked at Niall's stern profile. He looked as uncomfortable as she felt. But this was Niall. The boy she'd beaten in a bubble-blowing contest when they were eleven, the teen who'd taught her how to parallel park, the high school senior who'd celebrated with her when they'd been admitted to the same college, the young man who'd promised to write her every day from Afghanistan and then had stopped communicating with her altogether.

In crisp khakis and a white polo shirt that showed off his coloring and broad shoulders, Niall looked great. He was pale, probably from staying indoors as MaryAnne mentioned, but handsome. It felt as though she looked at him through the shifting lenses at an eye doctor's office. One minute she saw him as her old pal, and the next she glimpsed an unfamiliar man with experiences and secrets she no longer knew. How strange to feel as if she was meeting him for the first time.

He pulled out the curved wicker back of her chair before taking his seat across from her.

"It's good to see you," she began, her voice sounding strained. Niall's steady gaze was making it hard to concentrate. She hadn't expected to feel this nervous and tongue-tied around him. "I hope you're not here because MaryAnne forced you—"

"Let's order, shall we?" he cut in, and flipped open his menu, Kayleigh dismissed. He could have been a drill sergeant rebuking a private.

Her temperature rose, but she bit her tongue. Was it possible he was nervous, too?

"And how are you two today?" chirped a waitress with blond hair dyed blue at the ends. She filled their water glasses and smiled, bouncing on the balls of her sneakers.

"Fine." Niall lowered his menu.

"Would you like a table away from the kitchen?" Her eyes dropped to Niall's left leg, and her mouth turned down in a sympathetic shape. “I saw you come in, and I wouldn’t want the servers to accidentally knock into your prosthetic as they go in and out with food.”

Kayleigh winced. Her losses had shaken her view of herself and life. She could only imagine how losing a limb had impacted Niall.

“We’ll stay,” growled Niall, his expression ominous. “And when I need your concern, I’ll ask for it.”

The server paled beneath her heavy makeup. “Then, may I start you off with a couple of drinks?”

“I’ll have a diet soda, please.” The waitress returned Kayleigh’s smile, but her face fell when she glanced back at a grim Niall.

“And you, sir?”

“Water’s fine,” he bit out.

“Bottled—”

He held up his glass. “Any more questions?”

“Very good,” she quavered, and rushed away.

Kayleigh’s fingers tightened around her menu at his abruptness. With each passing moment, her memory erased a bit of the friend she knew and replaced it with this harsh stranger. She needed to get past his grim exterior and discover if the person he’d been still existed.

“Do you know what you want?”

You, she almost said out loud. What if he misconstrued it? Thought she insinuated something other than friendship? Before he would have known exactly what she meant, but now she wasn't sure.

"Yes," she said at last. "How about you?"

"Of course." His dark eyes looked straight into hers. "I always know what I want."

CHAPTER FOUR

RIGHT NOW, NIALL couldn't deny that he wanted to be here, with Kayleigh. Since he'd last seen her four years ago, the sweet, funny girl he'd known had matured. Her luminous gray eyes held the silver flash he recalled, and her long black hair still curled around her face. Yet there was something different about her. Gone was the girl he'd gone to camp with, and in her place was a stunning woman. Her green sundress set off her gold-toned skin and showed off curves that made it hard to look away.

How long since he'd held a woman? He gave himself a mental shake as he caught himself staring at her mouth. This wasn't a date. He'd come to advise and cheer up an old friend. Nothing more. And the sooner he ate and left, the better. So far, Kayleigh hadn't treated him like a charity case, nor did she know his hand in her brother's death, and he wanted to keep it that way. His strange reaction to her only complicated things further.

"Excuse me?" he asked when her soft lips moved.

"It's been a while." Kayleigh's uptilted eyes searched his. "Too long."

His fingers curled on his lap as he battled the urge to reach for her hand. "I've been busy." The feeble excuse hung in the air between them, and he opened his mouth to clarify his meaning, then closed it. Better to let her think the worst of him. Whatever it was, it couldn't be as bad as he deserved. He didn't want her thinking they would go back to being friends.

"I'm sorry about your injury. Do you want to talk about what happened?"

"It's in the past," he said, then gritted his teeth against the truth that rushed to escape him. Instead, he swallowed it down and the familiar, hard weight settled in his stomach.

"Where were you stationed?" Her voice was almost too low to hear over the loud background music.

His gut twisted as he recalled the acrid smell of explosives around the besieged, remote outpost on his last day in Afghanistan. The slick sweat of his skin beneath his body armor. The staccato fire of bullets and flares of light where grenades hit. The screams of wounded soldiers and insurgents, along with his commander's order to abandon the post. His hasty decision to double back and grab a hard drive containing classified information.

In the rush, he'd initially left it—a big mistake for a signal combat officer. It was his responsibility to maintain and protect communications. His eyes closed as he recalled the pain that'd ripped through his calf, how he'd been thrown several feet and grabbed by a Green Beret from the unit that'd been called in when the ambush began. When they'd staggered to the Humvees, they'd fallen by the wheels, the soldier's limp body on top of him. Reaching around the man's back, Niall's fingers had come away sticky and red and he'd realized, with horror, that his rescuer was dead.

It wasn't until Niall had regained consciousness, days later, to see his bandaged stump, that he'd learned a truth more painful than his injury. During his debriefing, his rescuer's name had been shared. Chris Renshaw. Kayleigh's brother.

His missing limb could never equal the loss of a family member. If he had grabbed the hard drive in the first place or left the post when ordered, Chris wouldn't have stayed behind to make sure he got out. Kayleigh wouldn't have lost her brother. Simple as that.

"Kunar," he said to her at last, when she repeated her question. He gulped his water, then forced himself to ask, "Is your brother still in Afghanistan?" Keeping this from her was even harder than he'd imagined. Especially when he remembered how much her parents' secrets had hurt her. No matter the time or distance, he still felt protective. Wished he could shield her. Ironic, considering he'd wounded her worst of all.

Kayleigh's eyes closed. "He's in Arlington Cemetery now. He was killed in a classified mission. That's all the army will tell us." She looked at him, her anguish as sharp as a knife to his gut.

"I'm sorry," he said inadequately, but meaning it with every part of himself. "You two were close."

Kayleigh rubbed her forehead and spoke from behind her hand. "I need to know what happened. But so far, my inquiries haven't gone far."

He sputtered on his mouthful of water and set down his glass. "Inquiries?"

"Yes. I've written to legislators and military staff. But I won't give up. Chris wouldn't."

He struggled to say something—anything—that wouldn't betray his emotions. She was right about the man who'd saved him. He wouldn't have quit.

But before he could speak, Kayleigh's drink appeared.

"Are you two ready to order?" snapped a heavyset older woman. He must have scared off the other girl. The one who'd been ready to serve him lunch on a gurney. Well, good. He'd rather be treated this way than have a pity party he didn't deserve.

When Kayleigh turned her head, his gaze ran over her delicate profile and the slight jut of her dimpled chin. She looked soft and vulnerable, and the desire to help this girl who'd lost her brother leaped in his chest. But he doused the thought and sipped more water.

Kayleigh smiled at the waitress. "I'll have the Five Leaves burger with gruyere cheese and bacon and a side of truffle fries. Oh, and could the cooks whip up some aioli sauce, please? A chef here made it for me once before. It's just garlic, olive oil, lemon juice and egg yolks. Maybe add a little mustard to spice it up? But the Dijon kind, not yellow. If it's yellow, then forget it. Please."

The older woman blinked at Kayleigh, then shook her head and wrote down the order. He held in a laugh. Her habit of demanding outrageous, off-menu items hadn't changed. At camp, she'd begged the cooks to make dim sum, offer hummus as a daily side and add

Cajun spice to the sour cream on taco days. In college, she'd demanded gravy and cheese with her fries after having the dish on a trip to Canada. The cafeteria workers had scrambled out of the way whenever she'd headed down the food line.

The server finished scribbling then turned his way, her expression hostile. "And you?"

"The plain burger, medium-rare, and a side salad."

"Coming up." The waitress grabbed their menus without refilling Niall's glass and marched away.

"Friendly," he drawled. "She'd be a shoo-in for Miss Congeniality."

Kayleigh's laugh spilled from her like a shower of silver coins. "You're terrible." She took a sip of her drink, then another and another until half of it disappeared before she set it down. Wow. He'd nearly forgotten Kayleigh's ferocious appetite, and thirst, always a shock given her petite frame.

She pointed her straw at him. "I mean it. And you probably scared our first waitress out of her station."

"If you can't take the heat, stay in the kitchen."

Kayleigh rolled her eyes. "We'll apologize

when we go and leave her a separate tip for taking our drink order."

He warmed to her, the familiar tendrils of their old friendship drawing him closer. But he forced himself to stay guarded. "Fine. We'll leave the tip. MaryAnne mentioned that you'd left your job and—" His voice dropped away as he studied her bare left hand. Another man had put a ring there. Strange how much that irritated him.

"Yes." Kayleigh cut into the awkward silence, her face glum. "I've been interviewing and making cold calls for weeks, but so far, nothing."

"But you've been a software designer for the top app producer in the country. Genesis Software Innovations, right?" His fingers swiped through the condensation on his glass. "You're a top candidate."

When she banged down her drink, the fluid sloshed up the sides of the glass. "My ex-fiancé, Brett, is spreading the word that I'm trouble in the workplace. He was my boss."

"He blames you for the breakup?" Niall pictured finding the jerk and beating some sense into him. Not that it was any of his business, but old habits die hard.

Her eyes narrowed. "Yes. Though he's the one who cheated."

He sucked in a harsh breath. "What an idiot. He lost the best thing he ever had."

A slow smile dawned and stole his breath. "Thank you, Niall." Then she sobered. "But we weren't compatible. Do you remember those lists we made at camp after my mother called about the divorce? We called them Must Traits, all the traits our partner must have in order to be compatible."

His heart skittered sideways. "Yes," he responded, remembering that evening by the lake, the night he hadn't wanted to end.

"If I'd used it with Brett, I never would have dated him in the first place. You know how honesty is in my top-five Must Traits for the perfect match? Well, Brett cheated at cards. That should have been a red flag. And he bypassed me for leadership positions…and being supportive is—"

"Number three," Niall broke in, recalling her list. All fifty items on it.

She pointed her straw at him, her eyes alight. "Yes! And being open is number one. Brett kept secrets from me, the ultimate deal-breaker."

Niall's gaze dropped from hers, and he battled the urge to blurt the truth about Chris. How much longer could he be around Kayleigh and not tell her what had happened? Orders or not?

"You know—" she tapped her fingernails against the side of her drink "—that would actually make a pretty good app."

"What would?" His mind was still in Kunar.

"The Must Traits list. What if it was an app that users could personalize? Wouldn't it be great if there was a program to create a compatibility score based on how many Must Traits you have in common with someone else?" Her voice rose in excitement. "Think about the heartache it would save people. How it would prevent them from wasting time on the wrong person like I did."

He glanced up and found himself unable to look away from her sparkling eyes. "Aren't there products like that already on the market?"

She shook her head. "I've seen features like that attached to dating websites, but no mobile versions."

"When you find your next job, you should pitch it."

"I'm starting to think that's never going to happen." She stared at the table for a moment, then looked up suddenly. "What if I created my own start-up company to produce it?"

He was shaking his head before she finished

her question, surprised. Kayleigh had always played it safe. Why the sudden shift? This new version of his predictable friend unsettled him.

"You don't want that risk. Three out of four start-ups fail. Besides, who would you get to invest, write the program?" He raised his glass for another drink, then lowered it at her prolonged silence.

He met her eyes, took in her measured look and shook his head. "No, Kayleigh. Not me. I've got other contracts."

She leaned forward, and the familiar smell of her, something light and floral, curled beneath his nose. "I'm not offering you a contract. We could be partners. A team, like the old days. Except I'd keep majority control."

"Have it all. I'm not the right guy for this. You'd need someone to help charm investors, schmooze at marketing events, give statements to the press and most of all, believe in this dating app. That's not me."

"But it used to be...." Her softly spoken words gutted him. Yes. He had been that guy once. But the events in Kunar had made working in the civilian world impossible. Especially with her.

Kayleigh crossed her legs, her features sharp with growing excitement. "Hear me out. It wouldn't be a dating app. It would allow people to input their own Must Traits lists and then synchronize it to others' lists to get a compatibility score. You aren't trying to meet people with it, just sorting out the good matches from the bad ones when you *do* meet someone. That way you have a better chance of starting a relationship with someone who's perfect for you."

"No one's perfect, Kayleigh," he muttered, feeling a phantom ache where his left calf had been.

Her lips pursed. "No. But there's someone who's exactly right out there for everyone. This app will make it easier to find that person and reveal the truth about what each wants right away. No secrets." He caught a pained expression in her eyes before she lowered her lids and sipped her soda.

After setting down her glass, she continued, "Dating websites and similar products are market pleasers." Her hand fell on his, and he jumped at the electric sensation. "We could create a viable business while providing a great service— reducing the number of broken hearts, maybe even lowering divorce rates."

He wondered how much of this had to do with her parents. "It's not that cut and dried. You're being idealistic and simplistic. A product like this is a long shot in a market full of ways to get singles together."

She snatched her hand away as if she'd touched a snake.

"I've been working in product development and app conception for over seven years in a Fortune 500 company. I know what the market will support. Besides, this isn't about getting people together. It's about ensuring that their relationship will last."

"Based on a checklist?" Surely she knew that there was more to love than that. He hadn't been successful in relationships, but his parents had shown him it was possible. Marriage took work, compromise and understanding, not an app with boxes to check off.

"You made a list that weekend at camp. You believed in it then, even though you never showed me what you wrote."

"There were reasons." He stopped himself from saying more. That was long ago, a different time. A different guy—a different him.

"So you didn't believe in it then either?" She took another drink, her eyes on him.

"I don't remember," he lied, and hated himself for it when the color faded from her cheeks. But he had to be firm. Not give her any false hope.

The server arrived, dumping their plates in front of them before stalking away.

"This isn't what I ordered." He contemplated the runny egg oozing out of the sides of an oversize burger.

"That's mine. Here."

They exchanged plates, and he watched with amazement as she lifted a sandwich bigger than her face and chomped on it, her cheeks bulging.

"Aren't you going to eat yours?" She dipped a clump of fries into a yellow sauce. Amazing how a girl who resembled a music box ballerina could eat like a trucker.

He lifted his burger. "I was, unless you want it, too."

Her face brightened again and she smiled. His pulse leaped as he took a bite. Despite himself, he couldn't help enjoying Kayleigh's company.

But an abyss of secrets and tragedy separated them, and he needed to keep his distance.

When Kayleigh's empty glass thumped to the tabletop, he hailed their passing waitress. "Another drink for the lady." She continued walking as though she hadn't heard him. "Please." His raised voice made her pause, and she nodded without turning.

"Thanks. I couldn't finish this without another one." Kayleigh gestured to her plate, and with a shock he realized it was half-empty.

"So other than this start-up idea, what options are out there? Do you have more job interviews coming up?" he asked after another bite, hoping to distract her from her crazy idea.

The light in her eyes faded. "None. Even the headhunter I hired is coming up short. If no one else will take a chance on me, then maybe I should take a chance on myself. And you should, too. We were good together."

He nodded, then caught himself. "It isn't realistic in an uncertain economy. You have to think rationally...look before you leap."

She gnashed on her burger, chewing with vengeance. When she swallowed, she said, "That's exactly what Brett would say. And I'm done with playing it safe. It's gotten me nowhere. The more I think about it, the more I'm convinced. I want to investigate this further. Give it a try. What do you say?"

He met her hopeful eyes and shook his head, hating the disappointment that made her mouth droop and her eyes dim. "I'm sorry. My best advice is to stay away from a sure fail."

She dropped her fry and hoisted her purse. He wished he could take back that blunt statement, but he owed her the truth. He'd promised

MaryAnne he'd help Kayleigh, and that meant saving her from her worst instincts.

"You're wrong." She fidgeted with the zipper on her pocketbook. "You may not believe in me—yet. But I'll change your mind. Give me a couple of days to draw up a business plan, and let's meet again to discuss it."

His mind raced over the impossible proposition. He could write the code, but the idea was flawed and lacked nuance. Kayleigh had grown up, but his earlier assessment was wrong—she hadn't matured from the girl who'd listed big-dog lover or chopsticks expert on her Must Traits list.

"I'm not interested."

She leaned forward, her expression determined. "This may be a gamble, but we'll beat the odds. Social technology is dominating the market. This idea is fresh, user friendly and has potential for spin-off products."

He glanced away from her and shook his head. His reasons for refusing went beyond business or his ability to explain.

"You want my help, and I'm giving it to you. My best advice is to find another job. One that pays benefits and has a 401(k). You don't want all this risk."

"What kinds of benefits do you earn working from home?"

He shifted under her piercing stare. "I get free medical with the VA, and I have my service pension. Plus, I invest what I make through contract work so I'm set. But you need more security than that."

When her gaze met his, her expression held a hint of disappointment in him. "I'll decide what's best for me, thanks."

Her words, delivered with quiet conviction, struck a chord in him. They both wanted to be independent, but for different reasons. She intended to leave her mark on life, while he wanted to pass through it without leaving more scars.

She flagged down their waitress. "Check, please!" she called, her eyes on him. "We'll speak another time. I'd like the chance to give you a full presentation."

But he'd heard enough. "You're wasting your time."

"So you're content to stay home and never take risks? Don't you want to go out in the world and live?"

Her words relit a fire inside. Yes, he'd always imagined a different life. But it'd been torn from him, along with his leg, two years ago. "I'm living the way I choose."

She looked for their absent waitress, then stood and studied him. "I'm not giving up.

Give this some thought before it's an absolute no. I'll contact you soon."

And without another word, she strode to the hostess's station, pulling out her wallet as she went. But before she could pay, he gestured to their server when she emerged from the kitchen and settled the bill. He hadn't given Kayleigh what she wanted, but he would pay for their meal. He returned her wave, then sat back against his seat as he watched her walk away.

Kayleigh Renshaw.

Yes, he'd keep her at arm's length. But just for a moment, he allowed himself to think about how much he'd missed her. And how much he always would.

CHAPTER FIVE

KAYLEIGH RETURNED A nurse's wave and tiptoed into her grandfather's oversize room. She heard him before she spied him reclining in a chair by a large window overlooking the lake. An open book lay on his chest, his eyes closed and mouth open as he snored. She glanced at her watch. Two o'clock. Given the Fourth of July festivities list she'd spotted on her way inside the building, he must be exhausted.

She hated to wake him up, but after a hard week, she was overdue for one of Gramps's pep talks. So far, the programmers she'd approached with the newly written business plan for her start-up company had been less than enthusiastic. Without job prospects or return calls from Niall, things were getting worse by the day.

Niall's dismissal of her app idea had strained the confidence she'd been patching together since leaving GSI. As an old friend, she would have hoped he'd support her. Instead, he'd acted like the kind of person she least wanted to associate with anymore—someone who told her what was best for her instead of hearing her out. Yet a part of her still held out hope that her old friend was in there somewhere, that he hadn't changed as much as it seemed.

At least here, with Gramps, she wouldn't be overlooked or ignored. With her grandfather, she always felt as if she mattered, and right now that meant so much. She peeked in his water pitcher, noticed it was nearly empty and grabbed it. At least she could make herself useful.

"Hey, Miss Kay, how are you doing today?"

Her grandfather's familiar greeting made her smile and turn.

"Hi, Gramps."

She set down the pitcher and hurried to his side as he struggled to stand.

"You don't have to get up." She kissed his creased cheek and inhaled the soapy floral musk of his pomade, his winter-white hair smoothed into a neat side part.

"Course I do. I've got to hug my only granddaughter, don't I?" His laugh lines erupted like a solar flare as he pushed to his feet, leaning on his cane.

He enfolded her, the feel as natural and soothing as ever. "It's good to see you, Kay. Sorry you're here instead of celebrating the holiday with that ex-fiancé of yours. What's his name again? Brad? Brent?"

She pressed her cheek against his heart, reassured by its steady thump. All was right in the world as long as Gramps was in it.

"It's Brett, and it's better this way." She strove to keep the catch out of her voice and failed. It still hurt to think of him, but a little less every day. Focusing on her new business idea helped. If only she wasn't coming up short in that area, too. She felt precariously close to proving Brett right, that she was a thinker and not a doer.

"Doesn't mean the hurt goes away." His unsteady hand slipped into hers, and he led her to a small sofa on the other side of his bed. "Breakups are hard on the heart."

"Thanks, Gramps. But I'm doing okay." She didn't want him worrying about her. After a life full of its own share of setbacks, he didn't need to be concerned about hers.

With care, she helped him lower himself to the couch, his other hand grasping his cane. Although his hip had mended from last year's injury, she dreaded a repeat incident. It'd been terrifying to see her feisty grandfather laid up for so long.

When she sat beside him, something sharp dug into her back. A red shoe with an orthopedic insert. She glanced at her grandfather when she pulled it out of the couch's crease and saw a flush creep across his weather-beaten cheeks. Interesting....

A nurse's aide bustled in before she could ask about it and grabbed the empty pitcher. She wore scrubs patterned in daisies, her hair in a French braid. "Hi, Kayleigh. Are you volunteering today?"

"Hey, Reanne. I'm leading water aerobics next week."

"Sounds good." Reanne smiled at her grandfather. "Is there anything else I can get for you, Mr. Renshaw?"

"If it's not too much trouble, would you mind delivering this note to Mrs. Larson?" He held out a folded piece of stationery and, with a smiling nod, the aide took it and left.

"Who's Mrs. Larson? Someone special?" Kayleigh couldn't resist teasing Gramps. "And shouldn't you have sent her this, as well?" She held up the shoe.

Her grandfather hung his head and then rolled his eyes up to meet hers, his hangdog expression making her laugh. "I would have, but I'm hoping she'll let me deliver it in person. She's not speaking to me."

Kayleigh wagged her finger. "You should

have told me you had a girlfriend." It felt good to tease again.

"Annette's not my girlfriend." Gramps took the shoe and held it on his lap. "I haven't dated anyone besides your grandmother in over fifty years. I'm making a mess of it."

"Who could resist you?" Kayleigh tucked a stray lock behind his ear. He really was the sweetest.

Her grandfather rubbed his jaw. "Annette's got one heck of a temper. Dumped a bowl of oatmeal over my head when I accepted Martha's extra bacon at breakfast."

"Sounds like a keeper." Her smile faded when her grandfather's face fell.

"She's not your grandmother, God rest her soul." He fumbled for the tissue box beside his bed, found it empty and blotted at his eyes with his sleeves.

"You still miss her." It'd been eight years since her grandmother had passed from lung cancer, and the ache of her loss flared up at the most unexpected times.

"I miss her every day." Her grandfather's chin folds sank to meet his collarbone, his voice a low rasp. "Every single day."

"I miss her, too." She scooted closer and put her arm around him. "But I know she's still with us."

"I can't hear her laugh anymore." He pressed his lips together and shook his head. "After she passed, I used to tell her jokes—in case she was listening. I wanted to hear her, and I thought I did...that little snort she'd make when she couldn't help herself. I heard it. But now, nothing. I think she's left me for good. Probably found some angel who can do the cha-cha-cha better than me."

Kayleigh returned his sad smile. "Gram is still with you, Gramps. She just knows it's not your time to join her yet." She rested her head on his shoulder, feeling his bones shift beneath her cheek. "Besides, I need you."

He stroked the top of her head. "I know, doll, I know. Your gramps isn't going anywhere. Unlike Brat."

She couldn't help but laugh at the mix-up over Brett's name and didn't correct her grandfather. Brat sounded about right. "Looks as if we're both having relationship troubles." She pulled back and met her grandfather's direct blue eyes. Paul Newman eyes, Gram had called them.

"It's his loss for letting go of a diamond like you." Her grandfather pointed at his mini-fridge. "Still got some of that diet soda you brought last week, if you want it."

"Thanks." She crossed the tiled floor and

grabbed a can as well as her favorite snack—white chocolate–dipped Oreos. She brought Gramps treats when she visited, and a few for herself.

"Funny how you drink that diet soda then eat all those cookies," he teased, his eyes twinkling behind drooping lids.

"Makes perfect sense to me. Then I can eat more." She tossed a treat in her mouth as she sat, her cheeks bulging.

"You'll catch lots of fellas with that kind of charm."

Despite the bad joke, she couldn't help but laugh. Something about being around her grandfather made her feel like a kid again. "You're not having the best of luck yourself." She picked up the red shoe and waved it at him.

He chuckled, the sound starting low and deep in his belly and growing louder as it erupted from his throat.

"Maybe I oughta quit while I'm ahead. What's an old guy like me doing thinking about romance anyway?"

"Looking for happiness. There's nothing wrong with that."

"Nope. But so far, I'm striking out." He chucked her lightly under the chin. "At least I've still got my hair and my teeth. Not bad for eighty."

"Life doesn't get better than that," she teased, then ate another cookie.

"Maybe for me." His face grew serious, and his eyes searched hers. "But what about you?"

She glanced out the open doorway and watched a couple of women shuffle by, their heads craning to peer inside her grandfather's room before they whispered and giggled together. These women had more going on in the romance department than she did. How depressing.

But lucky Gramps. He had a fan club, even if he didn't see it. As for her, despite Gianna's efforts to get her out to the clubs and tempt her to attend her family's Fourth of July party today, Kayleigh found it hard to get in a social mood.

"I'm hanging in there." She popped in another Oreo, sucking on the white-chocolate coating before it melted on her tongue.

"Barely, by the looks of it. You've got circles under your eyes. Besides your breakup, what else is bothering you?"

She swallowed the rest of the cookie and chased it with cold soda. "Still haven't found a job, but I got the idea to use one of my own app designs to start a business. Unfortunately I can't find an experienced programmer to write the software. Plus, I need an investor. Big money."

"Maybe your father—" began Gramps before he stopped himself with a head shake. "Forget it. His young wife has him on a tight leash. With four new kids, I don't imagine he's giving even Chris's family much help."

Kayleigh let the soda bubble down her throat before answering. "Just some checks on holidays and birthdays. Otherwise, my stepmother demands that he focus on his new family, not his grown kids. You know how he hates confrontations, so he gives in.

"As for Mom, she tries. The paintings she sends Beth to sell don't raise much money, if they're purchased at all." Kayleigh sighed, thinking of the framed canvases stacked in her closet. Her artist mother meant well and did the best she could. "It's up to me to make this work, for Beth and myself, since I help her pay for Josh's private school. But I'm failing."

A bent finger, one of the two he'd broken back in his days operating a cement truck, lifted her chin. Their eyes met.

"'Many of life's failures are people who did not realize how close they were to success when they gave up.' Thomas Edison said that."

She smiled at her grandfather's penchant for quotes. "Good one, Gramps."

Then the meaning of the quote hit her. Failure wasn't about not getting what you wanted.

It was about giving up. And she was not a quitter. No matter what others said, she was on to something.

Her grandparents had been happily married for nearly fifty years, and her grandmother's passing had felt unbearable. Yet despite losing his spouse, Gramps hadn't given up on enjoying life. The red shoe was proof. It didn't mean he'd forgotten her Gram. It showed that he wanted to find happiness where he could.

And wasn't romance what made most people happy? If Gramps still believed in it, then other seniors did, as well. If he was struggling to meet someone again, she was sure he wasn't alone. Her app could help them, not just young people. And many probably had smartphones, gifts from well-meaning grandchildren like her.

Youth didn't have a monopoly on romance. Everyone, of all ages, wanted it, and she could make it easier to find. But if she gave up, it'd be their loss as well as hers. She had to trust that she knew best and not quit when success might be right around the corner. This was an untapped market.

Her grandfather beamed when she pulled him close and squeezed. "Hey, what's that for?"

"Everything. You have faith in me."

His smile pushed up his skin folds and lifted his ears. “Of course I do.”

She thought about the cryptic note to Annette Larson and how he’d inspired her to expand her app’s market. “Thanks, Gramps.”

“Bingo starts in the lounge in five minutes,” the PA system announced.

Gramps straightened and ran a hand over his hair. “I promised Annette I’d be there. Of course, she might not be talking to me anymore, but I should go. You wouldn’t be interested in playing with a bunch of old fogies, would you?”

She opened her mouth to insist that she would, but closed it when she thought of Mrs. Larson. Maybe he was hoping to make up with his lady friend.

“No. I promised Beth I’d stop by and see the boys. You have fun, though.”

He grabbed his cane and wobbled to his feet. “You have fun, too. While we’re alive, we should make every day count. In the end, that’s what matters.”

Exactly. Tomorrow she’d redouble her efforts to get her business off the ground. Prove that she was taking herself seriously, believing in herself, even if others weren’t.

“Okay, Gramps. I’ll see you in a few days.”

To her surprise, he pulled his cell from his pocket. "Why don't I phone you on the text?"

A snort escaped her. "Gramps, you *text* on the phone."

"Huh?" He fiddled with his hearing aids.

She kissed him, and they strolled out to the hall together. "Why don't I call you, okay?"

He patted her shoulder. "Sounds good, honey. And keep your chin up. You're going to work this out."

She nodded, feeling more certain. "I know. Love you."

"Love you, too." He hugged her, then strolled down the hall lined with photos of residents taken at a variety of events. One even showed them in togas. Who knew the assisted-living facility was party central?

The key to business success was finding an unfulfilled need and supplying it to an untapped market like this.

Brett was wrong. She wasn't just a thinker. She was a doer. As Gramps said, success might be right around the corner.

Now she just needed to turn it.

"KAYLEIGH?"

She stopped in the hallway and whirled at the familiar voice. Behind her stood Mary-

Anne, her pink scrubs clashing brilliantly with her scarlet hair.

"MaryAnne, hi. Happy Fourth. Sorry that you have to work." She glanced down at her buzzing phone.

"Wait for me, okay?" MaryAnne said, ducking into the nurses' station.

Kayleigh scanned her screen. A text from Gramps read, I'm toning you. That's phoning you on my text. xo.

She chuckled and typed, xo X infinity.

MaryAnne hung her stethoscope on a peg in the nurses' station then rejoined her, carrying her purse. "Actually, I swapped shifts so I could be home for our family barbecue. Are you leaving?"

Kayleigh smiled. "I think Gramps has a date."

MaryAnne leaned in. "He's quite the catch around here."

"Well, I'm glad he's happy," Kayleigh said as they waited for the elevator.

The elevator chimed and they stepped inside.

"So what are your plans for today?" MaryAnne rummaged through her purse, pulled out hand sanitizer and squirted some into her palms. The astringent smell filled the enclosed space and made Kayleigh sneeze.

"I'm stopping in to see my sister-in-law and nephews before heading home. Nothing much."

"Why don't you come home with me? We're having a family party." Her eyes slid toward Kayleigh. "And Niall will be there. We could pick up your family and bring them."

The elevator door opened on the ground floor and Kayleigh stepped out, stunned at the unexpected invitation, her head feeling light at the thought of seeing Niall again.

"I wouldn't want to impose. Plus, I don't know if Niall mentioned it, but our lunch meeting didn't go very well." She could only imagine Niall's reaction to her being there. Then again, it was an opportunity to see him and make her case. Change his mind. Was this the corner she needed to turn?

MaryAnne pushed open the glass double doors, and they plunged into the bright, midafternoon sun. "Sorry, Kayleigh. Niall's a tough nut to crack these days, but I wouldn't give up. As for imposing on a Walsh family barbecue? Please. We'll have loads of food and not enough people to eat it. Plus, we have a pool for the boys. Even better, you'd be doing me a favor. Niall is so uncomfortable at parties. You could talk to him, keep him busy."

"Well—" Kayleigh considered. If there was a more perfect opportunity for her to approach

Niall again, she couldn't imagine it. And as Gramps had said, failure was giving up right before you succeeded. Here was her chance, and she'd be a fool not to take it. And she couldn't deny that she looked forward to seeing him again. Hoped she'd find her old friend this time instead of the stranger in the restaurant. "Okay. I'll call Beth. Ask if she wants to come and to have the boys ready. They love to swim."

MaryAnne beamed and pulled out her car keys as they crossed the cracked asphalt parking lot, the heat so strong it wove clear ribbons in the air. Kayleigh took off her overshirt, glad she'd worn a tank top with her shorts. It'd been a sticky bus ride from her apartment.

"Good. And I know Niall will be glad to see you, even if he wasn't on his best behavior. I can tell he enjoyed your lunch."

Kayleigh stopped for a moment, then hurried to catch up. She thought he wanted nothing more to do with her. "How? He wasn't willing to help when I shared some ideas with him." Had he said something to MaryAnne? Did he want to see her again? Her heart thumped at the possibility.

MaryAnne flicked a glance her way before they stopped in front of a blue sedan. "Because he has a Five Leaves matchbook by his computer, and all of your messages are saved on his answering machine. Usually he deletes them, especially mine, but yours he keeps. When I dropped off his laundry, I snooped a little before he kicked me out."

"Huh." Kayleigh mulled over what that might mean. Was he thinking about her start-up? Had he decided to help? Deep down she knew that they'd succeed at anything. He just needed to remember how great they used to be together. How they could be again if he'd give them a chance.

Her pulse raced. There was only one way to find out. Although, if he got on board, she didn't need another Brett telling her what was best for her. She needed her old friend. Partnering with someone who considered his feelings ahead of hers would be repeating history.

She'd come too far to go backward again.

CHAPTER SIX

NIALL SIDESTEPPED HIS older brother, Aiden, who rushed from the back of the pub and across their backyard bearing a hamburger-laden platter.

"Coming through!" shouted his brother, and the crowd parted as he dashed to the grills. Hickory-scented smoke rose from a far corner of the fenced-in yard, mingling with the aroma of grilled meat. In the still summer air, the chatter of Walsh family members, visiting and local, grew louder by the second. Niall's head ached. His leg throbbed. His eyes burned. He'd been outside for over two hours, and if it wasn't for an aunt or a cousin grabbing him every time he tried to duck inside, he'd be in his old room over The White Horse Tavern.

He leaned against a tall oak tree, taking the pressure off his prosthetic. Although the weather was warm and dry, he wasn't comfortable. Peace and quiet. That was what he needed. When a breeze tussled through the leaves, he squinted up at the limbs he and his siblings once climbed. Life had been full of empty promises then. Now he just wanted to make his excuses and take the train home.

"Happy Independence Day, soldier." His twin brother, Liam, saluted Niall, then held out a hand. "Thanks for keeping the world safe." His green eyes twinkled, and dimples created half-moons on either side of his smile.

Niall returned the gesture, feeling like a hypocrite. As a marine, Liam had fought on the front lines. He'd saved the lives of allied forces, not cost them. Still, it was good to see his brother again.

After cutting into a watermelon on the table beside them, Liam passed Niall a piece. "How's life?" He studied Niall as he chewed. It was a measured gaze, the kind Liam had worn as a kid whenever he'd scrutinized bugs under a magnifying glass.

Niall returned his brother's assessing stare. "Same." The fruit's sweetness barely registered as he bit into it and braced himself for a lecture. Liam only showed that much concentration when he was about to dissect something—in this case, Niall's life.

"Still holed up in your apartment?" Liam spit a few seeds into a napkin and dropped his rind into a garbage bag, his eyes never leaving Niall's, his expression serious.

Niall shoved his hair off his damp forehead. "Leave it, bro."

Liam stepped closer and lowered his voice. "Not a chance. As your older brother by three minutes, I want to hear that you're getting out, working with people, maybe even dating the next time I visit. Got it?" Liam gave him a light punch and tried to grin, but it slipped off his face before it stuck.

Niall glanced away and shrugged. He wasn't making promises he couldn't keep. "I heard you. So how's the new job? Saved any stranded campers yet? Tranquilized any bears?"

Liam's low laugh rumbled. "Being a park ranger isn't as exciting as that. Mostly I'm checking trails and filling out paperwork. You should come upstate. Visit."

"Maybe," Niall temporized. He missed his brother, but unlike his twin, he'd had enough of outdoor life.

"Shoot," Liam exclaimed as he angled his head and peered over Niall's shoulder. "Looks like Ma's upset." He started in her direction then stopped and turned back, his eyes direct. "We'll catch up later before I head back, okay?"

Niall nodded then watched his brother stride away. In the doorway to the family's upstairs apartment, his mother turned in circles and wrung her hands, her eyes wide. He held himself back, wanting to help. But the last time he'd visited, she hadn't recognized him. He wouldn't risk getting her agitated like that in front of her relatives.

His tense shoulders relaxed when Liam led her to a table full of her siblings, her sudden smile reminding him of the mother she used to be. How was it possible to miss someone who was still with you? Yet he did, more so now that she didn't always know him. Maybe she sensed he wasn't the man she'd hugged the day he'd deployed.

He turned away from his family and scooped a plastic cup into an ice cooler. As soon as he finished this drink, he'd slip away, hopefully unnoticed. But when he raised a jug of soda to pour, his younger brother Conner sprayed him with a water gun.

"Hey!" He lunged and Conner darted away, laughing.

"Got you, loser!" But the boy sputtered in surprise when Niall closed the distance and dumped his ice down the back of Conner's shirt.

"You need to cool off, kid." He ruffled Conner's bright red hair.

"I'll be back, old man," the teenager warned, stepping backward before turning and racing to join the rest of his cousins. Niall's lips twitched. When he'd been Conner's age, everyone over twenty had seemed ancient.

"Knock knock." His nine-year-old sister, Ella, rapped her knuckles against his leg.

He looked down and couldn't resist returning the wide smile that swallowed half of her tiny face. He tweaked her upturned nose.

"Who's there?"

"Rita." She clapped a hand over her mouth, but her giggle poured out anyway.

He tapped his chin, giving every appearance of thinking it over, though she'd told him this joke on Memorial Day.

"I give up. Rita who?"

"Rita lot of books!" She lowered her hands and the gaps between missing teeth showed as she snickered again. "Will you read to me at bedtime, Niall? Pleeeeeease. You do the Beast voice the best, and I want to read about Belle."

He pictured socializing for the rest of the long afternoon, making small talk into the evening before he carried his yawning sister up to bed. But before he could shake his head, he caught her pleading look and softened. He couldn't refuse Ella. Ever.

"Yes," he growled in his best Beast voice. "But you must promise to stay with me *forever.*"

He held her tight until she broke free, laughing, and raced away, calling, "Never," over her shoulder.

Kayleigh's laugh at their lunch the other day came to mind as he poured his soda. She'd seemed fine—strong even. He'd given her his best advice and had seen for himself that she was doing okay. Since he couldn't reveal information about her brother, there was nothing else he could do to help. Nothing except think about how good it'd been to see her again 'round the clock....

He bolted back his drink and returned Aunt Lucy's wave. A few times, he'd considered returning Kayleigh's calls about her business proposal before stopping himself. She hated secrets, and he held the biggest of all from her. Despite that, a part of him had wished things were different once he'd returned to his quiet apartment and missed her laugh.

But avoiding her was the right thing to do. By not encouraging Kayleigh to follow a dead-end path, he was doing her a favor. Like her brother, she was rushing headfirst into danger with her risky start-up idea. And while he couldn't take back what had happened to Chris, he could stop Chris's sister from making a fatal mistake.

So why, then, had he started researching

dating apps? Sizing up the market? Even purchasing a few to investigate? It must be idle curiosity, since he had no intention of accepting her offer.

Working with her wasn't going to happen.

Then, to his surprise, she appeared at their side gate. MaryAnne led the way, a tall woman with light brown hair beside her. Kayleigh, slender and graceful, followed holding hands with two boys, one too young to be in grade school. Were they her children? She'd mentioned an ex-fiancé, not an ex-husband. Something about the thought unsettled him.

Wearing a white tank top that showed off her smooth, sun-kissed skin, and jean shorts that topped lean legs, Kayleigh looked good. Better than good. Without thinking, he took a step in the group's direction.

"Oh, there you are, Niall!" shouted MaryAnne.

He flinched. Idiot. He should have bolted for the house the minute he'd spotted them. Later tonight, he'd set his sister straight about ambushing him with surprise guests.

Before he could duck away, another brother, Daniel, tossed him a beach ball. He chucked it back to the group of preteens sitting in an aboveground pool and returned their wave. When he glanced back, the group had reached him.

"Hi, MaryAnne." He forced his eyes to skim past Kayleigh when they wanted to linger. "Kayleigh."

Her hands rested atop the two boys' heads, and her eyes sparkled silver in the bright light. When a dark curl fell across her cheek, he watched as she tucked it behind her ear. "Hi, Niall. I ran into MaryAnne while visiting my grandfather, and she invited us over. It's nice to see you again."

His stomach rolled and he took a short breath before nodding, his expression neutral. It *was* good to see her again. But if he showed her any encouragement, she'd corner him with her business presentation. Better to put some distance between them, fast.

"Aiden's got hamburgers and hot dogs over there." He gestured to the grills. "Salads and chips are on the table."

"Hot dog!" the smaller boy shouted, and he bounced up and down. "I want one!"

The older boy made a disgusted noise, his expression sullen. His thin arms crossed in front of his narrow chest, his longish, light brown hair hanging in front of his eyes.

"Of course, sweetie. Give Mommy a minute." The tall woman held out her hand, her smile shy but warm. "I'm Beth Renshaw, Kayleigh's sister-in-law, and these are my boys."

She pointed to the older one. "This is Josh and my youngest is Samuel. Thank you for having us over."

"Niall." He gripped her hand, then released it, his mind racing over these facts. Kayleigh only had one brother. Chris. So if this was her sister-in-law, then that meant—

His eyes flew from Josh to Samuel to Beth. Chris's family. Seeing them cut like a saw through bone. He'd heard that Chris was married. Had children. He'd even thought about going to Chris's funeral to see them and to find out if Kayleigh needed support. But his emotions had been too raw. He'd worried that he'd lose control of them and spill his guts to the only woman he'd ever opened up to. Now here they were, the collateral damage of his thoughtless actions. Two boys without a father. A wife without her husband. His breathing hitched. He'd caused this, and the guilt slashed through his gut.

"MaryAnne mentioned you served in Afghanistan. My husband was in the service, too," Beth said softly, her large blue eyes dominating a narrow face. "We all appreciate your sacrifice." Her eyes skimmed over the prosthetic limb showing below his shorts.

"You're a hero," piped up the littler one. Samuel. He stepped close and reached for

Niall's prosthetic before his mother snatched his hand away.

"No, I'm not." His voice was more forceful than he intended, and the boy's eyes widened. The older son, Josh, peered at him through his overgrown bangs, his squint sharp and assessing.

"All soldiers are heroes." Samuel picked at a scab on his elbow. "Mommy said so."

Josh snorted, and Kayleigh shot him a dark look that made the boy study his shuffling sneakers.

Niall glanced from Beth, to Kayleigh, to a scowling MaryAnne. Time to go before he said more than he should. "Your dad was a hero." He turned to leave.

A tug on his shorts' hem stopped him.

"You, too. You, too!" Samuel jumped up and down. "Do you have a medal?"

Niall pictured the Purple Heart he'd stuffed in a sock drawer. He couldn't toss it, but he wouldn't look at it either. He opened his mouth then closed it, his tongue sluggish, his brain full of white noise. Kayleigh's hand fell on his wrist, and the warm pressure of her skin against his steadied him.

"My daddy has two medals," the youngster continued without waiting for an answer.

"It doesn't help us now that he's dead," Josh

burst out. His eyes were wild around the edges, and he shoved fists into his pockets.

Sam cried out, and Beth's chest rose with a sharp intake of breath. Instantly, Kayleigh let go of Niall and bent down to whisper something in Josh's ear.

Niall rubbed the spot where Kayleigh's hand had been, and silently agreed with Josh. Chris should have his life instead of medals, be with his family today. If not for Niall, he'd be celebrating his independence instead of resting in a cemetery. Regret sliced him like a sharp stone beneath swift water.

"He deserves them." It was inadequate, but all Niall could say, especially with Kayleigh's gaze on him. Facing her was hard enough. Seeing Chris's family, unbearable. It brought the same sick, breathless ache back to his chest whenever he thought about that day in Afghanistan.

Kayleigh gave Niall an approving nod, then touched the top of Sam's head. "Your dad was very brave."

"Or stupid," mumbled the older boy. He picked up an abandoned straw from a table and began bending the end and releasing it so that it whipped his arm.

"Josh!" exclaimed Kayleigh as Beth's hand rose to her mouth. "Never speak that way about your father." A deep sliver of anger ran through her patient tone.

"What? Only an idiot volunteers to get killed."

"Daddy went to heaven," cried Samuel before sticking his thumb in his mouth. Beth gently tugged it free and pulled him into her arms. Around them, the crowd hushed, and a few lowered their burgers.

"He left us, idiot." Josh whirled and stomped away. Before he ducked his head, Niall glimpsed pain underneath the boy's angry expression, raw and bloody, like a wound too deep for healing. He'd lost his father, and his resentment was palpable.

Kayleigh started after Josh while Beth picked up a shaking Samuel. "I'm so sorry, MaryAnne. We didn't mean to ruin your party. Maybe we should go."

"No. No," MaryAnne soothed. "Let's get this little guy a hot dog, okay?" She led the way, and Niall heard his sister say, "Do you like cotton candy or sprinkles on your hot dog, Sam?" followed by the kid's answering giggle. Leave it to MaryAnne to right all of the wrongs in the world.

He stared after Josh and Kayleigh. Despite not having a plan or a reason, he followed them. What could he do? It wasn't as though he could bring Chris back, reverse the past. Seeing the Renshaw family proved what he already knew. The wrong guy had died that day. A family had depended on Chris, while Niall had come home to…no one who'd really needed him. Fate had an ironic sense of humor he didn't appreciate.

Before they reached the entrance to the back stairs, Conner blasted Josh in the face with a water gun. Guffaws rang out amongst the younger pack, and Niall stiffened. Would Josh understand that they were just trying to include him?

But the boy lowered his red, dripping face and charged, his forehead ramming into Conner, knocking them both to the ground. Niall's military instincts kicked in. He rushed at the grappling pair and yanked off Josh before he landed another punch.

Josh struggled in Niall's arms, kicking the air.

"Let me go!"

A crowd gathered, Aiden pushing to the front of the pack. "Everything okay here?"

Niall gave his brother a curt nod. "It's under control."

Aiden put his arm around a protesting Conner and led him away, the rest of the kids following in his wake.

Ella remained and stomped a ballerina slipper, shaking her tiny fist at Josh. “Fighting is for sissies!” she yelled, then raced to catch up with the rest of the Walshes.

Beth shoved her way through the dispersing crowd and knelt beside her son. Her eyes searched Josh’s face for injuries. “What happened?”

“Nothing.” Suddenly, the fight left Josh like water poured from a bucket, and he sagged in Niall’s grip.

Beth held her son’s chin and forced him to look at her. “I told you. No more fighting.” Beth’s voice sounded more sad than angry, as if she and Josh had been through this before. Remorse forked inside. Chris should be here. Instead, Beth was on her own, parenting as best she could with a troubled kid.

“He shot me!” Josh’s voice wavered, full of anguish.

Sam flung his arms around Josh but staggered and fell on his backside when his older brother shoved him away.

A wail rose from Sam. “Josh pushed me!”

Beth’s eyes scanned one boy then the other, clearly conflicted on whom to comfort.

Kayleigh stepped up. “Beth, you take care of Sam, and I’ll talk to Josh. Okay?”

Sam clutched his mother's leg, his shoulders trembling as he sobbed. "No fighting!"

Niall flinched. Did Sam react so strongly to violence because he'd lost his father?

A cold trickle of sweat traveled down his back. His mind shied away from the memory, which settled in his stomach with a sharp twist. When he met Kayleigh's anguished gaze, he wished he could wipe away her hurt. Erase all of their pain. His actions that day had had a ripple effect, the rings of it traveling further than he'd imagined.

Kayleigh marched Josh through the back entranceway to the upstairs apartment, and he hustled after them. He still didn't have a clue what to do or say except that he couldn't stand by without helping. Chris hadn't left him behind, and he wouldn't leave the fallen soldier's family in crisis.

He climbed the back stairs, then paused at the top of the landing. Voices came from the kitchen on his right.

"I don't care if I get kicked out of school," he heard Josh say. "I'm not going to some stupid anger thing."

"It's not stupid. And it's called anger management. Your school said they won't admit you next year if you don't attend therapy to stop fighting. Do you want to leave your friends and go to public school?"

"Who cares? Besides, you quit. Why can't I?"

A floorboard creaked, and Niall pictured one of them pacing, probably Kayleigh. She always moved when agitated.

"That's different," he heard her say, her voice sounding uncertain. Was she second-guessing herself? "Sweetie, if you don't control your temper, no school will keep you. If we hadn't agreed to anger-management therapy, you would have been expelled."

Niall stooped to pet his family's snoozing cat, Grinch, stepped over him and drew closer.

"What's the difference?" Josh groused. "I heard you tell Mom that you might not be able to pay for school anymore. So why do I still have to go to therapy?"

In the long silence that followed, Niall pictured Kayleigh on the other side of the wall, struggling to answer. She'd always been a stickler for honesty, and she'd have a hard time leveling with Josh. And she hadn't been forthcoming with him either. Her jobless situation didn't just affect her. It impacted Chris's family, too, since she helped to support them. A cold anxiety slowly grew in his gut. It galled him to imagine them suffering more than they had already.

"That conversation wasn't meant for you to hear. And I don't want you to worry. Things will work out."

Her voice sounded less confident than her words, and Niall shifted his weight to his good leg, uncomfortable. He recalled all the unanswered voice mails she'd left. He hadn't wanted to make her think that he would consider her proposal. But now his certainty was shaken.

"Right." A loud thump sounded. The kid's fist hitting the counter? "Like the way everything works out. Dad. School..."

Niall understood where the kid was coming from. To a boy who'd lost his father, life wasn't his friend. Josh had a right to be angry, but that frustration should be vented on Niall, not on his mother, brother or aunt. He couldn't let Kayleigh take the brunt of it. He'd heard enough.

"May I speak with Josh?" Niall stepped into the large kitchen and Kayleigh's eyes widened, her hand rising to a red, white and blue cat pin on her tank top.

"Man-to-man," he added, sending her a reassuring look that he hoped reminded her of their old friendship.

She glanced between him and Josh, considering. At last her shoulders lowered and she shot him a grateful look that warmed him. "Sure. I'll be around the corner in the living room."

The boy's nostrils flared with each breath, and a hint of defiance touched his expression. He leaned against a counter cluttered with barbecue fixings, his light brown hair blending with the oak cabinets behind him.

"I don't have to talk to you." Josh ripped a sheet of paper from the fridge and began shredding it. Niall was pretty sure it was his grandmother's pecan pie recipe.

"That belongs to someone else, bud."

Josh shrugged, his expression defiant. "So." He threw the paper pieces into the air like confetti. "What are you going to do? Hit me?"

Niall felt a thud of concern. "Do people hit you?" He pictured soft-spoken Beth and couldn't imagine it.

"Fat chance."

But something in the kid's tone was off. He was hiding something. If Niall knew Josh better, he'd press the issue.

"I fought in the same war as your dad." Niall forced himself to look at Josh directly.

"Did you know him?" Josh rocked up onto the edges of his feet, then back to the flats, a light appearing in his eyes.

Niall drew in a deep breath, hating to lie. "No. But I know what it's like to be a soldier. Always on guard. Waiting for the next attack. Ready to strike."

"What's this got to do with me?" Josh's jaw tightened. His eyes scanned the ceiling, the cabinets, then the floor. Anywhere but in Niall's direction.

"You're not in a war." Niall caught Josh's eye at last and held his gaze. "Life isn't against you."

"Yes. It is," Josh blurted, then spun around, his thin back now facing Niall. "Just forget it," he said, lower. "I can handle it."

Niall turned Josh by the shoulders, feeling the boy tense beneath his grip. "No you can't. That's why you need anger-management therapy."

Could Kayleigh hear any of this from the living room? It amazed him that she still trusted him, saw him as her old friend and believed he could make a difference with Josh. He'd changed, yet she still wanted his friendship and help. It made him wish he could be that guy she'd once known. But the path to that person had closed long ago.

Josh studied him then blew out a long breath. "I already went once. It was some guy who wanted me to talk about my feelings." Josh made a gagging sound, and Niall could have joined him. But if the kid was in trouble, something needed to be done.

Niall opened the fridge, pulled out a couple of sodas and handed one to Josh. "What happened?"

The tabs popped, and they drank before Josh answered.

"He asked me how I felt, so I told him I wanted to punch him. Now I have to see someone else, except I won't go back. What's the point? My school wants me to do it, but Aunt Kay can't pay tuition anymore. I'm going to public school either way." His last words ended on a hiccupping sob, and Niall fought the urge to hug the kid.

After losing his father, Josh didn't need more upheaval in his life. Kayleigh's selflessness in helping Chris's family impressed him, while her decision to do her own thing and start her own company worried him. If she followed that path, there was a real possibility she'd let herself and Chris's family down, unless… Resolve tightened his jaw.

He'd offer Beth tuition money, but how would he explain the donation? No. There had to be another way.

"How about you and I spend some time together with your mother's permission? I can teach you some defense moves. Get your anger out that way. Then therapy won't seem so bad."

Josh recoiled, his upper lip curling, as he banged the soda can down on the counter. "You just feel sorry for me because my dad is dead."

"No. That's not how it is." Why would the kid assume that someone being kind meant he was being pitied? Then it hit him; he felt that way, too.

"Yes, it is. When my dad died, everyone was extranice because they felt sorry for me." His eyes were cold, dead and flat as he peered at Niall. "And I don't want it. I just want my dad, but that's not going to happen."

Niall's pulse sputtered, then stalled. Regardless of his own reservations, he knew what he had to do. He owed it to Chris.

"My offer stands whenever you're ready." Niall looked straight into Josh's eyes. "And you're not switching schools."

The boy laughed, skeptical, the sound of a child who's been promised much but received little. "They said my dad would come home. Grown-ups always tell you things that aren't true."

"I won't let you down, bud."

Kayleigh appeared. "Everything okay in here?"

Josh brushed by her and fled down the stairs.

"Fine." Niall raised his soda as if to toast her. "In fact, I was about to tell Josh the news. You and I are going to be business partners."

"That isn't funny." Her hand rose to her cat pin, her features tense, eyes unblinking.

"No. It's not," he agreed, though he found himself wearing a grin regardless.

CHAPTER SEVEN

A BAG OF muffins swung from Kayleigh's clenched teeth as she balanced a coffee holder and pressed Niall's apartment buzzer.

For the third time.

She glanced up at the brownstone's number: 573 Jefferson Avenue. Yes. This was the place he'd moved to, according to MaryAnne. She pulled out her cell phone. 9:00 a.m. Anyone would be up and about by now. And Niall had always been an early riser. So why wasn't he responding?

Feeling flushed and sticky in the morning humidity, she shook her hair back from her neck. Was Niall rethinking his decision to join her? After his announcement, he'd followed Josh outside, promising they'd talk another time.

She leaned her forehead against the cool stone beside the speaker. *Please don't let him have acted on impulse.* One he now regretted. Maybe she should have pressed him about his decision at the party.

Did Niall believe in her? She needed to understand his motives for agreeing to join her. As business partners, transparency was crucial. They'd always been honest with each other. Could she still count on that?

She ignored the nervous dance of her heart and glanced around Jefferson Avenue. The newly restored area was impressive, with stately rows of attached, earthen-toned, three-story homes, connecting wrought iron gates and fenced-in areas containing flower-filled planters. Stone facades contrasted with the leafy green sycamores lining the residential street.

At the foot of the building's tall concrete stoop, a man paused to let his terrier sniff a spent firecracker. It was peaceful here. She could see why Niall had little interest in leaving.

But no one should isolate themselves. Perhaps this business venture would help him as much as it'd help her. At lunch last week, she'd worried that he'd become too abrupt and rude. Yet from the touching exchange she'd overheard between him and Josh, that sensitive, considerate person still existed. Somewhere.

There was only one way to find out. She jabbed his apartment buzzer again, this time laying on it long and hard, followed by a series of short beeps. He might have lost interest in the world since his injury, but the world—namely she—wasn't about to leave him alone. He'd agreed last night, and she would hold him to it. She was done being ignored or dismissed.

"What?" a husky voice crackled through the intercom.

At last.

She ripped the bag from her mouth and leaned close. "It's me."

A long frustrated-sounding sigh came through the brass grid. "Not now, Kayleigh."

She poked the buzzer again for good measure. "You were supposed to say, 'Great. Let's get started.' But since you didn't, how about just letting me in, okay?"

Bass boomed through the street as a vintage 1970s car with gleaming rims cruised down the block. It slowed, and a male passenger leaned out and pointed at her.

"What up, girl! Lost your key? Need help?"

A window sash slammed open above, and Niall shouted, "Beat it!" as the entranceway opener vibrated. *Yes!* She pulled the iron grate and pushed through the heavy door.

Her visit this morning was a leap of faith that he'd want to get started right away. Oh, who was she kidding? *She* needed to get started right away. With no income and the clock tick-ing, she didn't have a moment to waste. Even on an ill-tempered hermit of a war veteran who'd rather waste his life than appreciate it. He'd promised that they'd talk later, and that time was now. It was her turn to call the shots.

When she reached his second-floor apartment, she stuffed the bag in her mouth again then raised her hand. But before she knocked, the door swung open, revealing a bare-chested Niall wearing low-slung gray army sweats. The muffin bag thunked to the floor.

Niall's smooth, broad chest tapered to a flat stomach defined by shifting muscle and small scars. Her lungs gave up any pretense of working as her gaze lingered on diagonal hip ridges that disappeared into his waistband. He was all lean muscle and sculpted lines. His was the kind of body featured in magazines, billboard ads and paintings, not hidden away in a Brooklyn apartment.

Yet here it was. He was. They were. She gulped, suddenly feeling self-conscious and regretful of the blueberry muffin she'd wolfed down on the bus ride here. No wonder she never shook those extra couple of pounds—or five...okay, ten if she was honest. But even if she ate nothing but salad and worked out every day, she couldn't imagine ever looking as cut as Niall, at least, not without the help of her Spanx. He was gorgeous, and she was—she discreetly lifted her arms away from her body—sticky.

"What are you doing here?" He pushed his rumpled hair out of his cocoa-brown eyes, his just-rolled-out-of-bed look making it impossible to think, let alone speak. What was wrong with her?

He peered down at her. "Kayleigh? You in there?"

A relieved laugh escaped her. She needed to hear one of their old jokes to put things back in perspective. This was Niall. Not some stranger to lust after. She'd known him when he'd been reluctant to take off his shirt to swim, unwilling to be teased for his scrawniness. Her eyes slid his way again, lingering on his broad chest. No chance of that now. She sighed and reined in her runaway thoughts. Time to shake off these weird feelings and get on with business.

"I'm here for our first meeting, partner." She scooped up the bag and straightened. "Plus, I brought breakfast."

"You should have called." Niall glanced over his shoulder, then leaned muscular arms on either side of the door frame, blocking an interior view. "Let's meet another day."

Kayleigh held up the coffee container, the sweet hazelnut smell filling the hallway. "Even just for a cup?" She had to get through that door. Until she did, Niall might back out. She had a limited liability corporation document in her shoulder bag, and she wouldn't leave until he explained why he wanted to be a part of her start-up and signed it, making their partnership official.

She pulled out one of the muffins she and Gianna had baked last night. "And I've got a chocolate-chip muffin. Your favorite, right?"

A hungry look entered Niall's eyes as they lingered on the treat, his nose flaring at the sweet, rich scent. Finally, he glanced away and shook his head.

"I'm sorry, but I'm really not—" A loud stomach rumbling cut off his words, making his face relax into a real smile that stole her breath.

"Fine." Amusement filled his voice. He lowered his arms and shrugged. "You win. But I haven't picked up, so don't mind the—"

She brushed by him, then pulled up short to check out the damage left by the hurricane that had blown through his apartment. It was a spare space, all the more cramped given that every surface was covered in newspapers, takeout containers and—of all things—clothes.

"Laundry day?"

"Nope. This is pretty much every day."

Before marrying Beth, Chris's place had looked like this. She gave Niall a sideways grin, hoping it hid the nerves that skittered through her stomach at his proximity. "Well. I like what you've done with the place."

"Sorry about the mess." His sheepish tone disarmed her. "I didn't know you were coming."

She followed him into the kitchen and set the bag and coffee on a clear spot on his counter. "I should have called. I assumed that we would—" When his eyes leveled on hers, she found it impossible to lie to him. Plus, she'd vowed honesty would be the rule in her business. "I was afraid you'd back out."

He pulled the coffees out of the cardboard holder and offered her one. "I gave my word."

Relief swept through her, and she nodded, removing the cover from her drink and ripping the tops off three packets of artificial sweetener before dumping them into the brew. Niall had never misled her and always kept his promises. She shouldn't have doubted him.

"So why do you want to be with me?"

"Excuse me?" he sputtered, lowering his coffee cup.

"In the start-up," she clarified, feeling herself blush.

He shrugged, his expression evasive. "Can't

a guy change his mind, or is that just a woman's prerogative?"

"Equal opportunity and honesty are the rules in this business. So why, exactly, are you joining me? You seemed convinced this would fail at our lunch."

He gestured to some papers by his computer, and when she wandered there she saw the Five Leaves matchbox and some printouts with notes in the margins about dating websites and apps.

"You've been researching."

He joined her, and she felt herself tense in awareness at his closeness. Why was he making her so jumpy?

"Yes." When he spoke, his warm breath touched her cheek.

She stepped away and tried not to breathe in the scent of him. It made her head swim. He was a friend and now a potential business partner. She couldn't—wouldn't—think of him in any other way. The last time she'd gotten involved with a business associate had ended in disaster. She'd let her emotions fool her once; a second time, and she'd be the fool.

Plus, Niall was like a brother and, after losing Chris, the only one she had left. She'd never jeopardize their relationship—now that she finally had him back—by giving in to some inexplicable attraction. Most likely, it'd disappear once they spent more time together and were comfortable again.

"And what conclusion did you reach?" she asked.

"That we could do better," he said, assurance filling every syllable.

She searched his eyes, looking for a lie in them, but saw only truth. He believed in her, saw the potential in her app. His quiet confidence erased every doubt that'd crept its way into her thoughts this week and she smiled, feeling slightly giddy. At last. A real partner. Better yet, her old friend. A person who wouldn't betray or mislead her as Brett had.

"I agree. So let's get started."

She wandered into his living room, cleared an area on his coffee table and set down her coffee and shoulder bag. "I thought we could go over the terms of our partnership agreement." She pulled out her LLC document. "Then I'll give you my market presentation, business plan and functionality layout to help you design the app. I have it in hard copy and—" she fished a flash drive from the bottom of her bag "—on PowerPoint. It's something we can use when meeting with potential investors. I've already lined up a meeting this week and two more next week, so the sooner we get—"

Niall held up a hand, stopping her word flow. “Just leave the information by my desk. I’ll go over it later.” Niall disappeared into a room off the back of his living room, and she looked down at her twisting hands and jittering knee.

One of today’s agenda items would be addressing his dismissive manner. Perhaps it was a side effect of being alone for so long? She’d try to understand, but she wouldn’t accept it. After being sidelined and overlooked at work, she wouldn’t let that happen in her start-up. Most important, as friends and partners, they were equals.

At last, Niall returned wearing a white T-shirt, his hair flatter and a bit wet, his clean, soapy smell making her breathe deep. Kayleigh forced her mind back to the meeting. He would not go over her materials without her. She wasn’t an employee to be sent away.

“Let’s iron out some basics to start.” She pulled out her notepad and a to-do list clearly outlining the meeting’s agenda. “First, we need to go over our LLC agreement, decide on a name for the app, discuss the functionality of the software, the markets we intend to reach, the best way to reach them…”

Niall took a bite of muffin and wagged a finger. When he stopped chewing, he said,

"There's a way this arrangement needs to work. If you want some ground rules, here are mine."

He held on to the couch's arm and lowered himself beside her. She opened her mouth to protest, then closed it when she saw the firm clench of his jaw. He was serious, and if she wanted his signature on their partnership agreement, she needed to hear him out. Besides, good leadership didn't mean talking over others. It meant listening, too.

"Okay. Go ahead." She munched on her cranberry muffin, the tart flavor making her suck in her cheeks.

Niall's mouth quirked, but his eyes didn't waver as they stared directly into hers. "We aren't going to work together in the physical sense."

Kayleigh swallowed her second bite too fast and coughed, feeling for her coffee as her eyes watered. What? How could they work together if they were never together? She must have heard him wrong.

Niall limped into the kitchen, then reappeared with a glass of water. She accepted it gratefully and waited for the cool liquid to soothe her burning throat before speaking.

"What do you mean?"

Niall shifted, and his knees brushed hers, a vague featherlight touch. "The majority of this work can be done remotely. We'll use email to communicate, the phone when we have to and Skype as our last resort." He held up her flash drive. "I'll review your business plan and presentations, make my own suggestions, then email it back to you. Once we've reached consensus, I'll sign the partnership agreement."

"We need to sign it together, in person, before a notary. Unless you can manage that remotely, as well." Her voice dripped with sarcasm. MaryAnne had warned her, but this was taking stubborn isolation to another level entirely. Did he really think they could run a business without seeing each other in person? Ever? He'd agreed to be her partner, yet he acted as though the less he had to do with her, the better. That wasn't how a friend behaved, and it dawned on her that his reasons for joining her had nothing to do with reconnecting personally.

Niall's brow furrowed. "Of course we'll meet for that. Otherwise, I'll handle the programming from home and email you with my input on how to represent us during finance meetings and marketing events."

Kayleigh's temper flared so hot and quick that she actually felt her skin flush. It started in her face and burned down to her chest and limbs. It made the hair on her arms prickle.

She took a deep breath. "So other than signing official documents, you and I—" She gestured between them, her motions jerky, an edge entering her voice.

"Won't see each other," Niall finished for her, looking pleased with himself. "Thanks for the coffee." He took another drink, and she clasped her hands to keep herself from snatching it away. He didn't deserve her treats or this opportunity. He wasn't a willing partner. He was a reluctant one.

Hot words boiled up, but she shoved them down with all the business finesse she could muster. "So you wouldn't be a true partner, then."

He shrugged, bringing his broad shoulders almost to his ears and back down. "More of a silent one."

Kayleigh shot to her feet and stuffed her papers in her bag. Meeting adjourned. She'd hoped to start a business and renew her relationship with Niall, but not on those terms.

"What are you doing?" Niall's voice rose, but she ignored him and slid the zipper closed. He wouldn't get another ounce of her attention. Bitter letdown drummed along the empty spaces inside her.

She slung her bag's handle around her shoulder and headed for the door. Just like Brett, he was treating her as if she was unworthy, not good enough, couldn't be trusted to think for herself. And she'd been there and done that. Niall was either all in or all out. She wouldn't accept anything less. Not anymore.

"You didn't leave the information for me to look over." Despite his prosthesis, his long legs helped him beat her to the door. He pressed a hand against it when she reached for the knob. When his eyes searched hers, the color was as dark as her mood, her defeat reflected in them.

"No need." Her voice sounded shrill. "Now. If you'll excuse me?"

She tugged at the door until he stepped back, and she opened it.

"I'm sorry this didn't work out, Niall." She stuck out a hand, and he looked at it. His dumb-struck expression would have been comical if her situation wasn't so desperate. She needed help, needed him, but Niall had smashed her hopes to bits today. He'd never be a real partner or her old friend. The war had changed him. Niall may have returned from the war, but her friend was gone as surely as her brother was.

"I thought that's what we were doing. Fig-uring this out." His eyebrows came together.

She shook her head and pulled the door wider. "No. You were dictating what you wanted while I was hoping to collaborate with an equal. Still am, apparently." Her lungs moved sluggishly in her chest. If even an old friend didn't want to work closely with her, then who? She might well and truly fail.

When he brushed his fingertips down the length of her arm, she shivered.

"What if that's all I can give?"

The confusion in his face touched her. But she needed more from him. When she took this high dive, it couldn't be on her own. If only Chris were here. Her heart ached as she imagined him pushing her out of Niall's apartment, insisting that she deserved better, promising her that she would find another way.

"I'm sorry. It's just not enough. Not anymore. Goodbye, Niall."

NIALL LEANED IN his doorway, frozen, and watched Kayleigh's curls disappear down his stairwell.

How had everything gotten messed up? Joining her business was the last thing he'd planned to do. But when he'd seen her again, learned that she supported Chris's family, he'd known he needed to help. And now she was throwing his offer in his face. Dismissing him.

He'd reached the bottom of the stairwell before he realized he couldn't let her go. No man left behind, Chris had said to him that day in

Kunar. He wouldn't abandon Kayleigh, no matter how hard she pushed him away. Yet she needed to compromise, see that he could be there for her in his own way.

With the program prototypes he'd provide, she'd be able to convince financers to invest. He'd study her business plan and put in serious hours to give her something flashy to show them. His work would do the talking. It would do a better job than he could. If he attended meetings and events, his unease would drive potential investors and consumers away. Kayleigh had to understand.

He watched her yellow skirt flutter down his stoop and yanked open the door.

"Kayleigh! Wait!"

A gray, tiger-striped cat streaked between his legs and bolted up the steps. He turned to grab it, but was too late. Animals weren't allowed in the building, but if he wasted time catching it, he'd miss Kayleigh. His gaze swerved back to the street, and he trod down the stairs after the lithe woman.

He followed, lengthening his stride until he caught up and cupped her soft elbow.

She rounded on him; her oval face, usually cheerful, was filled with such a cold anger that he stepped back.

"What, Niall?" Her voice was a tight coil of

fury. “Should I have brought more cream for your coffee? Sharpened some pencils for you? Refilled your printer cartridges?”

He rubbed his forehead, the bright sunshine making spots appear around the edges of his vision. “What? No. Why would I need you to do those things?”

She stepped close, and she smelled faintly of flowers, which he guessed was perfume, but beneath that was her own smell, like green grass, like the morning air after a light spring rain. It drew him, as did everything about her.

“Because you don’t see me as a partner. An equal.” Her voice rose and captured the attention of two women sitting on a stoop across the street.

“According to your—” she made air quotes “—‘ground rules,’ I’ll be a flunky taking directives via email missives instead of making decisions with you in person and working as a team. I need a right-hand man. Not another boss who wants to order me around while he sits back and gets the credit.” She swatted the air with her hand. “Forget it.”

“I won’t forget it.” He lowered his voice but kept it firm, with enough authority to keep her from leaving. Kayleigh was jumping to conclusions, misunderstanding him. “Listen. I want to be your business partner. Not your boss. Can we start over? Give me another chance to explain without sounding like Chairman Mao."

He held out his hands, palms up. When a light wind blew one of her curls in her face, he couldn't resist tucking it behind her small ear, the silky feeling of her hair and her vulnerable, astonished expression lingering. She was beautiful to him in the same way that'd stopped his adolescent heart years ago. Only that boy was gone, and he'd thought his ability to care had left, as well. Was he wrong? Kayleigh brought out feelings he had no right to feel, especially when she looked at him the way she did now.

A smile showed itself around the corners of her eyes, in the tilt of her head as she studied him. "Chairman Mao, huh?"

He nodded and waited, his thudding heart drowning out the singsong of a passing ice cream truck. And then she smiled. It was warm and sweet, like the unfurling of a flower, and suddenly he felt as though he stood on cracking ice. He held himself very still, worried that if he moved, everything would fall apart.

"Okay. But we're talking on the stoop."

His breath rushed out of him. "Fine." He fell into step beside her, distracted by the brush of her shoulder as they walked back.

Pigeons took flight when he opened his gate and gestured for her to precede him. Up on the landing, they seated themselves, and he stretched out his aching prosthetic leg. It was an older model, and ill fitting, according to the physical therapist. She'd insisted on upgrading, but he'd turned her down, not wanting any bells and whistles.

When he turned Kayleigh's way, he studied her profile, admiring the line of her jaw, the curve of her neck into her shoulder, the slight bump on the bridge of her short nose. Something about that imperfection added to the charm of her beautiful face. At least he'd thought so as a boy. Still did if he was honest. It made her more human, easier to talk to… only right now, he didn't have a clue what to say. Suddenly, he was arguing for a partnership he'd never wanted.

"I'm sorry, Kayleigh."

She examined her clipped, unvarnished nails, and the smallness of her hands struck him. How did such a big personality come out of such a petite person? No matter where she stood, she was the center of the room.

"And…"

His eyes roamed over the crown of her head, wishing he could read her mind and know what words she needed to hear. All he could do was speak the truth. And she valued that more than anything, he thought with a twinge as Chris came to mind.

"Programming I can do. Whatever you have dreamed up in that business plan of yours, I will make come to life. But as far as sitting in at the financial meetings and marketing events, I'm only going to hurt us. Not help."

She cocked her head and peered up at him, her expression oddly soft. "Why do you think that?"

His hands twisted in his lap. "I'm not the social type, Kay."

Her hand was cool and delicate as it slipped into his. "You used to be."

"That was before." He laced his fingers in hers, unable to resist before letting go. "I'll never be that person again. Too much happened and I—"

He broke off when an elderly woman appeared to water a potted shrub.

When his neighbor disappeared inside her building, Kayleigh turned, every feature fine and sharp. "I understand that you don't want to talk about what happened in the war. But know that you can tell me anything. Anytime."

The backs of his eyes burned. She'd been his best friend, the girl who'd listened and advised him, who'd stood up for him when she thought he'd needed defending from bullies.

Yet even she couldn't tackle this beast inside him. If she glimpsed it, it'd tear her apart, too. Shatter their new partnership. No. He'd keep managing on his own.

"That will never happen," he said honestly.

He felt Kayleigh recoil, and when she spoke, her voice sounded defeated. "So you'll never be your old self again."

It made him wonder. Chris had returned for him. Should he go back for himself? For Chris's family's sake? A sudden wish to find that person seized him, though he'd have to return to a bloody field in Kunar to find him.

"No," he said at last, and brushed away an ant that crawled across his ankle. Even to his own ears, he sounded uncertain.

"I don't believe you." A speculative gleam entered Kayleigh's eyes. "Come to tomorrow's finance meeting. See how things go. If you don't think you can handle it, then don't sign the partnership agreement. There's little chance of getting this financer anyway, as they rarely take on small projects like ours, but I thought I'd use the opportunity as a test. So no pressure."

There it was. A chance to step up with no strings attached. Kayleigh had asked for more than he could give, but this—this he could do. He owed it to her and Chris to try. Perhaps after she saw how miserable he was at this social stuff, she'd agree to go with his other option. Remote partnership.

"What's the address and time?"

Her laugh rang out, and she threw her arms around him, the warm feel of her making him aware of how much he needed to keep his distance from this gorgeous woman. She was the last person he had a right to be attracted to. He pulled back and saw her embarrassed flush.

"I'm sorry. I—I shouldn't have done that." She scribbled the address and time on her notepad, ripped off the page and shoved it into his hand before standing.

"I think this is going to work better than you imagine, Chairman Mao."

A man opened the door behind them and tossed out the gray tiger.

"Who's that?" Kayleigh ruffled its ears and slid her hands along the cat's arching back as it rubbed against her leg.

He picked it up and stood. "Don't know. Just a stray."

Kayleigh kissed the feline's pink nose. "I think you should keep him. Call him…call him…Chairman Meow. You two will make a pair." Her eyes sparkled. "See you on Monday."

He was still watching when she turned the corner to the bus stop.

"This isn't going to end well," he warned the cat. When he set it down, it lived up to its name and meowed in agreement.

"Smart cat." He gave it a final rub, then stared at the last spot he'd seen Kayleigh before she'd rounded the street corner.

When he slipped inside his dim apartment, he smelled her perfume in the air, the scent making him rethink his isolation for the first time.

How many days until Monday?

CHAPTER EIGHT

"ARE YOU SURE I can't get you any coffee? Tea?" the Capital Central receptionist asked Niall again. Her arms rested on the countertop separating them, her red lips stretched in a wide smile.

He glanced at his phone. How long before Kayleigh arrived? She was five minutes late when she should have been fifteen minutes early. Not the right impression for a finance meeting.

"No, thanks." When the receptionist's fingers slid along his forearm, he stepped back. "My associate will be here soon."

"And her name is Kayleigh Renshaw?" The woman scanned her computer screen, tapped a few buttons, then peeked at him through her tangle of false eyelashes. "Sorry, but I still don't have a record of the appointment. I hope she can explain."

Niall nodded. He needed an explanation, too. After maneuvering him into this meeting, would Kayleigh miss it? Impossible. "Does Mr. Carlton have another meeting at this time?"

The secretary blew on her mug's rising steam and held his gaze for an uncomfortable minute. "Not for a half hour, but he did leave orders not to be disturbed. Perhaps he set up this consult and forgot to let me know." She shrugged off her cardigan to reveal a silky red shirt and leaned forward. "So tell me about yourself."

He slid a finger along his dress shirt's snug collar. "I'll be sitting over there." He pointed to the high-backed, upholstered chairs beside Mr. Carlton's office door and ignored her disappointed pout. "Please let me know if Ms. Renshaw calls."

After taking a seat, he leafed through a sports magazine, then tossed it back on the glass coffee table. Where was Kayleigh? He rechecked his phone for messages then stared down a cubicle-lined corridor at two sets of elevator doors, willing one to open.

Men and women garbed in navy, gray or black hurried by him, chatting to one another and carrying files. In the climate-controlled air, the scent of coffee, cologne and air freshener mingled. The large, open space hummed with ringing phones, squealing fax machines and copy machines spitting out papers, the atmosphere electric and purposeful. Yet there was only one sound he strained to hear—the chime of the elevator.

He peered at the silver-metal doors again. *Come on, Kayleigh. Let's get this dog-and-pony show started.* The quicker he fulfilled his end of the deal, tried the partnership her way, the sooner he'd get home and continue working on the code he'd started over the weekend. The presentation she'd sent him had intrigued him more than he would have thought, her ideas more complex than he'd imagined. He'd even designed a mock-up of the app, which, although it didn't include her direct input, came close to what he believed was her vision.

At last, the elevator jingled and a diminutive woman stepped out, her dark hair scraped into a bun that accentuated her fine features, a severe business suit doing little to mask her curves. His pulse sped. Kayleigh. He'd been looking forward to seeing her more than he'd realized. Despite the lack of windows, the room brightened.

Her smile flashed when she spotted him, her hesitant stride lengthening. As she passed him, she waved crossed fingers behind her back, and he marveled. She was happy to see him. Relieved by the look of it. She needed him.

Wanted him near, not just for his tech speak, but because he'd once been her friend.

The thought woke something inside him, and it unfurled like a sleepy cat, stretching until the whole of him felt more alive than he had any right to be. He rose quickly, ignoring the scrape of his prosthesis as it moved, loosely, against the sides of his knee.

When she leaned on the counter, he noticed her wiggle a small, arched foot out of her black shoe before sliding it in again, a red blister on her heel. Had she gotten stuck in traffic? Chosen to walk? At least she'd made it.

His good humor evaporated when he saw the receptionist tap her pen before laying it down with an irritated sigh. Yes. Kayleigh was late. But she still had a right to the time left in her appointment slot.

"I'm sorry, but I can't let you in without an appointment. And since I don't have you listed under your name, or your business name—" the woman scanned her computer screen and frowned down at Kayleigh's card "—High Dive Enterprises, I can't allow you to disturb Major Carlton." She picked up the pen. "I can leave him a note with your business card."

Niall raised an eyebrow at the business name, wondering at its significance, before his mind snagged on something more riveting.

"But I spoke with someone last week," Kayleigh said, a hand smoothing the wisps of hair falling out of her bun. "And I apologize for being late, but a delivery truck blocked traffic so I had to leave my cab and run the rest of the way."

"Did you call Mr. Carlton 'Major'?" Niall asked, joining them in three anxious strides and interrupting whatever the irritated receptionist had been about to say.

The woman peered up at him, her face softer than it'd been with Kayleigh. "Yes. Sometimes I slip up and call him that. He just got back from his army reserves tour in Afghanistan."

The information banded around his chest and made it hard to breathe. "And was he stationed in Kunar?"

Her eyes widened, and Kayleigh looked at him sharply. "Yes. Do you know him?"

"I was a signal combat officer in Kunar." As much as he hated bringing it up, if it got them beyond that closed door, he'd do what it took—for Kayleigh's sake.

"I see," said the secretary primly, her face relaxing into friendlier lines. "Did you serve with him?"

"No," he forced himself to say as he willed back thoughts of that time. "But he'd be disappointed if he knew a fellow officer, Lieutenant

Walsh, had been turned away at his office." Or at least, he guessed so. Either way, it was an excuse to get the receptionist to bend her rules. If it weren't for Kayleigh, however, he'd rather see anyone else. The ghosts of wartime past assailed him at every turn.

The secretary's eyes grew round. "Hold on. I'll call him."

Kayleigh's gentle tug steered him away from the hushed phone conversation. Her eyes were as dark as slate and wide with concern. "Did you meet him before—ah—" She gave his left leg a fleeting look, then her eyes flicked up again, as fast as quicksilver. "Before you were discharged?"

He shook his head, mute, a stillness in his body and a terrible silence clenched between his teeth. Memories slashed through him, so clean and sharp he had to be careful not to cut himself. Reflexively, he drew away from them the way he would have pulled back from a fire, but they trailed him anyway.

He'd been another man then, sure of his mission, himself, his life. Now he wasn't certain about anything except that he wanted out of here. Giving Kayleigh's partnership idea a try was a mistake. He worked from home to avoid these kinds of encounters that brought back his past.

Kayleigh steered him to a fichus tree and lowered her voice, her gentle, determined tone a portrait of her soul.

"Why don't you go? If the receptionist lets me in, I'll handle the meeting on my own and call you with the rundown later." She twisted a small gold watch, the band narrow on her delicate wrist. "Or I'll email you, if that's better. Okay?"

Her tender voice moved through the deep places in his chest when she spoke. Something in her decision not to push him, to put his needs ahead of hers, affected him. *No man left behind.* Conviction tightened within like a cold fist. He straightened his back and set his jaw. He'd see this through.

Before he could answer her, a door opened behind them and a voice boomed.

"Lieutenant Walsh! My secretary just let me know a fellow veteran was here. Sorry for the wait."

Niall turned, his body growing numb. It felt as though he were trying to think through syrup. His prosthetic dragged on the industrial carpet, and Kayleigh's hand gripped his, steadying him before she discreetly let go, her angled body shielding the momentary awkwardness. He advanced toward the man and extended a hand that was caught in a firm shake.

"Always happy to meet a brother in arms." Major Carlton clapped him on the elbow with his other hand before letting go. Niall studied the tall man, whose clipped, salt-and-pepper hair and sharp, ice-blue eyes commanded as much attention when he was in a suit as they must have when he wore a uniform. The major's smile revealed large ivory teeth.

Niall forced himself to return the grin and relax the tension that made every tendon strain and stretch. His time in Kunar flashed in his mind's eye, Chris's loss punching holes in his guarded mask.

"We appreciate your time, sir." He gestured to Kayleigh, who stepped up beside him, her shoulder touching his. "And this is my business partner, Kayleigh Renshaw. There's some confusion about our appointment, and we'd be grateful for a few minutes of your time."

"Of course. And pleased to meet you, little lady." He thrust out a hand to Kayleigh, then dropped it after a perfunctory shake. He turned and beamed at Niall, not seeing, as Niall did, Kayleigh's slight frown. "I wouldn't miss this opportunity to speak with another officer. Come right in."

He gestured for them to precede him, and

Niall suppressed a groan as he waited for Kayleigh to pass him. Trading war stories with Major Carlton was like tossing a grenade. One wayward throw and the careful life he'd constructed would explode.

Kayleigh marched by, her set jaw and closed-off expression ringing alarm bells. She seemed angry, yet she should know that the business world was all about connections. Major Carlton's attention toward him wasn't an insult to her, yet she seemed to be taking it personally.

"Have a seat," said the major, who paced behind his desk, grabbed a bowl of cashews and offered them. The room was lined with dark wood, floor-to-ceiling bookshelves, an impressive view of the New York Stock Exchange and ambient light that reflected off polished surfaces. It smelled of old leather, coffee and cigars, one of which was burning in an ashtray beside the phone. The no-smoking rule didn't apply to men at Major Carlton's level, it seemed. "Where were you stationed?"

"I was a signal combat officer in Kunar serving with the 3rd Brigade Combat Team, 10th Mountain Division." Niall tossed back a few of the salty nuts despite his churning gut, his eyes returning to Kayleigh.

She sat beside him with her ankles crossed and her hands tightly clutching the briefcase on her lap. Her skin was the color of moonlight. She could have been a statue of herself, her expression stony, her body rigid. He hadn't planned on taking center stage in this meeting, yet with a fellow veteran, what choice did he have? Was it bothering Kayleigh? Why, if the end result was the same?

The major pushed on a pair of dark-framed glasses and cleared his throat. "Glad you made it back from the field. We lost too many good men over there, but you landed on your feet."

Niall coughed uncomfortably and kept a firm grip on his expression. If this conversation thread would lead into a discussion of Niall's civilian life, he needed to nix it, fast. He'd lost his leg, flunked out of rehab and now scraped by doing remote IT work from home. End of story. Until Kayleigh…

"Of course, sir," he said nonchalantly, but it came out almost strangled. Time to steer this back to his partner. "Which is what brings us here. Ms. Renshaw has a presentation to show you about a revolutionary dating app. We wanted Capital Central to have the first chance at funding what promises to be a best-selling product."

He nudged Kayleigh, who seemed to give herself a shake before pulling her flash drive from her briefcase along with a presentation folder labeled with Capital Central's logo. Impressive. A nice touch. He gave her a sideways smile, but she appeared not to notice. Well. He'd done his job. Now it was time to back off and let Kayleigh shine.

"Yes. You see," Kayleigh began in a brusque voice, "market research, as is referenced in my report, demonstrates that a growing portion of those seeking a partner are using technological means to do so. Our app will capitalize on this trend by allowing customers to determine their compatibility with one another, beating website-based programs because of its mobility and real-time interactive quality."

Major Carlton brushed his upper lip with his finger before he began, slowly, to speak. "That sounds like a promising idea, Ms.—"

"Renshaw," Kayleigh supplied, her crisp voice more serious than Niall had ever heard it. Being around the officer shredded him. But Kayleigh must be struggling, too. She'd said this was a test, and he wanted her to pass. Yet with the major practically ignoring her and forgetting her name, she must feel that she was failing.

"Yes. Well." Major Carlton puffed on his cigar, then blew smoke over their heads, the earthy aroma bringing him back to his war days and the nervous smoking that had helped his buddies pass the time. "Unfortunately, I don't have the time to go over your plans today. But if you'll leave your materials with me, I'll give them the consideration they deserve."

A quiet sigh escaped Kayleigh, who stood and held out her hand, every inch the poised professional. "Thank you for this opportunity, and please accept my apologies for the appointment mix-up. I'll look forward to hearing from you."

Her voice was like a sheet of smooth slate, without the barest hint of inflection or emotion to betray her disappointment. Her control was impressive. She was more than the woman who believed in magic lists and perfect men. This was a savvy businesswoman who deserved more respect than the major—or he—had given her.

The major stubbed out his cigar and got to his feet. When Niall joined them, he pressed his hand on his traitorous prosthesis. So far, he'd avoided any pity from the major, and he meant to keep it that way.

"Some of us vets get together on Thursdays for poker. How about joining us?" Major Carlton arched his back in a stretch, the muscles in his arms straining against his dress shirt. Then he relaxed with an explosive sigh and tossed another handful of nuts in his mouth.

Niall could practically feel the heat coming off Kayleigh, and her white-knuckle grip on her briefcase betrayed her. She was peeved, and for good reason. The major had dismissed her like a subordinate, choosing instead to focus on games rather than business. Niall's unease dissolved into irritation.

"I'm hoping to win your investment, not poker chips," he joked, although he was dead serious.

Major Carlton's bray of a laugh echoed in the high-ceilinged room. "Losing money at cards is a lot more enjoyable." This time Kayleigh's disgusted exclamation was louder, though the major didn't seem to hear it. Instead, he glanced down at Kayleigh's business card, then up at Niall. "Is your number on here?"

"Not my personal number. You see—"

A clicking sounded as Major Carlton raised a pen. "The guys are getting together next week. I'll call you with the details." He pointed at Kayleigh's materials. "We'll talk more about your venture then."

Niall opened his mouth, then closed it, formulating a polite refusal that wouldn't give away his ire. This was Kayleigh's brainchild, not his. Yet the major was behaving as though he was the point man. And he couldn't have been more mistaken. Besides, dealing with another officer was bad enough. A night of listening to glory-filled war stories from other veterans was not going to happen.

"The best person to follow up with is—" he began, but Kayleigh interrupted and gave the major his number. He stared at her, alarmed at her tense, determined expression. Why was she going along with this farce?

The reservist jotted down the number, then tucked the paper in his pocket. "Thanks, little lady. You've hitched your wagon to a good one here." Niall cringed when the major gestured his way. "Signal combat officers are expert coders. Wouldn't have known what to do without mine." His blue eyes shot Niall's way. "Perhaps if this venture doesn't work out, we can talk about you coming to work with me."

"Thank you, but we'd appreciate your time in evaluating High Dive Enterprises's business proposal." He slid his flash drive across the desk, fuming. He didn't blame Kayleigh, but this was exactly why he worked from home. One meeting had morphed into a poker night and a possible job offer from the kind of person he'd hoped to never see again.

"This is some preliminary code work and a mock-up template of what the app might look like, though it hasn't been fully approved by my partner."

Kayleigh gasped, then covered her mouth and shot him a withering look that made him swallow. Hard. He should have run it by her first, or emailed it to her. She'd said she wanted to collaborate. Have an equal partnership. Yet he hadn't considered that in his rush to get this done for today's meeting. This gesture of his was as dismissive as Major Carlton, and he winced at the false impression it gave her.

The major barely glanced at it while he re-checked his pocket for Niall's number. "You'll be hearing from me soon." They followed him to the door, shook hands and strode to the elevator, where a tense silence grew between them.

When the metallic doors slid closed, Niall turned to Kayleigh. She was close enough that he could feel the warmth of her, yet her remote expression left him chilled.

"I'm sorry for not telling you about the app materials," he began, his hands gripping the side of the elevator since its lurch made him unsteady. "I finished up after midnight, but I still should have sent them to you. As for the major, I apologize for that, too. If I'd known an Afghanistan vet was Capital Central's CEO, I would have warned you to leave me out of this one."

She moved to the front of the enclosed space,

her shoulders stiff. "I think it went very well. You and Mr. Carlton can play poker and arrange the universe for the rest of us *little ladies.*"

He let go of the rail, stepped forward and gently turned her toward him. "We fought in the sarne war, Kayleigh. He was just being friendly. That's all. He'll give your proposal his attention, and when he makes his decision, you'll hear from him."

Her eyes were a sea in a storm, and he drowned in them. "And what about your prototype of my idea? What if he likes it? Wants to go with a version that had no input from me?"

He nodded. "That was stupid, and you're right. He shouldn't see anything we both haven't approved. I figured bringing it was the lesser of two evils, better than trying to cram in a last-minute meeting between the two of us."

An errant curl sprung free of her bun, and she flipped it back. "The lesser of two evils? You think a meeting between the two of us is an *evil?* Conferences are a part of business. I'd hoped that today would show you that, but it only confirmed what you know and I need to learn. It's not how hard you work. It's who you know. Enjoy your poker game. And your new job. As for me, I have a water-aerobics class to teach."

When the elevator doors chimed, Kayleigh strode onto the marble-floored foyer teaming with people, her heels clicking. He hurried after her, pushed his way through the revolving glass door then burst out onto the sidewalk, nearly losing her in the milling crowd.

"Kayleigh!" He felt his prosthetic slip farther and cursed it for acting up when he needed speed. He ignored the sharp pinch and pushed himself harder. "Wait."

"For what, Niall?" She whirled and waited for him to catch up to her. He stopped fast enough to make a man bearing shopping bags swerve. Her expression was thorny; her eyes as hard as iron nails. "Go play poker. Or don't. It doesn't matter. I'm calling the shots in my life, and I'm not waiting for you to make up your mind or anyone else. Goodbye."

A snap judgment had him catching her wrist through a closing tunnel of people. Her surprised gaze flew from their clasped hands to him.

He opened his mouth and struggled to speak, his thoughts snarled. He couldn't let her go. Reentering the work world, seeing a veteran, had been tough. Yet Kayleigh made him see life, and himself, differently.

A protective instinct to shield Kayleigh from others, like Major Carlton, who'd underestimated her, took hold. She had a decent business idea that could set her and Chris's family up for life. He should be there to help. And that wasn't possible, he now realized, by sitting on the sidelines at home.

When she wrenched free, his words tumbled out. "You don't have to wait. I'm in. On your terms. No remote partner. No doing things without both of us giving input. Okay?"

Her pained look made cold sweat pool at the base of his neck, despite the summer heat.

"I don't appreciate being kept in the dark about things."

Despite her firm tone, something about her expression reminded him of the day her parents announced their divorce and how their secret-keeping had destroyed her. If she ever learned the truth about Chris's death…

No. He pulled his mind back from that brink. Declassifications could take years. He would have helped her business get off to a solid start and returned to his old life by then.

"Everything will be aboveboard from now on."

He felt a stab of guilt at that white lie, but to say anything less wouldn't convince her to keep him. He'd attended the meeting to change her mind about doing things separately, but had his beliefs shaken instead. Kayleigh deserved a partner. A real one. Not someone like Major Carlton, who'd dismissed her, or like her fiancé, who'd stolen her ideas.

She needed someone she could count on, and he now understood why she saw him, her old friend, as that person. He knew, deep down, he couldn't go back to the man he'd been before the war. Kayleigh made him want to go forward. To find out what kind of man he could become. And he'd never discover that holed up in his apartment. Maybe someday, when she learned about Chris, he'd explain his reasons and she'd understand. Her forgiveness, however, he didn't expect.

When a child jostled her, she bumped into Niall and put a hand on his chest. They stood together for a long moment, his eyes searching hers until her lids lowered and she backed away. For a moment, he'd imagined taking her in his arms and kissing her. Crazy.

"I'll give that proposal the attention it deserves," she said before vanishing into the crowd.

"STRETCH THOSE ARMS, Mrs. Larson. Mr. Tanner, straighten your back," called Kayleigh thirty minutes later. All around her, seniors swirled in the pool. They were garbed in a variety of swimwear, from Mrs. Perry's swim dress and floral rubber cap to—her brain shuddered—Mr. Jennson's lime-green Speedo. Needless to say, she hadn't given him much direction in today's water-aerobics session.

The music switched up to "Jailhouse Rock," and Elvis's growl echoed off the white-tiled poolroom and competed with the splashing seniors. The strong smell of chlorine burned her nose, the warm water loosening the tension that had filled her since this morning's crushing meeting.

"Roll your shoulders now. Let's do ten backward. One..."

She counted down, moving her muscles rhythmically as her mind wandered. There'd only been a slim chance that a major investor like Capital Central would take on a small start-up like hers. Still, she'd hoped to test her presentation skills, something Brett had always discouraged her from doing. When she'd asked Niall along, she hadn't expected the old-boys' network to leave her on the outside—again.

"We've done more than ten," warbled Mrs. Larson, who shook her arms, then slid them in an arc in the water around her.

"Sorry! Ten frontward shoulder rolls," Kayleigh called, her mind already drifting as she executed the moves for the group she led each week.

She'd thought her biggest challenge with

Niall would be to convince him to get actively involved. It'd caught her flat-footed when he'd taken center stage and she'd been ignored instead. Major Carlton had practically offered Niall a job and had paid the bare minimum of attention to her proposal.

Worse yet, Niall had handed over a program prototype he hadn't shared with her. As friends, they'd always been open with each other, yet he'd kept her in the dark about this.

How could she trust Niall?

"Can we switch to something else?" groused Mr. Tanner, his face red and puffing, strands of white hair dripping in his eyes.

"How about some pelvic thrusts?" Mr. Jennson's lime-green Speedo was a blur beneath the blue water, and a few of the women giggled while Mrs. Perry splashed water in his face. "Looks like you need to cool off."

"Hey. Just trying to get some exercise!" sputtered Mr. Jennson.

"That's not all you're trying to get!" retorted Mrs. Perry, who sprayed him again for good measure.

Kayleigh held back a smile. It really was impossible to stay in a bad mood on water-aerobics day. She loved volunteering at Gramps's assisted-living facility. In some ways, she felt closer to the residents than she did—with the exception of Gramps, Beth and the boys—to her own family. Now that Niall had come back into her life, she wasn't sure where he stood—close like he had in the past, or far away. After this morning's debacle, it seemed like miles separated them. Would they ever get back to the way things used to be?

"Everyone hold out your arms and twist your hips." She eyed Mr. Jennson. "A twist is a side-to-side motion, Mr. Jennson. Not a front to back."

"You could come over and show me." He waggled his silver eyebrows while he swiveled his lower half in the pool.

"That's my granddaughter, Pete!" Gramps shouted, and she exchanged a smile with him, noting that he looked pink from the exertion, his blue eyes, so like Chris's, sparkling.

Hopefully, he wouldn't want a nap after the workout. She needed to talk to him, ask his advice. She'd thought Niall was the right partner for her business, but now she had doubts. She wasn't sure if he would support her or take over. Tell her everything or disclose only what he thought she needed to know. When Niall expressed no interest in brainstorming company names, she'd settled on High Dive Enterprises because she didn't want to play it safe anymore, letting others take charge.

"Hey! Who's that?" hollered one of the seniors, and she looked up, wiping the fog from her swim goggles, to see MaryAnne walking beside a tall, muscular man wearing navy swim trunks. His body was as lean and sleek as a greyhound's, his muscles shifting under his skin with an animal grace. The group stopped along with her and watched as he dropped his crutches on the floor ahead of him, then swung his body forward, his biceps straining. Something fluttered into her throat and lodged there.

"This is my brother, Niall Walsh," MaryAnne called out. "Kayleigh invited him here to volunteer. He had a bit of trouble finding the center, but he's here now, so let's welcome him."

Kayleigh's astonished gaze flew from a sheepish Niall to a beaming MaryAnne, who was clearly oblivious to the fact that she'd been tricked into letting Niall in. Another fabrication. She met his eyes, his dark coloring contrasting with the white walls behind him. Why was he here? What did he want? She'd told him she'd be in touch, yet it seemed as though he didn't want to wait. She crossed her arms. Here he was, calling the shots again, deciding what was best for her.

A chorus of "Hi, Niall!" rose from the pool as several seniors, especially the women, waded to the edge and ogled him, their eyes wide enough to swallow him whole.

He nodded and, after waving aside MaryAnne's help, lowered himself to the side of the pool and dipped in his right leg, the stump of his left leg appearing at the edge of his trunks. It was her first real glimpse of his injury, and something softened inside her as she absorbed the fact that he'd exposed himself to seek her out.

Was he here to convince her that he was all in? If so, he was taking it literally. He shot her a wry look, slid into the water and dunked his head under. When he came up, water slicked back his dark hair. Droplets clung to his eyelashes and, for a moment, she found it hard not to stare. She forced her eyes away when she reminded herself that friends didn't look at each other like that. Or at least, they hadn't before…

"What moves do you have for us, Niall?" called Gramps, his all-knowing look flickering between her and her new water-aerobics partner.

Niall gestured her way. "I'm just here to support Kayleigh and anyone else who needs some help."

Several female hands waved in the humid air, and MaryAnne snorted before sauntering out of the room, the double doors making a loud click shut behind her.

"Ladies, take your places," Kayleigh said firmly, and pushed through the water toward Niall.

"What are you doing here?" she asked under her breath, working not to let her smile slip. "Let's all march forward ten steps, then backward ten steps." Her docked iPod shuffled to a Beach Boys' tune, and the group stepped mostly in sync.

"Like I said, I'm all in." Niall bobbed as he jumped forward the ten steps then backward alongside her.

"I told you I'd contact you," she huffed, and ignored his hurt expression to point at Mrs. Larson. "You're out of step, Mrs. Larson."

"So is Grace. She's all over Frank." Her grandfather's ladylove put her hands on her hips and pursed her lips.

"Everyone is too close to Frank, according to you, Annette!" shouted Mrs. Perry, who seemed to stumble, then batted her eyelashes when Gramps steadied her.

"You can march with me, Annette." Mr. Jennson put out his arms, and Mrs. Larson doused him with water.

"In your dreams, Pete."

"Only my best ones." Mr. Jennson blew her a

kiss, and she turned away and scowled at Mrs. Perry and Gramps.

Kayleigh couldn't help but return Niall's lopsided smile, her breath hitching as the amused glimmer in his eyes brought out their gold flecks. What was it about him that affected her this way lately? This new awareness made no sense and would be disastrous to their business relationship. If they still had one.

"Let's shuffle ten steps to the left, then back ten steps," she instructed, mirroring the move, impressed that Niall didn't miss a beat. He leaped alongside her, raising his powerful arms over his head and lowering them in time to the music. There was something endearing about his presence there, his strong, silent support of her.

"You don't have to do this," she murmured when he passed close.

He considered her for a moment. "Yes, actually. I do."

She forced herself to act nonchalant although she wondered what he meant. With a shrug of her shoulders, she continued the class and ended with a freestyle cooldown. Mr. Jennson finished with a flourish and spun Mrs. Larson until both she and Gramps protested. Sheesh. Middle-school drama had nothing on assisted-living facility antics.

The medical aides arrived and helped the residents from the pool. She waved to Mary-Anne, who was supervising, then watched as her grandfather limped away, Mrs. Larson frantically gesturing beside him. With a sigh, she turned to face Niall, but noticed he'd already pulled himself up to the edge of the pool.

He extended a hand. "Want some help?"

She ignored the offer and hoisted herself up beside him, the backs of her thighs scraping against the rough cement border. Her heartbeat pounded in her ear and she waited, wondering what he'd come here to say.

After a long moment, the silence grew between them. A tangible presence. "I'm sorry, Kay," he said at last.

"For what, exactly?" Her foot made an angry swirl in the water. It wasn't that she couldn't think of anything to accuse him of. She thought of too much. She needed him to say it.

His arms made a sweeping, overhead gesture. "For being rude, dismissive, offhand, inconsiderate and, basically, a jerk."

She couldn't hold in a smile. "Go on," she said, her mood lifting. It was nice to hear him own up to his wrongs—but did he really understand what he'd done or hadn't done?

Niall nodded, dark strands sticking to his angular jaw. "I'm not around people much lately.

Talking isn't something I do often and—" he rubbed the back of his neck and sent her an apologetic look "—not something I do well. I'm not sure what else you need to hear, but I'd say it if I knew."

"Some would say that's a matter of practice."

He caught her eye and held it. "I agree."

She studied a red caution sign above the exit door, glad for the reminder. "Look, Niall. I don't understand your change of heart, but even if you're all in, I'm not sure anymore how this would work. You're used to doing things your way, and I've spent too much time doing things other people's way. I can't follow that route again. I won't." Her voice trembled despite her attempt to sound confident.

The cool air on her wet shoulders made her shiver, and Niall wrapped his towel around her. "Here. I don't need it."

She handed it back. "No, Niall. You don't get it. I don't want you to come to my rescue. I'm not looking for a knight in shining armor. If I were a princess, I'd save myself."

Niall's leg circled in the water, making a mini whirlpool. "So tell me what a nonprincess needs," he said at last.

"Someone who brings out the best in me, supports me, values my opinion and, most of all, is honest with me."

"I'll do that, Kay." He looked sincere, and his insistent tone undid the wall she'd placed between them. "As much as I can. Let's set up our base of operations in my apartment, and we'll meet there tomorrow. I've got some things for us to go over, and nothing's final until we both approve." He pulled off her swim goggles, then trailed the backs of his fingers down the side of her face until they fell away.

Her breath hitched. That didn't feel like a "friendly" touch. And it definitely crossed professional boundaries. So why did she want him to do it again? To let his hand linger so she could press her cheek into his palm.

"We'll disagree at times. But I won't let anyone, like Major Carlton, act like you don't exist again."

She shook her head, trying to get her thoughts back on track. "I didn't think you'd noticed."

He studied his wrinkled fingertips, then lifted his eyes to hers, their tortured depths doing something funny to her heart. "I notice you, Kayleigh," he said quietly, almost to himself. "More than I should."

CHAPTER NINE

COOL AIR FROM the north had swept in overnight, leaving the morning fresh and dewy soft, the blue skies dotted with cirrus clouds that scuttled wherever the breeze blew them. Kayleigh could have floated, too, as she strolled through sycamore tree shadows on her way to Niall's apartment.

The weather, suited to fresh beginnings, energized her. Now that her partner was fully invested, she couldn't wait to get started. Once they secured financing, she'd breathe easier still. Most of all, she couldn't deny how glad she was to have Niall back in her life. Spending this time with him was filling up a part of her that had lain empty since Chris's death.

A loud bark jolted her from her thoughts, and she sidestepped the man and terrier she'd spotted yesterday. She paused to let a group of girls playing double Dutch jump rope finish, enjoying watching the game she and her friends had once played.

After a moment, she sauntered on, more

excited than she'd ever been for a business meeting. Was she looking forward to getting started, seeing Niall or both? Her mind shied away from the question. After yesterday's disastrous finance meeting, this was the boost she needed. Nothing more.

She unlatched his gate, climbed his stairs and buzzed his apartment. 9:00 a.m. A smile tugged at the corners of her mouth when the door vibrated instantly. He'd been waiting for her. Possibly anxious, too? She placed a hand over the thudding in her chest before pulling open the door and stepping inside.

I notice you. More than I should.

Niall's words returned to her as she started up the stairs, a shivering awareness dancing through her. Of course, he was right. They shouldn't notice each other. Attraction was wrong on every level. There was, of course, the old adage not to mix business with pleasure—a lesson she'd learned the hard way with Brett. Second, she was not the type of woman to jump from one man to another. She wanted to make it on her own and be an equal with a colleague, nothing more.

Her hand stilled on the first-floor landing's banister. Yet something about Niall's poolside admission, its raw honesty, had cut through her and melted her heart. Did she want more from him than friendship?

Impossible. She was mixing up the closeness she'd felt for him as a friend with this strange new attraction. One she needed to quash. Having Niall back in her life was a gift. If she gave in to her fledgling feelings and a romantic relationship between them didn't work, there was a chance—a big chance—that he'd vanish from her life forever.

No. She needed him as her business partner and as her friend. The part of her that wanted him on another level would have to do without.

She nodded to a man carrying a pair of inline skates and continued her climb. One thing was absolutely certain. She and Niall were in the business of helping others find love, not falling in love themselves.

Niall's door was ajar when she reached the second floor. He stood there, the top of his head just inches from the jamb.

"Good morning." The deep timbre of his voice unsettled her, and she clutched her bag of brownies. "You look nice."

She glanced down at her white capri pants and the rose-colored top that matched her lipstick. She had gone to a lot of trouble with her appearance for an informal meeting, even straightening her hair. "Thanks."

She did her best to ignore the clean, soapy smell of him as she neared, and the devastating way his turquoise polo shirt set off his coloring and lean torso. When she ducked under his arm, she pulled up short at his transformed apartment.

Every surface shone. A single newspaper lay on his otherwise uncluttered coffee table. A peek into his kitchen revealed a sink free of dishes and the percolating sound of a coffeemaker at work.

"You cleaned."

The locks turned with a metallic click and Niall joined her. "You mentioned bringing over office supplies, so I thought I'd get the place ready." He shrugged, and his eyes slid her way, his lopsided grin appearing. "Since I'm also the *office* custodian, do I get extra pay?"

She handed him the baked goods. "Will these do?"

When he opened the bag, his lids lowered and he inhaled deeply. "Barter works for me. These smell great. I'll check on the coffee."

She watched him disappear into the kitchen, touched. He'd said he was all in, and it looked as if he meant it.

"Set your stuff next to my computer." A current of excitement ran through Niall's offhand words. She swung her head around for a quick survey, and what she saw made her melt. He'd moved some of his hardware to the floor and cleared a desk for her. Her chest swelled. How sweet and thoughtful. Her old friend was back. Maybe now she'd be able to stop the traitorous thoughts that maybe he could be something more.

"This is great." She unpacked her supplies then froze when she saw a folded piece of paper with the words *Kayleigh—I like hamsters* printed on it.

She laughed, despite her efforts to maintain business decorum. But how could she resist? They were the words she'd once written on her summer camp name badge. Niall had remembered.

"I like my nameplate," she called, setting the Number One Aunt plaque Josh had given her next to it. "Very official."

Niall returned with a plate full of the brownies. "I thought it set the proper tone for High Dive Enterprises," he said solemnly, humor sparkling behind his long lashes.

She pressed her lips together and nodded. "Of course. How thoughtful of you, Mr. Walsh." She scribbled his name on a notepad, added his former camp introduction information and handed the folded paper to him. "Pizza Connoisseur."

He placed it beside his monitor. "Think nothing of it, Ms. Renshaw, Rodent Enthusiast."

Their light laughter rose then fell, and in its wake a silence descended that left them staring at each other for a long breathless moment.

"We should get to work—"

"The coffee must be almost finished—"

They spoke simultaneously then hurried off, Niall to grab mugs and Kayleigh to finish arranging her things on her new desk, contentment filling her. Minutes later, she placed her family picture beside her name card and stepped back to study the effect.

"I got some good news in the mail yesterday," she called, just to fill the quiet air between them.

The smell of something strong and Colombian announced Niall's approach. "What was it?"

"Senator Gillibrand is going to make higher-level inquiries into declassifying Chris's death. It's the furthest I've gotten with a politician, and she has a reputation for keeping her promises."

A harsh intake of breath sounded. Not so much a gasp as a long inhale through the nose. When she turned, Niall's face was white, and he swallowed hard enough to make his Adam's apple bob.

"Are you okay?" She took the mugs from him and guided him into the living room. They sat. Or she sat, rather. Niall's knees simply buckled.

He passed a shaking hand over his face. "Fine."

She lowered his hand and held it, concern filling her. "Liar. What upset you?"

His eyes flickered toward the desk and lingered before they dropped. "Don't mind me. Let's start the meeting."

"Is it Chris?"

Niall blanched, paler still. "What?"

"Does he remind you of Afghanistan?" It seemed like a loose connection, but it was the best she could come up with.

He nodded curtly, his expression pained as he gazed toward his curtained-off windows, where the drooping spider plant hung. Did Niall appreciate its reputation for hardiness? Relate to it? He may have survived, but he hadn't escaped the war unscathed. She should be sensitive to that.

She briskly strode to her desk and slipped the picture back into her briefcase. It'd go on her nightstand, Chris's encouraging smile the first thing she'd see when she woke. Better there than reopening old wounds for Niall. She headed into the kitchen, heart heavy that she'd gotten their meeting off to a bad start. After turning off the tap, she returned to the plant and dumped in a glass of water. Like its owner, it needed tending.

Niall's rigid shoulders lowered. "You don't have to put away that picture for me, Kay."

"I'm putting it away for both of us. We need to focus all of our attention on High Dive Enterprises. Think about the future, not the past. Starting now."

His face relaxed, and he leaned back on the sofa. "How did you come up with that name?"

She fumbled for the curtain cord and spoke without looking up. "Remember how you taught me to dive that summer at camp?"

"How could I forget?" To her relief, Niall's voice sounded normal again. "You practically gouged the board with your toenails before you let go of my hand and leaped."

Her fingers found the string, and she yanked, the curtains parting with a swish. "Exactly. That's what this start-up is for me. Letting go. Beginning again. Not playing it safe."

"Could you close those, please?"

She turned to one of the side windows in the three-window combination and parted the material, letting sunlight flood the dim room.

"Nope. We need light, Niall, just like that

plant. To grow. I won't work in the dark and neither should you."

He was quiet for a moment as she searched for the last curtain pull. "Okay. But consider this my first business compromise."

"First of many, I hope." She tugged, and the last curtain opened to reveal a small gray tabby cat on the fire escape. Its little mouth opened when it spotted her, the black pads of its paws pressed against the glass.

"It's Chairman Meow!"

Niall raised one eyebrow and cocked his head. "Who?"

She threw the sash up and struggled with the screen. The kitty's meows sounded hungry. "Help me, Niall."

"With what?" He began organizing paperwork into piles.

"We need to let in the cat."

"No." He joined her at the window and looked from the young cat to her. "Pets aren't allowed in the building, and this is just a stray. It doesn't belong to anyone."

"Hold on, Chairman Meow," she huffed, ignoring him as she strained to pull up the screen.

"Are we getting any work done this morning?" He sighed behind her.

She wiped her damp brow. “Once we give the cat a meal.”

Niall mumbled something about pushy women, nudged her aside and yanked the stuck screen. In an instant, a silver blur flashed through the air, landing on his chest.

“Hmmmph.” Niall stumbled backward when the feline climbed onto his shoulder.

“Chairman Meow thinks he belongs to you.”

“As we say in the IT world, that’s invalid data.” His muffled voice sounded through the feathery tail lashing across his face. “Can you help me with this?” He pulled the cat, but its nails were embedded in his shirt.

Oh, this was too rich. Niall, the bitter recluse, had been chosen by one of the most adorable strays she’d ever seen. “Sorry. I think Chairman Meow is now a permanent appendage.”

A helpless expression crossed his face. “I don’t want this cat.” A loud purring erupted as the animal butted its head into Niall’s neck.

It was hard not to laugh at a large man held captive by a tiny creature. “I don’t think you have a choice.”

“Please, Kay. Help.”

“Fine. But you are not tossing out that cat.”

When Niall gave her a noncommittal shrug, she filled a bowl with milk and returned, placing it on the floor by an end table. After rubbing Niall's cheek with the side of its face, the cat jumped away for the treat, its pink tongue darting in and out of the liquid.

She clasped her hands in her lap, itching to pet the stray. "I wonder if it's a girl or boy."

"A boy." Niall brushed cat hair off his shirt. "We got a bit intimately acquainted while you were gone."

She fought back a smile at his misery. "Hopefully, you won't need years of therapy now."

"Possibly." Niall raised his mug, his eyes laughing over the brim. "Can we start now?"

"If we must." Kayleigh gave an exaggerated sigh, then grabbed her briefcase. She started up her minilaptop and sipped her coffee while waiting for the desktop folders to open, furtively studying Niall as he got settled behind his own keyboard. He'd been an easygoing kid who'd turned into a hard-bitten man. Yet more and more, she saw flashes of the boy who'd made her laugh, and now a man who attracted her to no end.

She halted her wayward thoughts and opened a document labeled Must Traits. "I thought we could go over these, make a preliminary list for you to begin programming."

Niall nodded and drank more of his coffee. "Mind if I have a brownie while we look?"

"Of course. Gianna, my roommate, made them this morning to shake off last night's bad date. Some guy cut her steak for her at dinner then used baby talk to ask for a kissy-wissy." She grabbed a napkin and placed the chocolate square on it. *Poor Gianna. She really had the worst luck.*

"Baby talk, huh? Don't imagine that'll make our Must Traits list. And I'll have two, thanks." Niall held out a broad palm. When their eyes met, her mind went as blank as fresh paper.

The corners of his mouth quirked. "Unless you want them all to yourself?"

His prompt shook her out of her vegetative state. He should be careful when he smiled that way. It reached his eyes and transformed his handsome face into something special. Something that made her heart thump in a way that could not be construed as "friendly."

"Oh. Yes. Two coming up." She handed over the desserts and bit into one herself, the moist, dense bar melting on her tongue. It was her third of the day, but who was counting? She'd start her diet tomorrow. As usual.

His broad shoulder brushed hers as he leaned close and peered at the Must Traits document. "I have the latest version of this, correct?" His breath was warm against the back of her neck, making goose bumps rise over her whole body.

When Chairman Meow looked up from his milk, droplets of white clinging to his long whiskers, she scratched his sweet little head. It was a welcome distraction. She could hardly breathe for the nearness of Niall, the way he moved, the sound of his voice as it touched the air around them.

"It was with the original materials."

Niall lowered his brownie, his expression thoughtful. "Number twenty-three, forty-five, sixty-two and eighty are redundant, twelve doesn't make sense, and ninety-one through one hundred are unnecessary." He sipped his coffee then said, "In fact, if we could get this list down to twenty-five essential traits, it'd be more user-friendly."

She stopped stroking the kitty's arching back and gaped at him. "Every one of those is crucial."

"Dogs are mentioned three times. 'Must love dogs,' 'Must love big dogs,' 'Must love my dogs.' And cats are used five times. 'Must love cats,' 'Must own a cat,' 'Must have once owned a cat,' 'Must be willing to own a cat' and 'Must be willing to clean cat litter.'"

After swallowing another bite of brownie, she scooped up Chairman Meow and held him up before giving him a cuddle. "See how special he is? Like I said. Each one has an important nuance that is essential to finding the right person. A forever person. Your only love."

A strange expression came over Niall's face, and he seemed to look deep into her, not into her eyes, but through her eyes. As if he could see the thoughts clamoring to betray her. She glanced down then up again, finding it hard to look away.

"And you're certain your app will do this," he said, his face serious. "Help people find true love?"

Her hand stilled on Chairman Meow's white belly, earning her a prickly swat. She gave an emphatic nod. "Of course. Don't you agree?"

Niall frowned a bit. "No. I see it as a fun conversation starter, more or less."

She scowled. "So you're saying our product is some kind of joke? That users won't take it seriously? What's on your list? The one you made at camp. You believed in it then."

The question seemed to catch Niall unprepared. He sat still and awkward for a moment, his eyes scanning the room as if searching for a way out. Finally, he shook his head.

"I was a kid."

"But you'll make one now, of course." She added it to her to-do list so that she wouldn't forget to look for it.

"No." Niall waved Chairman Meow's tail

as the cat batted at it. "I compromised about the windows and the cat. But I'm not making a list."

Disappointment filled her. How closed off could he be? Sheesh. She was right to be firm with herself about not falling for him. They were great as friends, but couldn't be less compatible romantically—with or without a list, it was obvious.

After a long moment, Niall drew a deep, slow breath. "We're better off using traits from your list or ones we get from market samples."

Her eyes narrowed. "And why is that?"

He tilted his face, one corner of his mouth lifting in a wry half smile that didn't reach his eyes. "I don't exactly fall into your target audience." His stiff shoulders shrugged. "I'm not looking to meet someone."

"Oh." A heavy weight settled in her chest. Although her heart still broke when she thought of Brett, she knew that someday she'd be ready for romance. Something in Niall's tone, however, sounded bleak and definite, as if he didn't think he'd ever love anyone. Or worse, that anyone would ever love him.

In a breathless second, she almost asked him why he'd never consider love. She felt the question rising in her chest, drew in air then, hesitated. What could she say that wouldn't sound too personal? Take things to an intimate level that might endanger their fragile partnership? "Well, then, I think we should plan some market testing. I'll conduct some studies with people of various age groups and have the data back to you in a few days."

Chairman Meow arched his slim body before crouching for a leap that landed him on Niall's lap.

Niall studied the cat, then, with a shrug, ran his large hand over its ears, one of which was permanently bent at the tip. "Have you thought of promotional events? Places? People?"

"You met some of them." His closeness was sweet and sharp, making it hard to focus. Her fingers slid along the length of the tail whipping between them as she gathered her scattered thoughts. "The assisted-living facility residents."

He whistled, looking impressed. "I wasn't expecting that, but it'd work." An eyebrow arched. "Mr. Jennson would be an interesting target audience."

She bit back a smile. "Think of all of those singles living together, yet many having never dated more than one or two people in their lives. We could help them, and they could help us."

Niall nodded thoughtfully. "I like that. Their

Must Traits data will help us finalize the list. Once we have a prototype created, let's plan an event there, too."

Excitement bubbled. "Yes." She scratched the item off her to-do list. They'd made their first business decision together. It felt good. A step in the right direction for them. For High Dive Enterprises.

"Now, back to streamlining your Must Traits list."

His words made her heart sink. She'd wanted them to make joint decisions, but when it came to her list…? Her gaze lingered on his animated expression as he began to argue his case. At least she had a partner. She needed to give him a chance.

"So you see how the animal questions could be condensed to 'Must love dogs' and 'Must love cats,'" Niall said. "If they answer yes to those, the rest is a given."

She pulled her brownie away from a sniffing Chairman Meow. "I suppose," she admitted. He had a valid point. "But I don't see how anyone can misconstrue number one."

"'Must be open'? That's confusing. Open to what? BASE jumping? Learning to cook Thai food? Mimes?" Niall flinched when the cat climbed up his chest and wrapped itself around his shoulders and neck. "And I think Chairman Meow is part boa constrictor."

She leaned forward. "Let me help." She pried the cat's tail loose only to watch it encircle Niall's neck again. "I think you're going to have to accept your slow and inevitable death."

"Smothered by a cat." He blew some fur covering his mouth. "That'd be an interesting obituary. Anyway, back to number one."

"You're taking that trait too literally. I mean open as in emotionally, ready to accept and give love, to express how they feel. Not hide things." She bundled her hair into a loose bun, feeling warm under his scrutiny.

"That wouldn't translate well into a program like this." When he shook his head, his hair swished across his brow. "It's too vague. Concrete traits work best."

"You'll need to figure out how to make it work. It stays." She folded her hands on her lap and met his eyes. There was compromising and there was giving up her entire vision. She wouldn't do the latter.

"It's hard for you to get rid of it, but—"

"Why is this hard for me?" She frowned, her temperature rising. "You're the one who doesn't understand how to translate *open*."

"I understand that it won't work."

She ground her teeth. Before she could

think, she blurted, "Niall, you've closed yourself off from people and even yourself. And I get it, given everything you've gone through. But for some people, not being *open* is a deal breaker. It is for me."

Niall pulled the cat from his neck and placed it on the floor, his expression stunned. For a second she caught a glimpse of his dark brown eyes. Then he glanced away, shifting restlessly. In the awkward silence, her cell phone rang, Beth's image appearing on her screen. She brought it to her ear.

"Oh, thank God. Can you come over right away?" Beth's voice sounded high and panicked, and Kayleigh's pulse leaped. "Samuel and Josh got in a shoving match while I was changing one of the kid's diapers. Long story short, Samuel fell and hit his head, and now I think he has a concussion. Only I can't take him to the hospital because I have the children I babysit here, and Josh has locked himself in his room."

Kayleigh was already on her feet. "I'll be right there." She clicked off her phone. "We'll have to finish this another time. Beth has an emergency."

To her surprise, Niall followed her to the door after he placed the cat back out on his fire escape and shut the window.

"What are you doing?" she asked.

He grabbed his keys from a ring by the door. "Coming with you."

She waved him away. He'd reacted so strongly to Chris's picture. How would he handle an apartment full of them? "I've got this. You don't have to put yourself out."

He pulled open the door, his face serious. "Maybe I need to, Kay."

CHAPTER TEN

"OH, THANK GOODNESS, you're here," Niall heard Beth say when her Park Slope apartment door swung open. She gestured for them to enter, her eyes widening as he passed her in the narrow entranceway.

Inside, the air smelled of burned toast while cartoon voices floated down a short hall that led to a large, bright living room. Niall peered at a few children jostling each other at a plastic carpenter's workbench while others banged out discordant notes on musical instruments or zoomed on miniature tricycles.

His heartbeat drummed as he glanced around Chris's former home, fighting the urge to leave. Chris should be here. Not him. Guilt bit his gut, but he ignored it, needing to stay for Chris's family, for Kayleigh and—as she'd pointed out—for himself. On the bus ride over, he'd questioned his impulsive decision. What difference could he make? Kayleigh had said he was closed off, incapable of being open. And while he knew she was right, accepted it, something about her accusation had spurred him to action for reasons he couldn't figure out. He'd been comfortable in his insular world until Kayleigh came along. Now he didn't know what he felt or wanted.

Niall caught a questioning look between Beth and Kayleigh before Beth turned and gave him a tired smile.

"Thanks for coming," she said, hitching Samuel higher on her hip. The boy clung to her side, his legs wrapped around her waist, his head buried in her neck. Beth bounced on the balls of her feet, making the boy's lids snap open.

"Hi, soldier," Samuel slurred when he spotted Niall, raising his hand as they edged into the small kitchen. Low-hanging cabinets dominated the windowless space, a light fixture with one working bulb the only illumination. Beth should replace the bulbs, but with her hands full, chores like that probably fell to the bottom of her list. Regret filled Niall. As a single mother, Beth had to work twice as hard to keep her family afloat. At least she had Kayleigh, and now...him.

"How are you feeling, little man?" Niall tousled Samuel's dark hair and felt an egg-size bump above his left ear. It had to hurt, but the kid wasn't complaining. Admiration mingled with concern. The boy was as tough as his father, and war memories, sharp as a mouthful of glass, returned.

He caught sight of a drawing clipped to the fridge that depicted the boys and their mother, a stick figure with wings, labeled *Dad* flying above them. Sudden anxiety tied knots in his stomach. Was he ready for this?

"Can I take a nap now?" When Samuel angled his neck to look up at his mother, he winced and clutched his head. "Ouch."

"Not yet, sweetie." Kayleigh dropped her briefcase on the linoleum floor and smoothed her hand over the boy's red cheek, her fingers slow and deliberate. "Mommy needs to take you to the doctor."

"I don't want to go." Samuel's large eyes filled with fear. "Why do I have to go?"

"Because I'm all out of lollipops and Dr. Stein has the best ones." Beth tickled Samuel's curved belly, and his eyes brightened, his missing front tooth showing in a wide grin.

"I want a green one." His fingers twirled his mother's light brown curls.

"You can have all of the green ones they have as long as you're good. No sticking your hand in the fish tank." Beth's stern tone was offset by the kiss she pressed to his forehead.

Samuel returned her kiss with a loud smacking sound. "I'm always good. Josh is mean."

"You're both good, but Josh, well, he sometimes makes mistakes," Beth said cautiously, her eyes darting to a wall across the narrow hall. "And I'm sure he's sorry."

"Not sorry!" screamed a muffled voice from behind the wall. A thumping kick rattled an unseen door that Niall guessed opened onto another hall to the left. He shook his head at the flimsy materials that partitioned these older homes. Too bad the thin barrier let Josh hear the exchange.

"See! He hates me." Samuel's eyes watered, and when he brought his thumb to his mouth, Beth caught and kissed it, her expression stricken.

"He doesn't hate you." Kayleigh cupped the youngster's soft chin, the tender gesture doing something funny to Niall's heart.

A young boy wearing a Yankees cap tugged on Beth's pants. "Mrs. R! Austin smells bad."

"Poopy diaper! Poopy diaper! Poopy diaper!" a girl's voice chanted from the living room.

Beth made as if to lower Samuel, but the boy tightened his hold around her neck and a small choking sound escaped her.

Kayleigh handed Beth her purse. "We've got

this. Take Sam. Niall and I will stay as long as you need. We're a good team." Her eyes met his, and they stared at each other for a breathless moment. Finally, she smiled at his jerky nod. "Don't worry about a thing."

A rush of air left Beth. "Thank you, Kay." She whirled at the door, her eyes darting toward him. "Both of you. I appreciate this. The kids get lunch in a half hour, then nap time after that. Hopefully, I'll be back before they wake. I called the parents, so some might pick up their children. To be on the safe side, check IDs and, ah, I think that's it."

"We'll keep them safe," Niall assured her, liking the sound of *we.* Once again, his eyes met Kayleigh's. She'd called them a team, and her word brought back a forgotten sense of belonging, a feeling of being wanted, necessary.

It was like realizing he hadn't eaten all day, the rushing sensation of need taking him by surprise.

Beth stepped outside then turned again, her features pinched. "Oh—a couple more things. Kayleigh, your mom happened to call when all this was going on, and I haven't been able to phone her back. If you get a chance, could you let her know the grandkids are okay? And don't worry about Josh. He's fine in his room. I would have sent him there as punishment anyway, minus the video games. But since the door is locked, just let him play them. I'll talk to him when I get back." Her voice turned fierce, and she gripped her sister-in-law's arm. "Kay, we need to get him in the anger-management program."

Kayleigh gave Beth and Samuel a hug. "One thing at a time, okay? Everything will work out."

Beth stared upward for a moment, then pressed her lips together before nodding. Niall's hands tightened at his sides. He wished there was something he could say or do to reassure her about Josh. He was an angry kid. And he had a right to be. Life had dealt him a bad hand, and it pulverized Niall's insides to think that he was responsible.

The dark-haired beauty beside him shifted. When her arm grazed his, the small hairs on his skin rose. Kayleigh was loyal. Always had been. Until she was able to provide for her nephews, she would never quit. And he'd make sure she succeeded. He could help that way.

Beth wavered outside, her pale face as troubled as he suddenly felt. What if Senator Gillibrand got the declassification request approved before he finished the app? He shot an anxious glance Kayleigh's way and couldn't return her reassuring nod.

His body temperature dropped, and he grew numb. If they knew the truth about him and Chris, they'd kick him out of their lives. Kayleigh would be left with an unfinished product and a failed start-up. Beth would face even more financial struggles.

In the end, he grabbed a set of keys on the counter and handed them to Beth, his mind racing. He had to write the program fast. It was his way of being loyal. Supportive. Making amends, although that was only a small part of it. This wasn't about him. It was about helping his friend and a troubled family he was coming to care about.

Kayleigh gave Beth a gentle shove. "Go. We've got this."

Niall eyed the chaos in the living room and hoped so. The door had barely clicked shut before Kayleigh disappeared into the screaming hoard of kids. He trailed behind her, assessing the scene.

The sounds of the quarrelling children brought his childhood back to him. Hadn't his six siblings and he acted like this? Aiden had taken charge when he'd been twenty-one, and although he'd been young, he'd done his best. Looking back, Niall felt a new appreciation for his bachelor brother who'd given up so much to keep the family and their business together.

"Do you think you can handle them while I change him?" Kayleigh waved her arm at the milling children while she held a crying infant—Austin, he guessed. At his nod, she shot him a relieved look, mouthed, "Sorry" and headed for a back room.

The din grew louder still as two children screamed and pulled on opposite ends of a stuffed dinosaur while white fluff snowed from its arm. Another youngster grabbed the TV remote and ran from a screeching pursuer. One of the "musicians" repeatedly slammed a xylophone onto the varnished oak floor, making Niall's ears ring.

"Attention!" he said with a quiet, carrying authority that instantly silenced the group. The stuffed animal bounced to the ground, and the racing children skidded to a halt.

"Sit," he commanded, the familiar mantle of an older sibling settling over him. He'd frequently taken charge of the smaller Walshes when Aiden and MaryAnne had tended to the pub downstairs. The six kids scrambled to the floor and sat with crossed ankles.

A thin arm shot in the air, and he studiously ignored it. After a moment of eyeing each of the children until they stopped squirming, he nodded curtly to the waving girl.

"Are you the president?" A giggle wove

through her high-pitched voice, a polka-dotted ribbon unraveling around one of her uneven pigtails.

He bit back a laugh but couldn't stop the twitch that lifted the corners of his mouth.

"No. But I—I—" The feeling of levity vanished when he realized what he'd been about to confess.

"You're a soldier!" the boy in the baseball hat piped up, guessing the ending of Niall's unfinished sentence. The kid slid onto his knees then tucked his hands beneath his thighs. "That's why you said *attention*." He turned to the pigtailed girl beside him. "They all say that in the movies."

"Can we play war?" A freckled boy with bright red hair dug in his ear then examined his finger. "Everyone here is my prisoner."

"I want to be a Green Beret!" shouted a girl with hair so fine it seemed to float around her like a golden halo.

Something heavy thudded against Josh's door, snapping Niall out of his fog. "No war. Not in this house." He forced himself to point at a large picture of Chris that hung above a credenza. His rescuer was garbed in his dress uniform, his smile certain, his bearing confident. Niall opened his mouth to elaborate, but the words dissolved on his tongue like a bitter pill.

"Sam's daddy is dead," the girl in pigtails said in awed tones that carried in the sudden silence. Josh's door shook when another object smacked against it. Niall fought the urge to talk to the kid, but until he got this group under control, his hands were tied.

"He's a hero." The freckled boy puffed out his chest. "I'm going to be one, too, someday."

"Dead!" Josh's harsh voice came through the door. "That means you'll be dead, because heroes die."

"Pipe down, Josh," Niall ordered when one of the girls covered her face, and her shoulders shook. Distraction worked when dealing with crowd control. His eyes wandered the room and settled on a stack of books close at hand. "Who wants to hear a story about another kind of hero?" He grabbed one from the pile and sat on the sofa.

The children scooted closer on their backsides, their attempt to obey his order to sit making him smile.

He held up the book, and the little girls clapped while the boys groaned.

"*Beauty and the Beast.* Eeew. That's a girl book." One of the boys pulled his cap low over his eyes. "Wake me when it's over."

"Who said it's just for girls?" Niall growled in his Beast voice, and the kids squealed, and a couple fell backward, their legs kicking toward the ceiling.

"Do it again!" The girl with the pigtails bounced on her heels, her ribbon pooling on the floor beside her.

"Is everyone ready to hear the story?" he asked in his regular voice once the group quieted.

All six hands shot in the air, and one of the boys growled, "Yes," making them all laugh.

He launched into the story. Since it was the same version he read to his sister, he knew where to stop for dramatic pauses, how to switch up his voice from the braggart Gaston to the well-meaning elderly father to the prickly, growling Beast. His voice was the only sound in the room, and when he finished, a collective sigh rose from the group.

An appreciative whistle from the doorway brought his head around, and Kayleigh's light, approving eyes felt like warm hands on his face. With a baby in her arms, her dark curls tumbling around her long neck, she looked as beautiful and classic as a fairy-tale princess.

Longing seized him. Someday she'd be holding her own child. Whose? Unease roiled in his gut. Not his, that much he knew. She'd never forgive him when she learned what'd happened with Chris. He'd promised Kayleigh that everything would be aboveboard from now on, that he'd be honest. Although he'd tacked on *as much as I can* so that he wouldn't break the vow, the guilt of keeping the secret rushed back. It was the ocean that divided them. The riptide that pulled them apart.

"I didn't know you could do that." Her smile flashed, and she placed the baby in a swing before coming closer.

"I have three younger siblings." He shrugged as casually as her nearness allowed. "Nightly reading was the only way I could get them to bed."

She nodded appreciatively, a brilliant smile blossoming. Her admiration spread like a sweet heat in his chest, and he smiled. A real smile. The expression felt odd on his face, and he wondered how long he'd been scowling without knowing it. Yet when he caught his grinning reflection in the glass of Chris's framed photo, reality crashed over him. What had he done except entertain some kids? It wasn't as if he deserved a medal for it. His eyes flickered to Chris again.

"Do it again. Read it again!" shouted the girls, but the boys wanted him to read *Jack and the Beanstalk,* which, although he hadn't practiced it before, was easy to do since the Giant's voice was as loud and intimidating as the Beast's.

Kayleigh's foot accidentally brushed his from time to time, making him stumble over his words or lose his place. Being this close to her, without the invisible business barrier between them, felt personal and intimate. He admired the tender way she held a child who'd crawled into her lap when his voice grew loud. She was a loving aunt and a kind person. Always had been. Circumstances in her life had changed, but she hadn't.

He was glad she was still the caring, determined person he'd always known and, he couldn't deny it anymore, he was glad he was getting to know her again. Would he miss her when they parted? The certainty that yes, he would, gripped him, and he froze. He'd have to keep his guard up, or he'd end up wanting what he could never have. What he didn't deserve.

"I'm hungry," one of the boys said after Niall had finished.

Kayleigh stood, and a shaft of sunlight backlit her, gilding her in gold. "How's bologna-and-cheese sandwiches sound with carrot sticks and dip?"

"Can we have cookies, too?" The girl with

the fine hair leaped to her feet, blond strands streaming behind her like a parachute.

"If you eat all of your lunch," replied Kay-leigh, her voice soft but firm.

"Want help?" When he stood, he realized, too late, how close they were. Her breath felt warm against his neck.

She stepped back and peered up at him, the delicate lines of her eyebrows smoothing out. "No. I've got it. Why don't you entertain the kids?"

He looked around and saw them busily re-turning to a set of LEGO blocks while the girls thumbed through books. They seemed all right on their own.

"Actually, I'll go and talk to Josh." He nod-ded at the door. "He's been quiet in there too long."

She cocked her head and studied at him, her eyes unreadable. Surprise? Admiration? Cau-tion? All of the above? At last she dropped her gaze, her hair falling around her face like a curtain. "It can't hurt. Especially if you can calm him down before Beth and Sam get back. Thank you," she said quietly, making an odd fidgeting gesture with her hands. "I'm sorry if I made you feel like you had to come here. To prove something. I understand why going out isn't easy for you."

They studied each other for a long moment, until everyone else ceased to exist. There was so much he could say but much more that he shouldn't. Better to keep it simple. He forced a casual shrug. "I just thought you could use the help."

The color of her eyes was the silvery flash of fish in forest streams. "You helped a lot. I needed you." Her face reddened, and her lips made a wry twist. "I mean, I needed your help. Thanks."

"That's what partners are for, right?" he asked, steering the conversation somewhere safer and looking anywhere but at her lovely face. There was something about her expressive features, the shades of meaning she conveyed with the twitch of an eyebrow, a tilt of her chin, a lift of her lips that made it hard not to stare. With effort, he headed to Josh's room and knocked.

"Go away!" Josh's voice sounded hoarse, as though he'd been crying.

Niall leaned against the doorjamb. "Just making sure you're okay."

"I'm fine." But again, Niall heard something off in the kid's voice. He wasn't fine.

"I disagree." He pressed his forehead against the flimsy particleboard door. Such a small barrier, yet it insulated Josh from the hurts he'd inflicted. Did it buffer him from the ones he felt inside?

The rapid gunfire of a video game sounded, followed by a loud explosion that made Josh yelp. "I just lost this level! Leave me alone. You're ruining my game, and I don't want to talk."

Niall thought for a moment, having no other response but the truth. "Neither do I." Talking wasn't his thing, but he needed to make sure Josh was okay. He exchanged an anxious glance with Kayleigh as she led one of the girls to the bathroom down the small hallway.

"What did you say?" The video-game noise paused, Josh's surprised question loud.

"You heard me." Niall wondered what Chris would have said if he were here. How would he have handled this? He thought back to his own childhood brawls. Siblings fought, and sometimes one of them got hurt. If Josh would let him in, he'd tell him that he wasn't a monster. Not the bad guy, though it was hard to believe that when you unintentionally caused collateral damage. The kid was hurting, no matter how mad he sounded. "Now open up."

"No." The screams of fallen video avatars resumed, and Niall strained to catch the last of Josh's answer. "It's not bleeding so much anymore."

Niall's stomach filled with acid and ice. "What's bleeding?"

Kayleigh passed him on her way back with the girl. She gently steered the girl ahead, then stayed behind, her eyes wide. "Is Josh hurt?"

She raised her hand to knock, but Niall took hold of it, her delicate fingers soft against his palm. He let her go as fast as he stopped her, the feel of her lingering. "I think so. But it's better if only one of us talks to him at a time. Do you trust me?"

She swallowed hard and ducked her head a little, causing her long hair to cascade off her shoulder. "I always have." When her grave eyes met his, he couldn't look away, his lungs trapping his breath. It touched him that, despite everything, she felt she could depend on him.

A sudden ache, a wish that she'd never find out about what'd happened when Chris died, seized him. But she deserved the truth. To know that he wasn't a guy she should trust or admire. Once he finished the app, he'd give back his stake in the company and disappear from her life. It shouldn't matter that she'd think the worst of him, yet somehow it did.

At last, with a final nod, she walked away, leaving the fresh, springtime scent of her lingering in the air. He turned back to the door.

"Josh. Open up. Now."

"No."

He eyed the thin wood and knocked again, hearing a faint echo when he pressed his ear to it. A hollow core. "Then stand back from the door."

"What?" Surprise made Josh's voice squeak.

"Get away from the door. Now." He took a deep breath and let it out slowly. He squared his shoulders and loosened his muscles, readying himself for one of the dumbest things he'd ever do. But he was out of options with an injured kid he couldn't reach.

"It's locked, but whatever." Josh's casual tone didn't fool him. Hopefully, he was taking Niall seriously.

"You away from the door?" He shook the excess energy out of his arms as adrenaline rushed through him.

"This is stupid." Josh's voice sounded resigned and more distant, as though he had moved. "Yes. I'm not near the dumb door."

"What are you going to do?" Kayleigh's concerned voice reached him from the kitchen, but he barely heard her. His focused mind sank to a still, quiet place he'd found during his years of martial arts training.

He eyed the door, and his muscles calculated the force needed to kick it open. With a jab that was more instinct than thought, his right foot slammed into the space directly beneath the doorknob. The door crashed in and, too late, he realized that he'd balanced on his prosthetic leg, a poor prosthetic at that. His limbs felt loose, and his head spun. He staggered forward, off balance, but he managed to catch the edge of Josh's bedpost and kept himself upright be sheer force of will. Biting pain flared from his knee up to his hip, but he didn't cry out. In fact, the pain seemed to be coming from a long way off as he turned his attention to Josh.

Josh's eyes looked larger than his face could hold. "Wow," he whispered. "How did you do that?"

"Tae kwan do. What's bleeding, Josh?"

The boy held up his grazed elbow. "Are you a black belt?"

Niall examined the superficial scrape and relief flooded him. For the first time in several minutes, he felt like he was able to take a full lungful of air. He steered Josh to the hallway, a hand on the boy's shoulder. "Yes. Let's get this cleaned up."

Josh's words tumbled over each other as Niall led him to the bathroom. "Can you teach me how to do that? You were like a Power Ranger. Bet no one messes with you."

"What's going on?" Kayleigh hurried after

them, and Niall wiped the dampness from his brow before turning.

Josh glanced from one adult to the other, excitement dancing in his eyes. “Mr. Walsh was showing me some tae kwan do.”

Her eyes narrowed as she turned back and studied the broken doorknob. “That’s an unconventional approach. Josh, are you hurt?”

He held up his arm. “I banged it when Sam fell, but I didn’t want to show Mom because she was already upset. Plus, it was my fault.” His voice lowered. “How’s Sam?”

Kayleigh held up her cell phone. “I just called, and they’re finishing up at the clinic. You mom said that he only has a slight concussion and should be fine by tomorrow. I’ll phone Grandma and let her know.”

Josh’s defensive posture left him, and he sagged against the wall. “I’m glad he’s okay.”

“I know, sweetie.” Kayleigh wrapped an arm around Josh and pulled the unresisting boy close.

“Is lunch ready yet?” one of the kids called.

“Almost!” Kayleigh yelled over her shoulder, then let go of Josh. She followed them to the bathroom doorway, watched as Niall helped Josh rinse his arm in the sink and mouthed, “Thank you.” This time there was no denying it. She looked impressed. And he couldn’t deny that it felt amazing to be the good guy, even if it was another lie.

"So will you teach me how to do that?" Josh asked once Kayleigh disappeared to call her concerned mother.

Niall thought about his former martial arts center. How would they react if he came back after all these years? He couldn't stand their pity, and he was no longer the fighter he'd been. As for teaching Josh on his own—without a better prosthetic, he couldn't show him much. But if he had a better one, one tailored for martial arts, a voice whispered, he could do it....

He held out a towel and shook his head. "Impossible."

Josh's stormy gaze was reflected in the mirror. "You said you could teach me some defense stuff."

Niall held in a sigh. The kid was right. He had made that offer on the Fourth of July.

Then a thought occurred. One that could solve many of the Renshaw family's problems, though it'd force him further into the outside world he avoided. Kayleigh had said he needed to be more open. While he wouldn't do it for himself, he'd be there for Josh. "If you went to anger management, I'd consider it."

Josh dried his arm and stood still as Niall applied antiseptic and a bandage, his hair hanging in his face and obscuring his expression.

"Okay," he mumbled at last. When he lifted his gaze, Niall was shocked to see the shimmer of tears in the boy's eyes. Protectiveness swept over him, a fierce need to care for this angry, lost, misunderstood boy. Anger management was a step in the right direction, and if tae kwan do would be the carrot that led Josh to attend therapy, then Niall had to offer it.

"That's a smart decision."

"If you teach me tae kwan do."

He closed his eyes for a moment, thinking hard. He could get that better prosthetic, if only to help this kid. Chris's son. He'd take him to his old martial arts studio and work with him outside of class, too.

"I'll sign you up for lessons, and we'll practice on days you go to anger management if your mother approves. How's that sound?"

Josh grinned and kicked his leg through the open bathroom doorway. "Will you teach me to do that move?"

Niall followed him outside and dropped a hand on his shoulder. "Yes. But I've got something else to teach you first."

Josh's face looked bright, happier than Niall had seen it yet. "What?"

"How to replace a lock and a few lightbulbs."

"I'll get Dad's toolbox!" Josh scrambled farther down the hall, and Kayleigh reappeared with a platter of sandwiches.

"How'd it go?"

He grabbed a square off the pile, bologna never tasting better.

"I'd say he's back on track."

She let out a breath. "Good. Let's hope it stays that way." She laid a hand on his wrist, her touch hitting the speed pedal on his pulse. "I couldn't have done this without you, Niall. Thank you. For everything."

He nodded, a heaviness settling in his chest as he watched her walk away to join the children. As long as Senator Gillibrand's intervention didn't come too soon, things could stay this way.

But if it did…the news would ruin everything he was trying to do for Kayleigh and Chris's family. It would set off an explosion that would cause more casualties, he suspected, than the last.

CHAPTER ELEVEN

AT THE BASE of an arched, wooden footbridge, Kayleigh yanked Niall to a stop and pointed.

"Japanese water iris. They're so beautiful." She leaned over a slatted barrier and gazed at the purple blooms rimming a languid green pond. A summer breeze swayed the branches of Japanese maple trees and ruffled pink-blossomed bushes, the smell of apricots perfuming the air. Her eyes half closed against the afternoon sun reflecting off stone lanterns, and she sighed.

Only the pristine Adirondack Mountains and the Brooklyn Botanic Garden made her feel this peaceful. Nature swept away the stress, worry and doubts like a good spring cleaning. It was why she'd asked Niall to join her here for their weekly meeting. After rejections from each of their recent financial investment pitches, they needed to regroup. She did her best to ignore the part of her that simply wanted to walk outside with him on a beautiful day.

Niall rested his elbows beside her, the soft hairs of his arms tickling her skin. “Purple’s your favorite color.”

His breath whispered past her ear and made her shiver in awareness. “You remembered.”

Dark eyes slid sideways, a golden twinkle in their depths. “You used to wear it at camp every day.”

She shoved his shoulder, not budging him an inch. “Not true.”

He held up his long fingers and curled one with each word. “Purple shorts, purple tops, purple bathing suit, purple socks, purple headbands, purple backpack, purple-flowered flip-flops.” Her pulse raced at his teasing expression. He was so handsome when he let down his guard. “Am I missing anything?”

“It was a phase.” She followed his eyes to her purple tote bag and smiled. “Mostly. And you remember my flip-flops?”

He turned and stared directly into her eyes, his level gaze devastating. “I remember a lot about you, Kayleigh.”

“Oh.” Not her most articulate, but who could think when a gorgeous man focused all of his attention on you? It could go to a girl’s head—if she let it. And she wouldn’t. Niall was a friend and now business partner, she firmly reminded herself. Nothing more. Not ever. At what point, however, would her stubborn heart get the message? She hoped it'd be soon. The way he'd opened up at Beth's house had disarmed her. More and more, she saw facets of him that matched the kind of man she wanted in her future. And being around Niall was making it harder each day to hide her growing feelings.

She tore her gaze away and studied a pagoda across the water, its scarlet reflection shimmering against the pond's surface. "Did you know the Japanese Hill-and-Pond Garden was the first public Japanese garden ever created in America?"

Niall's eyebrow quirked, the left side of his mouth lifting in a way that stole her breath as easily as their stunning surroundings.

"Landscape artist Takeo Shiota designed it, and it opened to the public in 1915." His grin deepened at her scowl. "You're dealing with Otter Creek Camp's former Trivial Pursuit champion—"

Whatever she'd been about to say dissolved in her brain when he leaned farther against the railing, their hands touching. One more inch and she could slip her palm into his the way they had as kids, singing camp songs and holding hands by the bonfire. Yet that'd been harmless fun, and this felt much more dangerous.

"Look at that turtle," she said to distract her treacherous thoughts. When she started to edge away, his arm slipped around her, trapping her in a cage she didn't want to escape.

"There's a couple more sunning on the rock island."

She followed his pointing finger to a pile of pebbles curving out of the rippling water, forcing her mind to focus on the creatures rather than the exhilarating feel of him beside her, the clean, outdoorsy scent of him that reminded her of mountain summits and forest air.

"It's a good day for sun." She squinted up at the cloudless sky, grateful that the air felt light, an escape from the dense humidity that had gripped the city this week.

"Not a good day for a koi fish. Watch that crane."

A tall, white-feathered bird suddenly dived into the water and came up with a squirming, bright orange fish. In two gulps, it vanished down the bird's gullet.

"I think I know how that fish feels." She sighed and turned her back to lean on the fence. An uncomfortable look crossed Niall's face, and he snatched his arm from around her as if only now realizing where he'd placed it. "We've struck out with all three investors this week, and I need to put a deposit on…well…we need to get financial backing quick."

Niall opened his mouth, looking as though he were about to say something, then clamped it shut and crossed his arms over his chest. His deep green T-shirt blended with his surroundings, bringing out the burnished strands in his dark hair.

"We have another potential investor meeting next week." Niall's confident tone sounded reassuring, only she felt a pulse of fear when she imagined what would happen after that. She was running through funds fast, and without a capital infusion, High Dive Enterprises might close before it ever started up.

Brett would be right about her being an ideas-only person, and she'd realize her worst fears—that she never should have stretched herself, left her comfort zone and taken a high dive. Worst of all, she'd have no excuse to see Niall again. Would he at least still want to be friends? Spend time together?

An iridescent green dragonfly buzzed in front of her, its translucent double wings beating the air in a soft whirring sound. She froze, mesmerized. It hovered before her, then darted to her shoulder, alighting there.

"I think it likes me," she whispered, trying

not to move as its tiny legs crawled along her bare shoulder.

"How could it resist?" Niall's eyes dropped at her surprised glance.

"Can you take a picture?" She gestured to the small bag on the ground holding her iPhone, her pulse dancing in her veins at his unexpected compliment. "My mother is always looking for interesting portraits to paint." In fact, her mother's call this morning had included such a request.

Niall nodded, grabbed the sack and pulled out her device. The dragonfly crept closer to her neck, and she tried not to jitter at the feathery sensation in case she startled it away. As it was, her insides were a quivering mess given the intense way Niall studied her, moving to view her from different angles. It wasn't as though he hadn't taken pictures of her before, but somehow this felt different. Disorienting.

"Smile," Niall ordered when he'd found a spot that suited him. He raised the phone to his eye.

"I'm going for a mystical look." She schooled her features to look distant and faraway, tough to do when his scrutiny felt like a physical caress. But her mom liked painting fairies, and more than once she'd used Kayleigh as her subject.

After a few snaps, Niall raised his own phone. "Now smile for me."

And unable to resist, her mouth lifted at the sparkle in his eyes, a giddy feeling swimming through her bloodstream. He wanted a picture of her. In the recent past, it had seemed as though he saw her as an intrusion, but she'd seen a subtle change this week since they'd visited Beth's. He'd been less grim when attending the finance meetings, more willing to linger at coffee shops to analyze what had happened, and today he'd accepted her offer to visit the botanical gardens.

The dragonfly took flight from her neck, buzzed her nose and flew away, startling her from her thoughts.

"Would you two like a picture?" asked an elderly man wearing a wide-brimmed hat and a linen suit jacket despite the eighty-degree temperature. His craggy face was friendly, his deep-set eyes crinkling.

She glanced at Niall, who spread his hands and shrugged. Who could deny a sweet, elderly man? "Sure. That would be kind of you."

"Do you want me to set it up?" Niall handed the man his phone instead of hers, she noticed. Interesting...although she would have preferred to have the picture. A keepsake of this time if they went their separate ways again.

Over coffee, Niall had mentioned his plans to give back his shares. The thought had made her ache, as if she'd lost him already.

The old man's skin folds stretched into a vibrant smile. "My grandkids got me one of these things. I'm okay."

Niall handed him the phone and joined Kayleigh at the fence.

"Closer, you two," the man directed.

Her skin felt as though it glowed wherever Niall's shoulder touched hers.

The senior lowered the phone and frowned. "Put your arm around her, son. You two are in love."

She glanced sharply at Niall and met his surprised look. They stared wonderingly at each other before the old man snapped his fingers. "Time's wasting. And when you're my age, that's the most precious thing you've got."

Niall's arm wrapped around her with a solid warmth that made her heart flutter. His hand encircled her upper arm, drawing her close to his muscular side.

"Got it!" The stranger lowered the camera, his eyes shining. "That picture could be on the cover of one of those romance books my wife reads." He handed over the phone when Niall let go of her. An empty sensation crawled along her side when he left, as though a piece of her had been torn away. "Nothing does a body more good than to see two youngsters in love."

"We're just business partners. Friends," she blurted, needing it to be true, no matter what her heart whispered.

The old man's helter-skelter eyebrows lowered, and he shook his head. "You might be fooling yourselves, but I watched you two on the hike up here. You're not pulling the wool over my eyes. Been married to my childhood sweetheart for over fifty years. We were friends for ten years before that. I know a thing or two about love." He contemplated them for a long moment, then ambled away, leaning on a cane.

The lacy overhang of an exotic tree filtered the light, leaving Niall's eyes in shadow. The deep green of the leaves contrasted with the butterflies flitting from branch to branch, sipping from the tree's pale blossoms. It was a living kaleidoscope, and suddenly she felt dizzy watching it, and him. Did he think the older man was crazy? The lower half of Niall's face looked serious, his mouth in a firm, straight line. Was he considering the gentleman's suggestions? He certainly wasn't laughing at it.

As for her, she didn't know how to feel. Did the stranger sense what she'd been trying to hide, even from herself? Her feelings for Niall no longer seemed casual. They ran into deeper waters than she was ready to test. Yet there was no denying the butterflies she felt in her stomach whenever she was around Niall.

"Let's find a spot to sit and go over those marketing results," he said, coming no closer. A curl of wind brought in the sweet smell of summer grass and the sound of rustling leaves.

"Sounds good." She strove to keep the disappointment out of her voice. They were here for business. Nothing more. So why, then, did she want to linger in this bucolic setting with him, explore the surprises hidden in the garden's nooks and crannies, rather than tally up data?

"The viewing pavilion is over the bridge." She pointed to a wooden structure across the pond. "It's shady, and since it's a weekday, should be fairly quiet."

"Lead the way."

Her scuffling sandals on the wooden planks were the only sound as they crossed over the earthen-colored water. All felt serene, her restless heart settling, until a child scampered by, chased by a stroller-wielding father, a red balloon streaming behind them. She dodged, too late, and tottered when the boy careened into her. Before she lost her balance, a firm hand cupped her elbow, steadying her, and she peeked up at Niall.

Niall. He was always there to catch her before she fell. Affection for her old friend, now partner, rushed through her as she met his concerned copper-hued eyes, the bright light bringing out their gold specks. She'd spent so much of her life wishing for things that would never come true. That her parents wouldn't divorce, that she'd grow taller, that Chris would come home safe and that she'd see Niall again.

And here he was. Him and not him. Echoes of the boy he'd been mixing with the man he'd become. And while much of that version at first had seemed negative, seeing him with her nephew, the assisted-living facility folks and his family, was changing her mind. It made a case for her heart to trust itself. He could be her old friend again…so why wasn't she content with that? Some restless part of her demanded more, as impossible as it was.

They neared the open-sided building at the water's edge and Niall's hand dropped from her elbow.

"So you finished the study we discussed last week?" At her nod, he continued, "How many people participated?" Niall's hair slid across his forehead as he studied the hand that had held her before dropping it to his side.

"Two hundred and twenty-six." A bit of pride wove through her voice as she sat on the built-in bench that ran along all three sides of the pavilion. It was a decent market sample, especially for initial data analysis. She smiled to herself at the thought, then sobered when she remembered their urgent need for a financial backer. None of this research would matter if they didn't get funds.

When Niall peered out across the pond, the slanting sun outlined his chiseled profile. "What are the demographics?"

She took out her laptop, and the machine whirred to life while she pulled some numbers from her memory.

"I sampled from three age groups. The first, which comprises approximately fifty percent of our participants, are aged sixty-five and over."

Niall nodded. "MaryAnne mentioned that your grandfather organized some discussions and went door-to-door to collect questionnaires."

"He calls himself our CEO. And my number one fan." She smiled at the thought, then glanced up from her screen to catch Niall's intense look.

"I believe it." He stretched sculpted arms on either side of him. "Family's important."

She winced inside, remembering how she'd always thought of Niall as her brother. Yet the term no longer seemed to fit given her confusing new feelings for him.

She pulled the heavy mass of hair off her neck and swirled it into a loose bun. "The remainder is split at twenty-five percent in the eighteen-to-thirty-five and thirty-six-to-sixty-four age groups."

Niall whistled, impressed. "So you were able to use the social media sites you'd mentioned?"

A yellow-and-gray bird flew into the pavilion and perched on a vaulted rafter. It opened its beak and cocked its head, as if joining the conversation. "Yes, and some in-person work at events this week."

Niall lifted an eyebrow. "You didn't mention those."

She rolled her eyes. "Let's just say I went to a lot of speed-dating events, cafés and singles clubs. And the self-help section in the bookstores was also very useful."

"Speed dating? Singles clubs?" Niall's brows crashed together.

For some reason, Kayleigh felt apologetic. Why did he look angry? "With no funds, I had to get creative."

Niall scowled. "I don't want you going to those. They're—they're fake environments with unreliable data. And we're supposed to make all business decisions together."

"True. It's just that Gianna offered to take me, and I couldn't pass up the chance to get free research. But, Niall." She laid a hand on his arm, then withdrew it when a strange look crossed his face. "We can't run any marketing events, promote or manufacture the product without financial backing. Creativity only gets us so far. Major Carlton and next week's meeting are our last hope."

His expression hardened. "I heard from the major."

Excitement rushed through her. The man had been a condescending jerk, but if he was willing to back their product, she'd never think a bad thought about him again.

"And—"

Niall blew out a long breath. "And he offered me a job, but passed on High Dive Enterprises."

Her shoulders fell. With only one meeting remaining, there was a real chance the start-up would fold. Then she'd know she shouldn't have left the shallow end of the pool after all.

The rest of Niall's words replayed in her mind, and sour doubt settled in her gut. She might be about to lose him, too.

"What kind of job?"

"Setting up internet-protection systems for the city police department, managing their communications and so on. They have a new contract and need someone to head it for them. Look, let's focus on High Dive." He ran a hand through his hair, then dropped it back to the rail.

But she couldn't let it go. "How much did they offer you?"

"It doesn't matter, Kayleigh. Tell me more about your findings." He peered at the computer screen until she lowered it.

"It does matter." Her heart plummeted when she imagined him leaving for a better opportunity. Yet she wouldn't hold him to a doomed partnership.

"If this is a better opportunity for you, then you should take it," she made herself say, despite the burning in her chest. Her mind ran over the salaries the GSI IT guys had confessed to earning. "I bet Major Carlton offered you six figures."

Niall's eyes slid from hers, and his shoulders lifted and fell. "We signed our LLC partnership agreement. There's nothing more to discuss."

Her eyes widened. Since he didn't deny it, she must be right. "You turned him down?"

"Our start-up is a better option for me." His eyes bored into hers, and she found it hard to swallow. He'd said *our.* Somehow it made him seem more invested than ever.

"From a business perspective," he amended.

"But we don't even have financing."

He stilled her fidgeting hands, his fingers lacing with hers for an electric moment. "We will, Kay. Have faith. And I'm not going anywhere."

A rush of wetness made her squeeze her eyes shut. Relief, joy and hope jockeyed inside. He had a guaranteed, six-figure-income offer, and he was choosing to take a gamble on her. She couldn't begin to measure how much that meant to her. He supported her, something Brett had never done.

"Now, if you look at this screen, it's a rundown of the most popular traits. I've cross-referenced them with their ethnic, social class and age demographics."

His face was so close to hers, she could feel the faint prickle of hair along his jawline. After several minutes, his chest rising and falling beside hers, his eyes running left to right, he finished clicking through the screens and looked up.

"The most common Must Trait for seniors is 'Adventurous'?"

She bit her lower lip to keep herself from smiling at his shocked expression. "Makes sense to me. Don't you remember them in the pool?"

He rubbed his chin, his expression thoughtful. "They were having a good time." He tapped the computer screen. "And you proved that people do value partners who are open."

"Of course they do." She folded her arms across her chest, happy that he'd seen this all-important trait affirmed.

"Over seventy percent of participants want a partner who has that trait. Good thing I didn't bet you," he teased.

She placed her hands on her hips. "What would I have won?"

"Told-you-so rights."

She sucked in her cheeks. That had been a coveted prize…when they were kids. "I'd rather have you make a Must Traits list.

"Oh…um—" His gaze flew around the space as if he was searching for an escape route. "Did I mention I was taking Josh to my dojang?"

"I heard." She smiled at him. "Josh talks about it nonstop. Thank you for that. Smooth change of topic, by the way."

He shrugged, looking sheepish. "The kid needs to get away from those video games and do something positive. It's no big deal."

"It's a huge deal. Until you offered, he'd turned down every one of Beth's suggestions."

"It's nothing. Glad to do it. Now, let's get back to the research." His index finger began scrolling through the screens again.

"Of course." She sighed, glad for Josh, for Niall and for herself. Things were precarious financially, but if he could help her nephew control his temper, it was worth a hundred failed start-ups.

"So what exactly do you think seniors mean by 'Adventurous'?" He raised his brows, and the gleam in his eyes was so attractive, she stared. "Bingo past 8:00 p.m.?"

She pictured Annette Larson's red shoe in Gramps's couch. "If it was strip Bingo..."

His mouth dropped open.

"Oh, it's not over until it's over." She grinned and tabbed down a few more spaces. "See. They also ranked the traits 'In Shape,' 'Healthy' and 'Spontaneous' highly, too."

"So you're saying senior residents are on the emotional dating wavelength of middle-school kids?"

She shook her head. "No. Just that after surviving everything they have, they're looking for some fun. Isn't that the point of living? Of making it through hard times? To appreciate the life you've been given? What you have left?"

He returned her significant stare, but his eyes seemed to look more inward than outward. She hoped he was thinking about his own life and considering not wasting it by being so reclusive.

"The middle-aged groups are interested in 'Loyalty,' 'Honesty,' 'Morality'..." he spoke into the silence.

"That makes sense. Many have gone through breakups and even divorces." She paused and pulled down the hem of her shorts. "They want guarantees that they won't deal with that hurt again." She could relate.

He relocated a caterpillar undulating across his leg and looked up. "There are no guarantees, Kayleigh."

She moved restlessly under his scrutiny. That was the point of her app. Besides making money to support herself and Beth, and proving that she was more than an ideas person, she wanted guarantees—for herself and others. It bugged her that Niall didn't get that. Sure, the concept was a bit simplistic and unsophisticated to use on its own. But it could be another piece of the puzzle that helped singles make sense of their love lives.

"This app will come as close to a guarantee

as possible." She powered down her laptop. "People will know, up-front, that they want the same things, that they're compatible."

"Unlike your parents."

His quiet words cut her. He remembered the reason for her parents' divorce.

"It's not the whole story, but sure, a compatibility score might have made them look closer at their relationship. Steered them in different directions."

"Then they wouldn't have had you."

The skin on her arms rose in small bumps. That was exactly what she'd once said to her mother.

Niall's eyes searched hers, and he covered her hand with his. "Good things can come out of bad."

She leaned against him and rested her head on his shoulder, so close that she could hear him breathe. His hand toyed with a curl beside her cheek, the feeling too intimate to be right, yet she couldn't move away. How many times had they been this close, as friends, and she'd felt nothing? She wished for those days back.

"We still need to do what we can to help people make informed decisions, especially when their choices affect others." She thought of Chris's sudden decision to enlist after their family had fallen apart. If her parents had stayed together, would he have become a Green Beret and died?

Niall stood and shoved his hands into his pockets, his body tense. "Agreed. It's better to prevent problems than cause them."

"Then why won't you make a Must Traits list? If you ever meet someone, don't you want to know if there'll be problems in the future?"

He stopped pacing and looked down at her. "Sometimes you just know when it's right."

She shoved her computer case into her purple tote and stood. Once again, he was running down the very product he was programming. Their product. "If you're so sure of yourself, then why are you hiding out in your apartment? Not spending time with anyone?"

"I don't need to be around other people," he said drily, his gaze never leaving hers. "Except you."

Heated blood rushed through her. That was treacherous thinking—for both of them. "But if you used the app, you'd find the right girlfriend. Want to be with her. You can't waste your time on someone like me. I'll never be more than a friend."

He closed the distance between them in one stride and eyed her. "Sure about that?"

And suddenly, he pulled her into his arms, his strong body enfolding her. His lips lowered then paused, his heated eyes questioning. Was he waiting for her to refuse him?

Her bones melted against him, and her resolve to keep things professional crumbled. She wanted this kiss as badly as she'd ever wanted anything. She stretched up on her tiptoes and heard him groan as his lips swept down and captured hers, the caress as feather soft as the dragonfly's wings.

He pulled the band around her bun loose, and her hair tumbled down her back, his hands burying themselves in it. When he deepened their kiss, his mouth slanting firmly against hers, her skin heated. Their hearts pounded together, and she breathed in his minty breath, tasting the strawberries they'd eaten earlier. Wanting him closer, she traced his bunching back muscles, loving their hardness and strength.

When his lips left hers and traveled along her jaw, she fitted herself against him closer still, needing to feel all of him. As his lips slid along her earlobe then down her neck, the world tilted and spun madly in the wrong direction.

She cupped his face and brought it back to hers, wanting his mouth again, the caress deepening into a demanding kiss that left her breathless and clutching on to his shoulders when her knees weakened.

At last he stopped, and they stared at each other, chests heaving, breath coming in fits and starts.

“Still sure?” he murmured, his eyes searching hers.

Struck dumb, she nodded automatically, her gesture making him scowl, disappointment in his eyes. When he strode out of the pavilion, her fingers traced her swollen lips.

How had she let that happen?

CHAPTER TWELVE

When Niall and Josh entered his former martial arts academy, he removed his shoes and nudged the boy to do the same.

"Niall! Good to see you," exclaimed Niall's former sparring partner, Brennan, his voice low so as not to distract the students training in the dojang. He sat on a bench outside the training room, fanning himself with a towel.

"Same here. Just finished?" Niall pitched his voice low, as well. The students needed 100 percent focus. He scanned Brennan's red face, watching the guy's forehead bead with sweat as fast as he wiped it.

"Been here since six." Brennan flipped the cap off his water bottle then gulped before leaning forward, elbows on his knees. "Haven't seen you in years. Where you been?"

Niall stretched out his new prosthetic, still marveling at the articulated movement in his bionic Genium ankle and foot. After committing to Josh, he'd phoned his therapist and gone through with the measurements and fittings.

He rotated his ankle, then flexed his foot. What a difference. His limp was about gone, but the changes felt deeper than that. Did he deserve it? He glanced at Josh. The kid needed his help. That was what mattered.

"Afghanistan and—" he trailed off, wondering himself. Where had he been? He thought back to the past two years spent in his apartment and realized he'd been nowhere. But instead of feeling satisfied, the thought unsettled him. Until Kayleigh, he hadn't realized that he'd missed getting out.

"Around," he continued after nodding at a sympathetic interjection from Brennan. He wanted to bypass any comments about his "sacrifice." "I'm working on a start-up company with an old friend."

There. A positive direction. The first he'd taken in years—if Kayleigh was still talking to him. After their unforgettable kiss, she hadn't returned his calls, texts or emails in days. It had been a rash, stupid thing for him to do, and he wanted to apologize. Needed to. But she was avoiding him, and although he usually liked being left alone, he missed her. She'd burrowed her way into his life, and her absence left a hole he wasn't sure he could stitch back up.

He knew he was on borrowed time with her, but he wasn't ready to end it. Doubted he ever would be. But with Chris's declassification a real possibility, the time would come. His gut wrenched.

"You and Aunt Kayleigh were friends?" Josh's hair floated in every direction when he pulled off his Yankees cap and hung it on one of the pegs behind them.

Niall nodded. "Yep." A part of him wondered if, after their kiss, it was still true. He'd been wrong to catch her off guard, but her smug certainty had gotten to him. He'd wanted to shake her confidence that they were only friends for reasons he couldn't explain to himself. Why start something he knew they'd never be able to finish? Yet he couldn't deny his feelings for Kayleigh. Could he control them and not scare her off again?

"A start-up? Is that like a new business?" Brennan wrapped his towel around his neck and tied his shoes.

"Yes, but it focuses on using the internet and social media in new ways." When Niall pointed, Josh trudged across the space to pick up the sneakers he'd kicked off. At Niall's nod, the boy slid them over shoe holders beneath the large front window.

"Come again?" Brennan stared at him quizzically, and Niall remembered that he managed one of his family's hardware stores. He probably didn't need to know much about social media.

"Like one of those couples-compatibility sites, but for your iPhone."

Brennan's thick eyebrows spread apart, understanding dawning in his close-set eyes. "Sounds like those horoscope things my wife reads. Whenever she's mad at me, she calls me a Taurus. As if anyone believes that crap."

At Niall's narrow-eyed look, Brennan waved his hands, his face turning scarlet. "No offense, buddy."

"None taken," Niall said evenly, then turned toward Josh as the kid flopped on the bench beside him. "And your aunt and I met at summer camp when we were eleven. Your age."

"Random." Josh peered around Niall, his eyes tracking the action in the training room. But for his shaking knee and clenched hands, he acted like he couldn't care less.

"Some things are," Brennan responded then pushed to his feet. "Good seeing you, Niall. Will you be back again?"

Josh's head whipped around, his eyes on Niall.

"Depends on how things go today." Niall gave the boy a significant look. If Josh didn't follow the directions he'd given him earlier about showing respect and self-control, they'd be kicked out on their first day. For good reason. Martial arts were more about self-discipline than fighting, a lesson that Josh needed to learn.

"Good luck to you, then." Brennan pulled on his sunglasses and pushed through the front door, letting in a burst of morning-traffic sounds and bright sunshine. The light glared off Josh's pale face.

"You ready for this, kid?"

Josh's tense shoulders belied his nonchalant shrug. "I guess." He crossed thin arms over his narrow chest, his expression defiant.

What a change from his earlier excitement. He'd been practically bouncing off the apartment walls, telling his grandfather, Chris's dad, about their plans when Niall picked him up. Then Beth mentioned a one o'clock anger-management therapy appointment, and the boy had grown quiet and sullen.

Niall handed Josh a water bottle. "That attitude isn't going to work here."

"Whatever." Josh grabbed the metal canister. "I just want to learn to do that kick that knocked in my door. Then no one will mess with me."

There it was again, that hint that something else was wrong in Josh's life.

Niall tried to catch Josh's eye. "Who messes with you?"

"Only people who wish they hadn't." Josh laced his fingers and popped his knuckles.

"Kids at school?"

Josh's face grew pinched, and he sprang to his feet. He stomped away, then halted at the arched entrance to the dojang training area. "Are we going in now or what?" he demanded without looking back.

"What." Niall slowly pulled out a pair of towels as if he had all the time in the world.

Josh turned, surprised. "Huh?"

"What," Niall repeated calmly. He grabbed a sweatband and fitted it around his temples. "That's my choice. I'm not taking your bad attitude inside. You either leave it at the door, or you stay behind."

Josh blew out a long breath and his shoulders lowered. "Fine. May we go inside?" At Niall's raised eyebrow he added, "Please?"

"Better." Niall got to his feet, marveling at the rolling motion of his new foot as he padded to the entranceway. Inside the cavernous space, lines of students went through a series of opening stretches and poses. Was he capable of those now? Excitement stung him, as if a part of him that had fallen asleep had woken.

Together, they walked along the wooden

floor's perimeter, listening to the muffled sounds of students straining to keep their balance and the muted commands given by the class leader. When Josh opened his mouth, Niall's head shake kept him quiet.

He breathed in the old smells of sweat, rubber and, oddly, fresh laundry, as their air vents adjoined a dry-cleaning business. Despite the windowless space, the whirring ceiling fans, bright artificial light and air-conditioning were invigorating, and a wish to take charge of the hardworking students on the mats seized him. He'd become an instructor when he'd earned his purple belt and had continued—until he'd left for the war—as he'd gained in rank to become a five-time black belt.

As they strode toward a compact man wearing a white dobok, a black belt around the V-neck jacket of his uniform, Josh whispered, "Do I have to wear those lame pajamas? Those kids look like losers."

Niall eyed the colored belts around the children's waists. They were far from losers. "Those kids could kick your—"

"Greetings, Master Walsh. It's been too long since we've had the pleasure of seeing you."

Niall returned the man's bow, noting that his black hair was now sprinkled with gray, but as close-cropped as ever.

"Greetings, Master Jung. May I introduce this novice, who seeks your permission to train?" He nudged Josh forward.

The boy's eyes were wide as he watched the older man bow to him. Josh put his hands together and clumsily repeated the gesture.

"I'm Josh."

Niall coughed and shot Josh a long look until the boy flushed and stammered what they'd practiced on the bus. "Master Jung. I would like the honor of learning your craft. I hope to be worthy of it."

Pride spread its warm tentacles in Niall's chest. Josh's tough-guy, apathetic persona was an act. Niall was more certain than ever that bringing him to the dojang had been the right move. It might be a dangled carrot to get him to agree to attend anger-management therapy, but it would also help him rein in his emotions. And it would give him a safe place to belong, as it once had Niall.

Josh held himself stiffly as Master Jung's eyes searched his. At last, the older man turned to Niall.

"He has much Han."

Niall returned the nine-time black belt and one-time World Champion's stare impassively, knowing it would only hurt their chances if he argued about Josh being, as Master Jung astutely noted, angry. In fact, Han was much more than that, and its meaning in Korean culture summed up Josh in many ways. Han was sorrow caused by heavy suffering, injustice or persecution, a dull lingering ache in the soul as it waited for vengeance.

But Josh wasn't waiting. He was getting revenge against the world that had stolen his father by using his fists and his rage. Guilt scratched Niall from the inside out. The man who'd brought Josh to this dojang deserved his anger, his revenge. No one else.

But his lips were sealed, as much as it pained him not to share what had happened. Instead, he'd do his best to help the kid get a handle on his temper.

Josh moved restlessly beside him and rose on the balls of his feet. "What's Han?" He glowered at Niall, his hands fisted at his sides. "Is this dude making fun of me?"

Niall shook his head firmly at the boy, silently conveying the need for him to simmer down. Josh was not helping their cause. When his heels hit the floor again, he unfolded his hands and lowered his head.

At last, Master Jung's tight mouth relaxed, and he nodded. "Yes. There is much to teach and much to learn. If he applies himself, he'll gain what he's missing. However, to stay, he must control his temper."

Josh opened his mouth, then shut it at Niall's sharp glance.

"We bow to your wisdom, Master Jung," he said gravely, relief sweeping through him that they'd made it this far. Now, if Josh could keep a lid on his temper, they might join after all.

Master Jung's narrow face stretched wide as he smiled. "Josh, as you are not in uniform, go to the back of the group and follow Master Thomas's directions."

"But they're just stretching," Josh protested. "I want to learn how to fight."

"I suspect you already know a bit of that skill." The smallest smile lifted the edges of Master Jung's mustache but didn't reach his eyes. "Tae kwon do will teach you to be master of yourself. The best weapon of all. Now go."

Master Jung's last words rang with such authority that Josh scurried away without a backward glance. Niall watched him join a few other kids in street clothes and begin lunging. Good. The boy might run roughshod over others, but he wouldn't get away with that here.

He smiled as he recalled his older brother, Aiden, signing him and Liam up for classes shortly after their father's death. It'd helped get them through that tough, confusing time, turning their anger-fueled teenage fights into controlled sparring matches. Tae kwan do focused them on building skills rather than hurting each other.

Much of the frustration he'd felt over losing his dad had been contained when he'd practiced self-restraint and moved up in belts. It'd given him peace and pride. Hopefully, that would happen for Josh.

Could he apply the same self-discipline in reining in his runaway thoughts about Kayleigh? He had to try. Given the impossibility of their situation, he couldn't afford to let himself think about her as anything other than a business partner, no matter how much their kiss had blown his mind.

"Shall we fill out his forms?" Master Jung inclined his head, and Niall followed him back to the reception area, bypassing the desk and heading into a small office. An electric waterfall dominated a corner of the room, clear liquid burbling down its greenish stone. A wall calendar flipped to July revealed a stunning picture of Seongsan Sunrise Peak, piles of moss-covered rocks strewn around the ancient volcanic crater. A traditional Hanbok robe was encased in a large glass box that showcased its simple long lines and rich scarlet-and-orange fabric. The smell of incense rose from a stick burning in a burnished-copper tray beside a small bonsai tree with green, glossy leaves. So much had changed in his life, yet here, it seemed as though time stood still with only the changing calendar pictures to mark the passing days.

Niall accepted the pen and stack of papers passed to him. “Thank you, Master Jung. This is a great opportunity for Josh.”

“And your relationship to the boy?” Master Jung’s offhand question froze Niall’s hand as he filled in information. How to explain that? Josh was the son of the man who’d died saving Niall. In a strange way, Master Jung, of all people, would probably accept that explanation if Niall were allowed to give it.

“He’s my friend and business partner’s nephew.”

“And his father is—”

Niall’s numb fingers dropped the pen, and he fumbled for it near his feet.

“Dead,” he made himself say. Funny how often he thought about it, but saying it out loud was still tough.

“You knew this man.” Master Jung slid him a cup of tea he’d poured from an electronic kettle. The smell of ginger and lemon filled the room.

Niall nodded and sipped the brew, his

tongue blistering when the scalding, tart liquid splashed over it. He'd known Jung too long to outright lie.

"I'm sorry for the loss of your friend."

"Oh. He wasn't my—" Niall cut himself off. It felt wrong to call Chris a stranger. "I knew him briefly."

"But his passing troubles you enough to help his son."

Niall dodged Master Jung's all-seeing eyes. This was beginning to feel more like a counseling session than a business transaction.

"I'm concerned about his anger. He's been fighting at school and may get expelled."

Master Jung pressed his palms and the tips of his fingers together and peered over them. "I remember a boy who came here once, angry over his father's death."

Niall nodded. "That boy is grateful to you."

"But there's new anger in you, as well. You should rejoin us."

Niall leaned back in shock. He'd planned to bring Josh, sit on the sidelines, perhaps work on the Must Traits code on his laptop, demonstrate a stretch or pose or two when they got home to reinforce Josh's lessons. He wasn't up to the mental and physical rigors of the dojang.

"I—" He opened his mouth to refuse, and hesitated. Wasn't this exactly what Kayleigh meant about being more open? Working through his issues had helped him once before. It was unlikely that it would change his feelings now, given that he was squarely to blame for Chris's death. However, refusing seemed churlish given all Master Jung had done for him.

"I accept." He picked up the small porcelain glass and drained the cooling liquid.

Master Jung pushed aside a vibrating cell phone, his eyes burning into Niall's. "Very good. You'll find an additional form in the papers for you to reenroll. Once I've judged your level, I'll assign you classes to lead."

Niall swallowed hard. He'd planned to be responsible for Josh and now...he would be in charge of dozens. The more he opened up, the more life poured in. Would he sink or swim?

"Very good, sir." He picked up the pen when Jung left the room to handle a customer at the front desk.

As he filled in the information, his mind wandered, running over the timeline of events that had gotten him here, stopping on the botanical gardens kiss a couple of days ago.

It'd stirred up feelings he hadn't thought he was capable of. The feel of her in his arms, the sweet taste of her, the way she'd responded... It drove him crazy remembering it. He shouldn't have kissed her. Wouldn't have if the look in her eyes hadn't said yes, if she hadn't reached for him...yet given her stony silence, she'd regretted it in the end.

A few minutes later, his phone vibrated against his hip. His heart pounded when Kayleigh's name flashed across the screen.

"Hello?"

A long snuffling sob sounded in his ear.

"Kayleigh?"

A hiccup interrupted her skipping intake of air. His fingers tightened around his phone. He'd been worried that his actions at the garden would drive her away. Was she about to call off their business arrangement? Suddenly, he realized how much he wanted it for himself, not just to help Kayleigh and Chris's family.

He should have kept himself in check and not thrown back the first lifeline that'd been tossed his way. If he could keep her from giving up on him, he would never go near her again. Hard as that might be, the thought of not seeing her at all was too difficult to swallow.

"Talk to me, Kay."

His words were met with a long silence that was broken when she blew her nose.

"I'm sorry." He lowered his voice and glanced through the doorway to see Master Jung talking animatedly to a mother and her two sons. "I should never have kissed you.

It was rude and thoughtless. It won't happen again."

"No, it won't." When she spoke, her voice sounded more tired than he'd ever heard it. His forehead dipped, and he shut his eyes. He'd known the kiss was wrong, but to have her agree so readily wounded him.

"Now that we've got that behind us," he said brusquely, wanting her to trust that he could be the professional partner and friend she needed, "let's plan on going through our presentation for our next finance meeting—ForwardTech Ventures, Inc. All signs point to them investing in this product. They're progressive, not risk adverse—"

"None of that matters now."

"I see." He'd royally screwed up if she didn't want him involved at all. He'd known, since the war, that he wasn't a hero, no prince to rescue a damsel in distress. So why the heck had he acted like one, sweeping her into a kiss she clearly detested?

"No, no, I do care. I mean, it's not about that." Her words jump-started his heart. It pounded hard against his rib cage.

"Then, what?" he asked faintly, relief pushing the air out of his lungs.

"Brett."

Instantly, he grew tense. Was her ex trying to get Kayleigh back? Niall noticed his clenched hands and forced himself to unfurl them. If so, the guy would have a hell of a fight. Niall couldn't be Kayleigh's boyfriend, but as her friend, he'd make sure she didn't waste her time on a jerk like Brett.

"Block his number and email. Tell Gianna not to let him in if he comes over. Better yet, I'll come by and tell the idiot to stop bothering you."

His belligerent tone garnered a small laugh. "He's not after me," she said. "He wants our app."

Niall stopped pacing and stared at the intricate design of the framed ceremonial robe. It was a complicated pattern with unexpected shapes and directions, much like this conversation.

"He can't have it," Niall said harshly, possessiveness for Kayleigh and this product they'd created taking hold.

"He already has."

Niall froze. "What do you mean?"

"Gianna called me from work and said Brett announced his new idea for an app in a department meeting and described ours perfectly."

An angry exclamation escaped him. He scooped a handful of smooth polished jade stones piled on a small golden platter and let them fall through his fingers, a pinging sound filling the room.

"That's impossible."

"That's what I thought. I never told anyone about the idea except you, Gianna and our potential investors."

"And you're sure of Gianna?" He hated to ask, but how else could the information have been accessed?

"She's on her way home because she quit."

"Oh." His mind raced along other possible channels and stopped on one that seemed so obvious, it couldn't be possible.

"Would you have sent anything to Gianna at work?"

A harsh intake of air confirmed his worst suspicions.

"No. But she's been messing around with our prototype at home. Maybe she brought it to work and they found it in her files."

"Someone could have detected the unfamiliar program and alerted Brett. Or he looked through her files."

"I can't imagine it, but yes. It's the only way he'd know about our app." Kayleigh's voice sounded distant, as if she'd moved the phone away from her. When her next words came, he had to strain to hear. "I didn't think he'd have the nerve to steal my ideas outright. Up until now, he's only taken most of the credit for them."

"You said yourself the man didn't want you to succeed. He was making sure he was right."

"I told him I would be developing apps within the month. Giving him competition."

Her tone sounded furious, and he burned inside, too, wishing he had Brett in front of him. What he'd do—

"With his team of specialists, he'll have the code written and sent to the patent office before we do. They'll get the rights ahead of us, and we'll be shut out. It's over, Niall." Her last words quavered, but instead of sharing her sense of defeat, a cold determination filled him.

"We decide when it's over. Not Brett."

"He has top-notch programmers who will work plenty of overtime to get this done quickly." Her voice sounded colorless, lost. "I've seen him beat out other companies for similar programs."

"You have a top-notch programmer, too, Kay," he said quietly, rubbing his thumb over a jade stone for good luck. "One who will work night and day. We will get this in to the patent office before he does. We need to send them the first twenty-five pages of the code and the last twenty-five."

"And you're what? Almost halfway done?"

"Yes." He would be farther along if he hadn't wasted time remembering the details of their kiss and checking for her messages instead of coding. But he'd make it up. He had to. Time to focus. He strode back to his chair and flung himself into it. "Did Gianna give you any more details? Like how long he's been working on it? If the programmers have started coding?"

"No one would talk to her once she quit. Apparently, she called them a bunch of thieves." Her voice was louder now, steadier.

Good. He'd need her to be strong over the long workdays ahead. Every minute suddenly felt critical. They were in a tight race with the biggest app developer in the country, and they had to win.

"I'm coming over." He checked the time on his phone screen. Josh's lesson would be over in fifteen minutes.

"I don't want to quit."

"Neither do I. We'll salvage this."

Her short laugh was hard. It reminded him of the soldiers who'd peered into the black night, looking for an enemy they sensed but couldn't see.

"You don't know who you're going up against."

"Neither does he," Niall said grimly. "We're an unbeatable team."

A watery laugh sounded. "Yes, we are. Now hurry."

CHAPTER THIRTEEN

WHEN NIALL STRODE through her apartment door, Kayleigh flew into his arms and clung to him as if he were a lost piece in her broken world.

Forget that he'd shaken her to her core with his kiss in the garden, and that avoiding him hadn't stopped her from thinking about him every waking minute. Dreaming of him during the rest. She needed him. As a friend, a business partner and— Her thoughts screeched to a halt before they tumbled off that cliff.

He was here, and she needed him. That was what mattered. She pressed her ear against his chest, the drum of his heart steadying her, tapping out a rhythm that everything would be all right. The broad hands stroking her back stopped the trembling that'd taken hold of her since Gianna's call. She fit herself against him, inhaling the fresh, clean smell of him, loving the tight feel of his arms around her.

How could everything have fallen apart just when they'd been coming together? In hindsight, she shouldn't have given the program to Gianna, but her roommate had been so excited to play with some of the codes as a former programmer herself. Kayleigh hadn't imagined a possibility where Gianna might have brought it to work.

Maybe she wasn't capable of leading a team and handling the myriad details that went into creating a successful product. Security was essential. She should have safeguarded their product, protected the work they'd done. Instead, they were compromised.

Niall eased back, leaving a respectable distance between them, and she fought the urge to close the space. His solid, warm body was the strength she needed as doubt cracked through her. For a moment, she wished she could drop her worries and simply slip back into his arms. Enjoy a moment with him, a port in the storm life waged against her. But the reality was that she deserved his criticism, not his comfort. More important, they couldn't—and shouldn't—act like a couple. Especially after their kiss. Now more than ever, she needed her best friend. Niall.

"I'm sorry," she croaked, meeting his deep brown eyes, the concern in them nearly undoing her.

"This is not your fault."

She relaxed. He didn't blame her. His opinion of her mattered more than she'd realized. "I should have protected our start-up and app."

"You couldn't have predicted piracy on that level." Her hopeful heart rose at his sincere voice. He meant what he said and wasn't just trying to make her feel better.

"There's so much I don't know." Her eyes searched his, and suddenly she wasn't talking about the business app but about them, their kiss. She could see he knew it, too, in the way his features sharpened, his gaze growing intense.

"Kayleigh," he murmured, and he seemed to be holding himself back, his arms rigid at his sides.

"Nothing makes sense anymore." Their eyes met.

"Life isn't always logical." Niall looked away, his eyes darker than she'd ever seen them. "And neither is love."

A long moment of silence stretched between them. It hung dangerous in the air, like the calm before a summer storm. This was exactly what she'd been obsessing over since their kiss. If only Niall was a stranger and not her closest friend, someone she couldn't afford to lose if things didn't work out romantically.

"Yes." She sighed, her voice no longer

sounding as certain as it used to. "It can't be controlled."

"Not from where I'm standing." His longing gaze felt like warm arms around her, the ones she dared not rush into again. If she did, she knew she'd never let go.

"Ahem! Am I interrupting anything? Market research?" Gianna's teasing voice sounded behind them, and Kayleigh's hand covered her mouth. Niall looked shaken as well and turned away.

"Are you okay?" Kayleigh embraced her friend, then took her box of personal belongings and put it on the table beside their front door.

"Tell us what happened." She led her friend to an off-white couch filled with floral-patterned cushions. "And this is Niall. Niall, Gianna." The two shook hands, and Niall sat in a rose-patterned chair, his masculinity incongruous against their feminine decor.

Gianna's earlier amusement dropped away, leaving a simmering anger in her brown eyes, along with remorse. "First of all, I'm sorry that I took your program to work and didn't tell you. I thought I'd help a little, try it on the systems at work since they're the most up-to-date. I only had it on my computer one day, but that must have been enough for our IT guys.

Maybe they were doing a backup? Either way, they got it, and now Brett is claiming it's his. I feel terrible, Kay."

Kayleigh held Gianna's hand. "You didn't mean for this to happen."

Niall's hair fell across his forehead when he leaned forward. "What did Brett describe in the staff meeting?" A current of rage ran through his restrained voice.

Gianna's gaze darted Kayleigh's way before she continued, "He gave a presentation on an app that would allow singles to input the qualities they most desired in a partner and later interface that list with someone with a similar app to check their compatibility score."

"Sounds like our app." Niall lunged out of his chair and walked across the room in long strides.

Kayleigh seethed, furious at Brett for lacking any sort of ethic—personal or professional.

Gianna nodded, then said, "Since I was technically still part of the IT department, I was able to look at their program before I had to leave."

Niall whirled from their large front window. "How much code did they write?"

Gianna ran a hand through her hair, leaving its short ends at odd angles. "It's hard to say. They're not as far along as you."

Niall strode back to the chair, and Kayleigh felt her muscles loosen with relief. So it wasn't over. They were still in the game.

Gianna wandered into the kitchen that opened off the living room. "I found where they stored your program and deleted it from their system," she called over her shoulder. "It's only fair, since it doesn't belong to them. At least now they can't copy any more of it. It will buy us a few more days, at least."

"Us?" Kayleigh peered at Niall, and his expression, though calmer, seemed inward, fierce, determined. Was he planning his strategy? He looked as if he was going into battle. Never before had she glimpsed the warrior in him.

Three glasses and a pitcher of lemonade thunked onto their oval coffee table when Gianna rejoined them.

"I quit, and you two need help if we're going to beat Brett. I want to join High Dive Enterprises."

Kayleigh breathed in the lemony scent before setting down her drink. "You don't have to do that, Gia."

"Of course I do. If it's okay with Niall?"

Niall nodded, a small smile beginning on his handsome mouth. "Can you program?"

"She did a combined BA/MS program at

Yale in five years and worked in our IT department before she moved to software design. Gianna can do anything."

"I don't know about anything, but I want to make up for what happened." Gianna hugged Kayleigh, then eased back.

"Then welcome aboard." Niall gave her a lopsided smile and extended his hand. "We'll need every bit of help we can get beating GSI to the patent."

"THEY'RE CALLING THE app Tingle?" Niall peered over Gianna's shoulder at the notes she'd taken during the staff meeting at GSI.

"No one is going to buy a product that makes them want to visit the restroom." Gianna's eyebrow arched.

"Wrong word, Gia," Kayleigh chimed in and sat beside him, her subtle perfume making it hard to concentrate.

"So what's your app called?" Gianna bit into a peanut-butter cookie.

Kayleigh's silver eyes slid to him, her soft curls falling around her beautiful face. "We haven't agreed on an official name yet."

Gianna, now garbed in sweatpants and an old Yale T-shirt, tucked her bare feet beneath her. "What have you got so far?"

"I like The Must List, Perfect Match and

Forever Yours," Kayleigh said. She nodded her head for emphasis, her hair moving across her shoulders like drifting shadows. She was dressed for comfort like her roommate, the fresh-faced, no-fuss look appealing to him even more than her dressy outfits.

Gianna snorted. "Those sound like bad romance titles. You're up, Niall. What do you have?"

"Compatibility Quotient, Relationship Databasics and The Common Denominator."

He crossed his arms and leaned back in his chair. At last, a voice of reason in the group who would settle this argument. He waited for Gianna's praise, but she scowled instead and nibbled on another cookie, her appetite as voracious as Kayleigh's.

She quit chewing and swung her finger between the two of them. "You two couldn't be further apart. Niall, yours sound like workshop titles at a tech convention. We need something catchier."

She strolled to the window and gazed out, a finger on her chin. He glanced at Kayleigh and she shrugged. It took every ounce of willpower not to brush away the cookie crumbs clinging to the inner curve of her mouth. Had Gianna not interrupted them earlier, would he have given in to temptation and kissed her again?

Convinced Kayleigh that they could be more than friends? If he had, it would have been a huge mistake. He'd let down his guard at the botanical gardens and had to be extravigilant now.

Gianna turned and snapped her fingers.

"How about Mesh? It's catchy, captures what we're doing, shows how well people *mesh* together and has some edge. What do you think?"

Kayleigh leaped to her feet. "It's perfect! I love it. Niall?" She turned his way, her eyes shining.

He nodded slowly. "One-word app titles gain name and brand recognition faster. Plus, it says it all. Works for me."

Kayleigh squished in beside him on the chair and threw an arm around his shoulders. "Finally. We agree on something."

He turned to face her, her nearness driving away whatever he'd been about to say. He felt the warmth of her touch, inhaling the smell of her, which reminded him of green leaves and the air before dawn. Everything about her affected him lately—her clever mind, generous heart and quiet beauty. He hadn't known how much he craved this, her, until now. But how to pursue a doomed dream?

Kayleigh stared at him for a moment, then moved away. "I can already hear people asking one another to *mesh* with them. That'd even be a good advertising tagline."

"Good idea." Niall looked across the room at Gianna. "If you'll finish coding the Must Traits, I'll begin programming the share capabilities. Once we have that, we'll test it and, if it works smoothly, we'll send it into the patent office. It sounds like we're ahead of them, but with more programmers at their disposal, it'll be a close race."

Kayleigh's hands tightened in her lap. "We can't let them win."

"We won't," Niall said with quiet conviction, though worry twisted his gut. He didn't doubt Brett had his top people on it.

But he'd work faster. Smarter. Harder. He'd get it done and copyrighted before them if it meant not sleeping for the next couple of weeks. Although he knew it was improbable, a part of him hoped if he did this for Kayleigh, she'd hate him a little less when she learned about Chris.

"It's over if we don't get financing. Either way." At a faint scratching sound, Kayleigh raced through an open doorway in the back of the small, neat apartment. When she returned, she carried a calico cat.

"We have a fire escape cat like you." Although the lower half of her face was obscured by orange, black and white fur, a smile filled her voice. “This is Pringles.” Kayleigh waved Pringles’s front paw at him. “How’s Chairman Meow?”

“Bugging the heck out of me,” Niall said, not feeling annoyed at the cat’s visits at all, actually. He’d been on his own for so long. The fact that he searched for the feline in the mornings, let the stray nap in his room and bought cat food showed that despite apartment regulations, Chairman Meow was his. Kayleigh had called him closed off, a label that was seeming less and less applicable.

“Sounds like me.” She laughed, then pressed a kiss to the top of the feline’s head. Niall’s chest tightened. How could a grown man be jealous of a cat?

“So you have another finance meeting this week?” Gianna asked after disappearing into the kitchen and returning with a bowl of cat food. The calico leaped from Kayleigh’s arms and wove in and out of Gianna’s legs as she set it on the floor.

Kayleigh sighed and sat beside him. “It’s our last, but our best shot. ForwardTech Ventures has invested in other pop-culture apps, and Mesh seems like the kind of thing they’d be interested in. We have to get them because, patent or no, without money, High Dive Enterprises is dead in the water."

Niall flinched at her choice of words.

Gianna glanced at him, her straight, dark eyebrows meeting over her nose. "You agree?"

He thought of the funds they'd need for marketing and promotional events, advertising, development and the long list of business expenses ahead.

"Yes. Spec investors are still risk adverse, and although Kayleigh's idea is unique and marketable, her lack of a track record, along with mine, makes us a hard sell."

"I'll go to the next meeting if you think that will help." Gianna pulled on black-framed glasses that dwarfed her thin face.

Kayleigh shook her head before he could respond. "Better if you keep coding. We need to stay ahead of GSI."

Gianna nodded. "Niall, why don't you bring me up to speed on your program, and I'll start today. Once I finish inputting the coding, I can begin some of the design work. We'll need a great logo, splash screen, tab icons…"

Kayleigh stopped picking up the empty cups and plates on the coffee table. "I have preliminary sketches for those, but what are we supposed to pay you with?"

"Brownies?" Gianna's eyebrow quirk didn't seem to amuse Kayleigh. He knew they were hemorrhaging funds. Paying for another worker would only strain things further....

Kayleigh reached for Gianna's shoulder. "You should get another job. Or ask for your old one back."

He marveled at Kayleigh's unselfish offer. If they stood any chance of beating GSI to the patent office, they needed Gianna. Badly. But he'd give her the same advice and admired Kayleigh for putting her friend first.

Gianna rested her hand atop Kayleigh's. "I'm joining you, and you can pay me when you get financing. Until then, I have some savings squirreled away."

Kayleigh sighed and hurried to the kitchen, her arms full of dishes. "All right. But I hope you won't regret this," she called over her shoulder.

"I'd regret it if I didn't help." Gianna took off her glasses and peered up at Kayleigh when she returned.

Kayleigh studied her then smiled. "Will you two be okay if I leave and make a phone call?"

Gianna had already sat down beside Niall on the couch and waved her away with a casual hand flip. "We've got this, oh, mighty leader."

KAYLEIGH SMILED AS she eyed the two people who had come to mean so much to her. Her best friend and her… She turned on her heel and headed for the bedroom, shutting the door behind her with the back of her foot. Better not to give Niall a label. Nothing fit anymore.

She flopped onto the Amish quilt covering her four-poster bed and punched in the number she'd vowed never to dial again.

"Kayleigh!" a hateful voice crowed, the smug tone making her clench the thick fabric of her bed cover. "I knew you'd call."

"I bet you did, Brett, after you stole my app idea." Too fired up to remain stretched out, she sat cross-legged in the center of her bed.

"I don't know what you're talking about." His voice turned questioning and innocent, but she wasn't falling for it.

"I'm contacting my lawyers about the Must Traits app as soon as we hang up." Though who that was and how she'd afford them, she hadn't a clue. Only she wouldn't stand by and do nothing.

Brett made a clucking sound. "Kay. We both know that the app was on GSI's software, worked on by one of our former employees. The IT department will back me up on that."

She gasped at his distortion of the facts. "That's a lie."

"It's the truth, and I'm prepared to swear to that in court."

Her skin felt as though it were covered in fire ants. How dare he? Brett was disgusting. Somehow, this betrayal hurt more than the cheating, though how that could be true seemed strange. Had she ever loved him? It was hard to imagine given all she knew about him now.

At the scratching on her door, she let in Pringles, who streaked across her room and leaped for his favorite nap spot, one of her pillows. She stretched out beside him, feeling the cat's claws dig into her stomach, a low rumbling burbling from its throat.

"It will come to that if you keep going ahead with this," she warned. "The app is my intellectual property, and you have no right to it."

"We once said we'd share everything." He sounded wounded, and Kayleigh felt like choking. *Brett* was playing the victim?

She squirmed onto her stomach. "That ended when you cheated on me. I'm going to make this work, Brett, no matter how many stunts you pull."

"It's not just me, Kayleigh. GSI loves my compatibility-app idea. They're putting all of our resources behind it, and we expect to have the patent shortly."

Worry tiptoed across her shoulders, but she forced herself to stay—and sound—strong. "It'll be too late."

Brett laughed. "You forget whom you're dealing with."

She slid off the bed and stomped to the window, contemplating the attached three-story homes on her block, the children jostling for control of a soccer ball, the old woman straining to wheel an overloaded shopping basket behind her, a couple of men haggling over the price of a car, their gesticulating hands waving in the air. These were her people. Brooklyn. They were tough. They were fighters, and she was, too.

"You're forgetting whom *you're* dealing with." She took a deep breath and tried to keep the shaking out of her voice. "Or maybe you never really knew her."

"I know I still love her." Brett's sigh came through the phone, his gentle tone disingenuous. "And I would do anything for her."

Kayleigh picked up her family picture and traced Chris's smile. "Prove it," she implored, knowing it was useless. "Stop writing my app."

"I can't do that, Kay. The company's invested too much. But if you come back to GSI, I'll give you your old job back and make you the team leader."

Her blood stilled, and she shivered at this tempting offer.

"Imagine it," he continued, his voice strengthening when she didn't interrupt or protest. "The chance to see the app produced by a top team that you'd control. No more risk. A sure thing. I even believe it will win a Shorty award, and I'll let you give the acceptance speech."

She wavered. High Dive Enterprises was one more funding refusal away from folding. If the start-up failed, she would let down Chris's family, a possibility that looked increasingly likely. Should she let pride keep her from being the provider she'd vowed to be? Her eyes met Chris's in the photo. It would be selfish. He would have wanted her to take a risk, and she'd done that. But he wouldn't want her to go all in on a bad hand.

"What about Gianna? Would she have her old job back, too?"

"There's no real harm done there." Brett's irritated tone belied his words. "I haven't sent her resignation letter to Human Resources yet. If you give the word, I can tear it up, and both of you can come back to GSI tomorrow. It would be as if none of this had ever happened."

Her knees shook as she made her way back to the bed. If none of this had ever happened,

Niall wouldn't be a part of her life again. And she couldn't bear the thought.

"As for the two of us," Brett said, "I won't push anything. We'll take it one day at a time with no expectations. No pressure. Please consider it, Kay. We need you. I need you. Why do you think I haven't filled your job yet? I knew you'd come back."

She felt herself weaken further. Gianna had quit out of loyalty to her, putting her own career in jeopardy. Did she have the right to turn down this chance to put their universe to rights? She thought of Niall and imagined not seeing him. Pain ripped through her when she imagined her life without him. But perhaps it would be for the best. He'd be happy to disappear back into his quiet life. She'd be letting him off the hook and making his world right again, too.

Yet it all felt wrong. She knew what the logical thing to do was, but her gut said otherwise.

After a long moment, she spoke again. "No deal. Be prepared to pay your programmers some overtime. With Gianna on my team, we'll have the app submitted for patent very soon."

A stunned silence followed her pronouncement, and she could imagine Brett adjusting his tie, a nervous tick that betrayed him.

"I hope you'll reconsider." Fury coated his

voice. "You won't hear a better offer, or have another chance."

She strode to the window fan and let the air blow her hair off her flushed face.

"I don't need another chance or your offer. I'm counting on myself." She nearly said goodbye, then changed her mind. "Oh, and, Brett?"

"Yes, Kay?" Hope buoyed his voice, making him sound like his old self. A man she no longer cared for, if she ever had.

"See you at the Shortys. Bye."

She clicked off and blocked his number before he could call her again. After making her way back to the bed, she absently ran her hand along the cat's spine. What had she done?

The door creaked open, and Niall's handsome face appeared. "You okay?"

She brushed dampness from her cheeks and forced a smile. "Fine. Peachy. Couldn't be better. Really."

He was at her side in two strides.

"You're not okay," he said, a fierce note in his voice. "Were you talking to Brett?"

She almost laughed. He knew her so well. "Yes."

Niall sat next to her. "Want to talk about it?"

"Not really." She put her hand beside his on the quilt, his nearness lending her strength. "He offered to give me my old job back. Gianna, too. Said I'd be the team leader on Tingle." Her nose burned as she imagined Niall telling her to do it.

He stiffened. "And what was your answer?" His tight voice was flat, and she couldn't tell if he cared.

"To look for us at the Shorty Awards."

His bark of laughter sounded relieved. Was he happy that she'd resigned him to more weeks spent working on this project with her?

"Good one."

When her eyes wandered upward, they met his. The affection she saw there nearly undid her. It'd been a heck of a day. "I'm sorry that I shot him down without checking with you first."

He brushed an eyelash from her cheek, his fingers lingering on the side of her face, his touch tender, before he quickly withdrew his hand. "Why?"

She shivered at his gentleness. "You only did this as a favor to me, and if you want to back out, well, I have Gianna, so it's not like you'd be leaving me in a lurch. In fact—"

He pressed a finger to her lips, stopping her nervous chatter. She was all too aware of being here, alone, with him. She'd thought of it far too much, and the reality was making her head spin. Her surprised gaze caught the admiration glinting in the depths of his brown eyes.

"I told you before, Kay. I'm all in, and I'm not going anywhere. Whatever happens, I'm seeing this through with you to the end."

Gianna entered the room and sat on the bed beside them. "Count me in, too." The cat climbed onto her lap, surveyed the group, then meowed, making them laugh.

"I didn't mean to eavesdrop, but I heard the part about Brett offering me my old job back. Kay, I wouldn't work for him again no matter how much he paid me."

She took Kayleigh's hand and twined her fingers in it. "The place wasn't the same without you. You were the heart of that division, just like you'll be the driving force of High Dive Enterprises. I believe in you, Kay. This isn't just a friend's loyalty. I'm betting on a winner. You."

Kayleigh fought back the rush of happy tears. With Gianna and Niall beside her, she felt capable of anything. Perhaps going with her gut, instead of logic, was the right move. She peeked at Niall from beneath her lowered lids, taking in his firm jaw and the angular planes of his face. Would it work out if she applied that strategy to their relationship and went for it?

She shook away the thought. Better to focus solely on business. The stakes were never higher or more important.

"So what are you two slackers doing in here, then?" she joked, though her voice cracked at the end. "Get to work."

Gianna leaped off the bed, tucking the cat against her chest. "Yes, Captain." She used Pringles's tail to salute then left.

Niall chuckled and stood. "Gianna's got a handle on her end of things, so I'll head out and work from home. Are you sure you're okay?"

She got to her feet and peered up at him. "Better. Thanks for coming over."

"I'm always here for you."

She almost sighed at the earnest look in his eyes.

"You always have been."

His hand slid from her shoulder to her fingertips, the feel of his touch lingering long after he disappeared out the door. Her toes dug into the rag rug beside her bed, and she fought not to run after him. She wanted him to stay, but what excuse could she give him? Give herself? Her feelings were a tangled mess—all the more reason she needed to shut them away before they caused either of them harm.

Despite her resolve, however, she couldn't deny it anymore. She needed him…and not just as a business partner or a friend.

CHAPTER FOURTEEN

"THAT WAS QUITE impressive, Ms. Renshaw."

Kayleigh returned the CEO of ForwardTech Ventures's smile and clicked off her presentation. She sat back in her conference chair, her spine rigid against the plush fabric. Cautious optimism mingled with relief. At least she'd done her best. After finance-meeting reactions that had ranged from indifference to skepticism, disapproval and, the worst, discouragement, this was the most promising response yet. And she desperately needed it to be. As her start-up's last real hope for financing, ForwardTech had to invest in Mesh.

"Thank you, Mr. Cantwell." She peeked at Niall out of the corner of her eye and glowed at his knee nudge and approving grin. Though things had been awkward since last week's kiss, their push to finish coding ahead of GSI had kept them too busy to address it. And maybe it was for the best. With their worries over getting the patent ahead of their competitor and securing the funds they needed to go forward, romance had to be on her back burner, no matter how much she thought of him. And that kiss.

Niall leaned forward, the gold buttons on the sleeves of an unfamiliar navy jacket gleaming. Was the suit new? She'd never seen him look so dressy, or handsome, in a crisp white dress shirt and crimson tie that set off his dark coloring.

"Let's talk numbers. Here's a rundown of the expenses that details High Dive's projected costs." Niall slid a folder to the executive.

When Mr. Cantwell snapped his fingers, the dim lights in the glass-walled room brightened, and the screen on which Kayleigh had projected her PowerPoint rose. Impressive. ForwardTech might be a small finance firm, but they invested in innovative technology. Would they see the same potential in her product?

When her leg began to jump, Niall's warm hand folded over her knee, and her worries faded to the background. They exchanged a small smile, his "we've got this" expression making her want to laugh. He'd worn it whenever they'd teamed up to play Capture the Flag at camp. But that was the overconfidence of kids. In the adult world of business, it was too early to tell if they'd succeeded.

She gazed over Mr. Cantwell's bent head

and out the large windows comprising the far wall. Pigeons took flight from a stone gargoyle adorning a building across Broadway. The muffled sounds of the Financial District traffic reached this fourth-floor suite and she marveled, as she always did, at the electric pulse of this city, its people. They flowed through its arteries, carrying information, products, finances and services to keep this metropolis thriving. It humbled her to imagine that, if things went well here, she'd be contributing to that system, diving into the flowing course instead of watching from the sidelines. A thinker and a doer.

As the waiting continued, she contemplated the arch of Niall's strong neck, the way his hands moved when he talked. She breathed in his spicy cologne, another change from his usual soapy, masculine scent. It was different, but she liked it. And, now that she thought about it, weren't his bangs shorter? Had he gotten a haircut? Why all of these improvements? Not that she disapproved.

At last, Mr. Cantwell pulled off half-moon glasses and ran a hand through his thatch of gray hair. He was a fit man for his age, mid- to late fifties, she'd guess. In his expensive Italian suit, shiny loafers and a diamond-studded watch, he practically screamed success. She pushed back her shoulders and discreetly held her arms out from her sides, needing some air beneath the jacket that topped her sleeveless red sheath dress. It felt as though her entire future, along with Josh's, Sam's and now Gianna's, hung between them, a fragile entity that would disappear at his rejection.

His neutral expression gave nothing away. "I read over the market research and business plan you'd sent earlier and conducted some of my own research through private channels."

She felt a rush of excitement in her chest, followed by a knot in her stomach. Mr. Cantwell was taking their idea seriously if he'd invested his own time before meeting with them. Perhaps he had already made up his mind and planned to invest? She didn't want to jinx herself with the thought, so she pushed it away. Niall's warm glance showed he was as hopeful as she. This was it. She sensed a decision. *Please, please, please let it be a yes.*

"And what did you find?" she asked, keeping her tone businesslike despite her quivering insides.

"My daughter-in-law works for a company you're familiar with, Ms. Renshaw." He carefully closed the folders but made no move to slide them back. A good sign. He wanted them. Maybe. Perhaps planned to use them as they forged a deal? She tamped down her rising excitement.

"Which is...?" *Cut to the chase, Mr. Cantwell,* she silently added. Good news was coming. She could practically smell it like an overdue thunderstorm.

"Genesis Software Innovations."

Niall shifted beside her as she struggled to hide her dismay. Why was her old company being mentioned in their meeting? A feeling of unease took hold, and she thought about the last name. Cantwell, she mused... Was it someone she knew? The name had sounded familiar when they'd been ushered into the leader's conference room.

And then it hit her.

Stacey. Stacey Cantwell. An IT programmer. Could she be working on the rip-off version of her app? Had Stacey heard about her dramatic exit from the company? What exactly had Stacey told her father-in-law? Kayleigh's breath hitched.

"I recently left GSI to develop my own app. As I hope you agree, this idea shows great market potential."

Mr. Cantwell smiled, revealing overlapping front teeth. His eyes bulged from beneath thick eyebrows, his pointed chin making him resemble a badger.

"Yes, it does. In fact, when I received your initial inquiry and packet of information, I looked forward to this meeting and what could be a promising business venture for us."

Her fingers reflexively tightened around themselves. Had they done it? Secured financing and saved their start-up?

"Would you like to begin with a discussion of the itemized list of costs?" Hope crept into her voice, raising it half an octave.

Mr. Cantwell's smile faded around the edges. "There's no need."

"So our estimates are in line with your cost calculations," Niall spoke up. The tense way he held his mouth told her he was still feeling cautious given these mixed signals.

"You misunderstand me. There's no need to go over your financing requirements, as ForwardTech will not be funding you."

Kayleigh's hope fell from some place in her chest and landed around her feet, shattering like a glass jar tipped from a high shelf. She mentally scratched off "meet with ForwardTech" from today's to-do list, then pictured ripping the paper to shreds.

"And why is that, Mr. Cantwell? We appreciate your honest feedback, of course," she forced herself to say, keeping the disappointment out of her voice. There'd been enough meetings in which she'd witnessed winds firmly blowing in one direction only to see them shift at the last minute. It might not be too late to turn this around. Perhaps she could change his mind.

His blunt fingernails drummed on the long mahogany table. "Yes. Honesty. That is key. Tell me, did you conceive of this app while working for GSI?"

The blunt force of his words struck like a blow, and she struggled to speak. So Stacey had been working on Tingle. Had mentioned it to him. And now ForwardTech's CEO saw her as an intellectual-property thief.

"If you are suggesting that I stole this idea from my employer, the answer is no," she said coolly, despite the heat creeping up her neck and into her cheeks.

"Mr. Cantwell," Niall said firmly. "With all due respect, GSI maliciously appropriated our app idea from a former employee, who now works for us. She'd mistakenly brought in the program to try it out on GSI's more advanced operating systems, and it was discovered when they did a backup."

"Malicious? That seems a rather strong word for the number one app-producing company in the world." Mr. Cantwell sniffed as if smelling their guilt. "Why would GSI need to take another idea when they have an entire department devoted to creating apps? They've won a Shorty for Best App the past six years in a row." When Mr. Cantwell shook his head, the skin beneath his chin wobbled.

Niall's chair scraped back and he bolted to his feet. "Ms. Renshaw was the genesis for those award-winning ideas while working for GSI. When she left, she took her talent, creativity and progressive ideas with her. Any idea linked to her would be very attractive to GSI."

Despite the cocktail of disappointment and fury mixing in her gut, she felt a jolt of pleasure at Niall's compliments.

"I understand that Ms. Renshaw was a valued employee, but it stretches credibility that a company with GSI's reputation would act unprofessionally." Mr. Cantwell readjusted gold cuff links, his eyes narrow with suspicion.

"My boss was also my fiancé." She stood beside Niall and peered down at the small balding patch at the back of Mr. Cantwell's head.

Confusion flickered in his eyes, along with disapproval. "I see. So this is a personal matter."

Kayleigh nodded, a jerky, tight movement, feeling this chance slipping away with every moment that passed, carrying her hopes and dreams with it. Capitalists were risk adverse. Even a progressive company like ForwardTech

Ventures wouldn't involve themselves in a squabble with the potential for lawsuits.

"Then I wish you well. Both of you." Mr. Cantwell slid their folders back to them; Niall snatched them up and stuffed them in his briefcase, his shoulders stiff. "But I'm afraid our interests are not compatible." He gave a short laugh that neither of them returned. "Excuse the play on words."

She didn't. In fact, her temper was as hot as a bar of molten iron. It seared her as she accepted his perfunctory handshake, then followed Niall to the elevator. It burned her as she and Niall stood, side by side, wordless, as the glass elevator delivered them to the lobby. It smoldered as she stalked outside, shoving through the gold-metal–framed doors and onto the crowded street. Professionals filled the sidewalk, eating and drinking as they conducted lunch-hour business on their cell phones.

When she spotted the pretzel vendor, she froze. It was the same one she and Gianna had eaten at every day when they'd worked at GSI. An angry sound escaped her. She'd chased after independence but had tasted defeat instead. Unlike the men and women easily navigating these streets, she felt flattened. She should never have left the shallow end of the pool. She wasn't a risk taker, and this venture had been a horrible mistake with serious consequences.

"Are you hungry?" Niall's deep voice behind her startled her.

"No. I—I—I want to—" She turned in a slow circle, taking in a large bronze bull sculpture that seemed ready to charge but was really going nowhere. She could relate. What did she want? Life didn't give you do overs. There was no rewind button. She was out of options.

A firm hand settled on her back, and Niall led her to a crosswalk. She waited numbly for the red-lit walk signal to turn green, then followed him through the gated entranceway to Bowling Green park, a large fountain surrounded by a circle of scarlet petunias at its center. Tall trees shaded the fenced, wrought iron perimeter lined with simple wooden benches. They were packed with tourists, bankers and college students taking advantage of the free Wi-Fi. This innocuous space, the oldest of the city's parks, was where much of the world's business was conducted. An epicenter. And she realized, with a sinking heart, that she was wrong to ever think she'd be a part of it.

At the fountain area, they spotted an empty bench. A man slept on the ground beside the fountain. Newspapers were spread neatly beneath him, a dog curled across his head, one eye opening as they approached.

"I'm getting you something to drink. Don't move." Niall let go and backed up, his eyes on her until she nodded. She watched him turn on his heel and head back to the street, her gut sour, her thoughts thick and sluggish.

Losing Brett hadn't been nearly this painful. The demise of High Dive Enterprises meant so many endings. The end of her ability to help Chris's family, the end of her chance to prove that she was a doer, not just an ideas person, and the end of spending time with Niall. Somehow, that last thought hurt most of all.

She dropped her head in her hands and listened to the water as it shot into the sky before falling to earth. Just like her, it could only reach so high. Without Mesh, there was no Niall. He'd planned to sell his shares and go back to his solitary life when the app was done, and now he'd only leave sooner. Without him, her future felt bleak and empty, a shadow-filled place in sepia tones.

Her feet slid out of the tight heels she now regretted wearing. She might as well have worn flip-flops for all the good it would have done her with Mr. Cantwell. She wished he'd simply called off the meeting, but she supposed he'd wanted to hear her out before turning her down.

She reached up and untied her confining bun, letting the waves tumble in front of her face.

"Here's some coffee."

A to-go cup appeared in her line of vision. She studied Niall's concerned face and could have cried. Was this the last time she'd see him? With no way to move forward with their business, there was a good chance that he'd slink back to his man cave and never contact her again.

"Thanks." She took the cup and set it beside her, staring listlessly at a singer strumming his guitar beneath a tree, a small crowd gathered in a half circle around him.

On the street beyond the black wrought iron fence, cabs whizzed past, buses rumbled by and pedestrians breezed along, all hurrying to some important destination. Or at least it seemed that way. But where could she go? Brett had out-maneuvered her. If Stacey Cantwell was talking about her, then others were, as well. Even if she could drum up more options, there was a good chance other investors would hear of the controversy and turn her down. Even if Brett didn't beat them to the patent, he'd defeated her anyway.

She ground her teeth and must have made a noise because suddenly Niall scooted closer.

"It's going to be okay," he murmured, his voice gentle, as though speaking to a spooked three-year-old. She was sick of men talking down to her—Brett, Major Carlton and now Mr. Cantwell. Sick of her accomplishments overlooked and her dreams going nowhere. Suddenly, all of her fury turned on Niall.

"No. It's not going to be okay." Her loud voice made the musician stop playing and his fans glance her way. "It's over."

Niall frowned and opened a packet of sweetener before handing it to her. "There are hundreds of investment firms. We'll find someone else."

She put down her coffee and ignored the artificial sugar. "When, Niall? How soon? Because I don't know about you, but I'm just about out of money and have a family to help out. Did you know I supplement Beth's expenses?"

To her surprise, he nodded. Had Josh said something? Not that it mattered. "I know you have a lot of responsibilities, and they'll get taken care of. Don't worry." He laid a hand on her arm, and she shook it off, not wanting his understanding. She needed to rage and wished he'd be furious with her. His attitude set her teeth on edge. He was just like Brett. Like her parents. Thinking he knew best.

"You don't even know what responsibilities are," she spat, and continued despite his surprised flinch and the sense that she was acting irrationally. But this overdue rant could not be stopped, regardless of who stood in its path. "When have you ever worried about anyone other than yourself?"

He opened his mouth then closed it, his face paling beneath the color it'd recently acquired from their outings.

"Exactly," she continued, needing to vent. "You put yourself first, and who cares about the consequences."

"I do care," he said quietly, his eyes large. "I don't want to see this fail."

She flung herself off the bench, unable to be near him in her vortex of conflicting emotions.

"Why do you care? You can have everything back the way you want it. No more leaving the apartment, talking to people, playing by other people's rules. And no more putting up with me. This is good news for you, isn't it? You're off the hook."

He squinted up at her in the bright sunshine. "That's not what I want."

"Right." She snorted derisively, then shouldered her bag, ready to get this painful parting over with.

Niall stood and held out a hand she ignored. "You're wrong."

She squared her chin and glowered. "Then, what do you want?"

His fingers twined with hers. "You."

His simple answer ignited the fireworks exploding in her head. She simply couldn't take it in. Wasn't able to process what he meant. Did he want her as a friend, or more? Her feelings were much too strong to hear him say he wanted them to stay "pals." When they'd reunited, she'd wanted his friendship. Now it wasn't nearly enough.

"Don't say that. Don't. Ever." She backed away and nearly tripped over the homeless dog's leash. Niall's stricken face stayed with her after she whirled and sprinted for the street, searching for the subway stop that would take her away from here, away from it all. Though she knew there was no escaping her worn-out heart.

NIALL MOVED AUTOMATICALLY through one of his old routines at the dojang, working through the pain of Kayleigh's rejection. Why had he said anything? He'd known she only saw him as a friend and business partner. And with his involvement in her brother's death, he didn't deserve her either. Didn't deserve love, period.

Yet, like a fool, he'd told her he wanted her. What had he expected? That she'd jump into his arms and tell him that she wanted to be with him, too?

His foot lashed into the air before he pivoted, dropped to his knees and punched. He stood, then sank into a lunge. He'd vowed to help her, not fall for her. Yet he'd done it anyway. She was beautiful, strong, smart and funny, yet it was at her vulnerable moments that he wanted to carry her away and never let her go. Perhaps that was what had tripped him into saying how he felt. Seeing her so hurt had triggered his instincts to take away her pain. But he should have known that confessing his feelings would only complicate things, not make her feel better.

He sank into a sitting stance, and his hands punched the air at blistering speed, loosening up tight shoulders and upper-back muscles. When he rose on his artificial foot's tiptoes and held the position for three minutes, he marveled. Good had come from this time spent with Kayleigh, however.

Because of her, he'd come back to the world, or it had returned to him. Although he still felt terrible about what had happened to Chris, somewhere along the line he'd stopped wishing he'd died, too. And he couldn't deny that Kayleigh was the reason he was glad to be alive. He thought of her every night before he went to bed, imagining her beside him, talking about their company, their day, their tomorrows… together. Every morning he looked forward to seeing her beautiful face.

He executed a quick succession of moves, then bent his prosthetic leg back at a forty-five degree angle, holding the L stance until he was sure of his stability before kicking again. Ironic that now that she'd helped him regain control of his life and himself, Kayleigh was slipping away. He unclenched his jaw and forced himself to relax as he alternated between still, strength-training positions and fighter moves.

He needed to focus on technique if he was to regain Master Jung's approval to work with students again. It wasn't until he'd brought Josh, and begun tutoring him this week, that he'd realized how much he missed it. The kids had given him much more than he'd ever given them. Would they accept a one-legged teacher? Would Master Jung approve once he saw him in action?

An hour later he stepped out of the locker room, refreshed from his shower, his mind still in turmoil. Today had been full of failures—their rejection at ForwardTech and, even worse, Kayleigh's disgust at his confession. He wouldn't be surprised if she ended the company and her time with him. His body ached at the thought of a life without her. But hadn't that always been the reality? Eventually, she would find out that he'd caused Chris's death. Whatever they started was doomed to fail.

"Master Walsh. Welcome."

Niall pulled the towel away from his dripping hair and returned Master Jung's smile. "Hello, Master Jung. It's nice to be back." Under other circumstances, when he hadn't just had his heart handed to him, it would have been.

Master Jung gestured toward the front of the dojang. "Will you join me for a moment in my office?"

Niall hid his disappointment. He'd planned to call Kayleigh now that he'd cooled off. See where things stood.

Master Jung's compact form disappeared inside his office, and Niall followed, sitting in the chair that he always felt two times too big for.

"I've worked out today, Master Jung, and in a few weeks, I may be ready to be tested."

Master Jung waved graceful hands. Niall knew how much brute strength lay in them. "No need."

"Sir?" Niall blinked in surprise. Had Master

Jung changed his mind about having an amputee for a leader?

"I watched you earlier."

"Oh." Niall mentally ran over his performance, critiquing it. Master Jung's standards were high, and he demanded perfection. And if there was one thing Niall was not, it was perfect. A wave of disappointment rolled through him. He'd been looking forward to working with the kids again, but he had to abide by Master Jung's rules.

Master Jung reached behind him and handed Niall a set of white robes and a black belt. "You'll be needing these when you teach next week. Will Mondays and Wednesdays at 4:00 p.m. be acceptable?"

His mouth opened and closed, words dying on his tongue. Overwhelmed, he ran the familiar belt through his fingers, thankful for this second chance.

"I didn't think I was ready."

"You're ready to teach." Master Jung nodded and his eyes gleamed. "Ready to learn, too. That's more important."

"Yes. I've lost flexibility, and my balance is off. But I hope with time I can—"

"No." Master Jung's hand sliced the air and came down flat on the desk. "Like young Josh, you have much Han, yes? Since you returned from the war."

Niall sat back in the chair as though the words had pushed him. Master Jung's perception never ceased to amaze him.

"Yes." He met the leader's eyes and held himself tight. There was no sense in hiding what the man would see anyway.

"Accept this pain and think of it as a lesson instead of a burden. Study your wound, then cast out the shadows. That's how to be rid of your Han."

Niall's chest expanded as he absorbed Master Jung's advice. He was right. He couldn't—shouldn't—avoid his pain, the blame he cast on himself, his life. A strong man would learn to accept what he'd done. And if he opened up to Kayleigh and she didn't accept him, especially after hearing the truth about Chris, then he would bear that, too.

He contemplated his prosthetic leg. His mistakes would always haunt him. Better to face them directly. As soon as he finished coding, he'd reveal what had happened to Chris. Although Niall would be breaking military code, he cared too much about Kayleigh to hold back the truth any longer. Once the product was complete, he'd tell her everything. If she sent him away, at least he'd know she was taken care of. Had a working app that would provide for her and Chris's family.

He hoped that she'd find a way to forgive him. The more he'd gotten to know her again, had seen her giving and generous spirit, the more possible it seemed. But if he was wrong…

He shook the doubt from his head. They'd cross that bridge when they reached it.

Until then, he would not run away, and he would not hide.

Not anymore.

CHAPTER FIFTEEN

KAYLEIGH'S GAIT SPED up as she passed the nurses' station at the assisted-living home. Even though it was midafternoon, and Mary-Anne was nowhere in sight, Kayleigh didn't want to risk running into her, didn't want to deal with questions about the start-up or Niall.

He told me that he wants me, Kayleigh might blurt out. It'd been all she'd thought about since leaving him in the park. Did he mean he wanted her as more than a partner? More than a friend? Because she really, *really* wanted to know.

But the less she dwelled on his ambiguous confession, the better. She had other, important things to worry about. Namely her failure to develop her app, to finance her company and to provide for Chris's family.

Her fingers tightened around her purse handle and she forced a smile at the residents she taught in her water-aerobics class. When she peeked into her grandfather's room, she found it empty, and sighed in disappointment. He must be doing an activity. She put away the treats she'd grabbed after her subway stop, then set off back down the hall. This time she did run into MaryAnne.

"Hi, Kayleigh. How'd your meeting go today? Niall was telling me—"

Kayleigh's eyes fled MaryAnne's shrewd gaze.

"I'm so sorry, but I'm in a bit of a rush. Would you know where my grandfather is?"

MaryAnne reached for her hand. "You're so cold, and you look pale. How about some coffee to go? It's already made in the break room."

Kayleigh clamped down on the temptation to follow MaryAnne. She didn't trust herself to keep her tangle of emotions to herself.

"Next time." Kayleigh gave her a wan smile. "Okay?"

After a moment, MaryAnne nodded slowly, a line appearing between her brows. "I'm guessing your grandfather's in Annette Larson's room, 228. If not, then playing Ping-Pong. Would you like me to have him paged?"

Kayleigh could only imagine the alarm that would raise. "No. And thank you."

"Stop by on your way out if you want to talk," MaryAnne called as Kayleigh waved and set off.

Down another hall and around a corner, she

heard raucous laughter and a Buddy Holly tune coming from one of the open doorways. She glanced at the number. 228. Was she about to crash a party?

Inside, the seniors were focused on a board game set up on a folding table in the center of Annette's room. Six folding chairs were pulled up to it.

"You didn't shake the dice hard enough. Roll again. That twelve doesn't count!" hollered Mr. Jennson, his red polyester dress shirt open at the collar, revealing several gold necklaces and a patch of white chest hair.

"It counts," grumbled Mr. Tanner, whose thin wrist appeared below a loose cotton sweater as he moved his piece around the board. "And I'd like to buy Boardwalk, please."

"Any chance I can buy it from you, Michael?" purred Mrs. Larson, her silky cream dress shirt and pearls contrasting with her bright red lipstick. Mr. Tanner gaped at her without answering. "I already own Park Place." Her glossy lips parted in a smile to reveal perfect white teeth, her green eyes gleaming.

"I—I—" Mr. Tanner stuttered, seemingly paralyzed by Mrs. Larson's smile.

"Aw, come on, Michael. That's a bad deal. Don't do it." Mrs. Perry grabbed a handful of M&M's and tossed them into her mouth, her floral housedress complementing the pink in her cheeks. "And stop flirting your way to a win, Annette."

"The property's his, dear," Gramps said quietly, his voice barely carrying to the doorway. But apparently Mrs. Larson heard it loud and clear because she nodded and withdrew the money she held out to Mr. Tanner.

"Pete, it's your turn," she said, and handed Mr. Jennson the dice. He brought them to his lips and kissed them. "Now that you've touched them, I'm bound to have some luck."

Kayleigh watched the small smile that passed between her grandfather and Mrs. Larson. Interesting. The two seemed to be close, the squabble over the bacon long forgotten. Perhaps Gramps didn't need her compatibility app after all. She blinked back the sting in her eyes. Now that she'd lost her last shot at financing, he wouldn't have gotten it from her anyway.

She must have made a sound because suddenly it grew quiet, and when she looked up from the tissue she'd retrieved from her purse, all eyes were on her. Gramps used his cane to push to his feet, concern deepening the lines around his mouth.

"Kayleigh. I wasn't expecting you until tomorrow. Is everything okay?"

Her nod turned into a head shake as emotions welled. "I'll come back tomorrow." Her voice broke, and she swallowed hard over the lump in her throat. "I don't want to interrupt your fun."

Annette reached her before Gramps, the smell of Chanel No. 5 enveloping her. "Sweetheart. Come in. We don't mind being interrupted. Besides, Mr. Tanner's been cheating the entire time."

The thin man's eyes bulged. "That's not true."

"Oh, shut it, Michael," drawled Mrs. Perry, pushing to her feet to join the circle of arms now surrounding Kayleigh.

"Can I get in on that hug?" called Mr. Jennson.

The group shouted an emphatic "No!" and dissolved into laughter as they led Kayleigh to an oversize futon couch covered in a denim rose print. Gramps sat on one side and Annette on the other, both holding her trembling hands.

Mrs. Perry pulled her chair up beside them and Mr. Tanner and Mr. Jennson turned around to watch the action, but not before Kayleigh noticed Mr. Tanner sneak a five-hundred-dollar bill into his pile. If she wasn't in such a terrible mood, she would have smiled. He really was a cheater.

"What's wrong, Kay?" Gramps's blue eyes delved into hers, and Annette squeezed her hand.

"Man trouble," pronounced Mrs. Perry. She tightened the knot on her head turban and nodded emphatically, her chins wobbling. "Don't know why I wasted so many years on them. Worthless creatures. Whoever he is, you're better off without him."

"Hey. We can't help it if we're irresistible," protested Mr. Jennson, undoing another button on his shirt and winking at Mrs. Perry.

She waved a heavily ringed hand. "Close that up, Pete. No one wants to see it."

"Can still do fifty push-ups and a hundred sit-ups a day. Want to see my six-pack, Grace?" His hands rose to his buttons again but were stopped by another loud "No!" from the group.

"You don't know what you're missing," he groused, and subsided back into his chair.

An iPod in a dock beside Annette's bed shuffled to a slow song, the crooner wailing, "Moon River."

"This song always makes me want to dance, which reminds me, when are we going to have that party for your company? The one where we get to try that thing on our phones," Mr. Tanner asked. "I was getting jazzed about it."

Kayleigh looked at their expectant faces

bleakly. When they'd graciously taken part in her market surveys, she'd promised to hold a marketing event here. Only that wasn't going to happen. Not now. She wondered if GSI's version of her app would take into account the thriving dating pool in the sixty-five and over group. She hoped so. Everyone deserved love. If only she'd been able to help them find it.

Her chest burned at all that she'd lost today, and when she shivered, Annette and Gramps wrapped their arms around her.

"Can't you see she's upset?" accused Mrs. Perry, passing Kayleigh the bowl of M&M's. "Stop pestering her about a party."

"There's not going to be a party," Kayleigh managed. "In fact, the compatibility app is over."

"Over?" Annette leaned back and studied her while Gramps pulled her close and kissed her cheek.

"What happened?" Mr. Jennson buttoned his shirt up to his neck, his cocky smile gone.

"Folks, I'm going to take my granddaughter back to my room. Please excuse us. I'm sure she'd like a word in private." Gramps put a hand on his cane, but Kayleigh stopped him before he rose. The kind faces surrounding her stopped the sensation of free-falling that'd taken hold earlier.

"It's okay, Gramps. I want to stay." Her words quieted the protesting seniors. "I don't have a big family, but you all feel like part of it."

Mrs. Perry's eyes grew moist, and she leaned over to hug Kayleigh. "We feel that way about you, too, honey. Tell us what happened."

"I see more of Kayleigh than I do my own grandchildren," muttered Mr. Tanner, whose chair scraped the linoleum floor as he pulled it closer and patted her knee. "We're all ears, toots. Go ahead."

Kayleigh clasped her shaking hands and spoke. "The last finance company on my list turned me down today."

The group looked at her blankly, as if waiting for her to get to the bad news. And maybe it wasn't the worst part. Niall's hurt face flashed before her eyes. She'd lost him, too.

After a beat, Gramps squeezed her hand. "Sounds like it's time to make a new list, then."

She shook her head miserably. "It's not that easy. These were the only companies that agreed to meet with me. I could cast the net farther, but I'm out of time. And besides, my app idea got stolen by Brett and GSI." She scanned the group. "They're my old employer, and Brett was my—"

"Cheating ex-fiancé," snorted Mrs. Perry,

pounding the table with her palms and making the game pieces jump. "Annette told me. What a fink. Like I said. It's man trouble. Sorry, sweetie."

A murmur of sympathetic noises and agreement rose from the crowd, and Kayleigh nodded glumly. Yes, she supposed at the heart of things, it was. She filled them in on the rest, Gramps's steady back rub helping her go on until she ended without mentioning Niall. If she couldn't figure out her feelings, how could they understand?

"So you'd need funds to pay the new programmer you hired," Mr. Jennson said, glasses now perched on the end of his nose.

Kayleigh glanced at him in surprise, as did the rest of the gang. "Yes, and—"

"Capital to get it approved by Apple, connect it to the iTunes store, hosting and servers, marketing events and advertising campaigns with the biggest fee, of course, going to your lead programmer, who will charge a pretty penny to create this layered program." Mr. Tanner pulled a green see-through visor over his head, his eyes sharp beneath its brim.

"Watch out, Pete's put his old CEO hat on," cackled Mrs. Perry, grabbing a ball of yarn and knitting needles from a bag by her feet. "I think better when my hands are busy."

"I may be retired, but I'm not dead," Mr. Jennson protested, pointing a pencil.

"The only thing he likes more than women is money," Annette whispered, leaning across Kayleigh to speak to Gramps. Her grandfather's eyes twinkled at her.

"So how much is this fella charging you?" Mr. Jennson stopped scribbling on a paper pad and assessed her.

"Niall is a partner, so he's doing it for free."

Mr. Jennson pursed his lips and whistled. "You've got a good one there. Those guys can charge thousands of dollars. He must believe in this app to give up payment for potential profits."

Kayleigh's heart stuttered to a stop. Niall did believe in her. Brett never had, but Niall... He'd been there for her. It'd taken him a while to warm up to the idea, but once he'd come around, he'd been "all in." Did that include his heart, too?

Sure they'd quarreled, disagreed, scoffed at each other, but at the end of every day, they were still a team. And wasn't that what counted? They'd known each other for so long that she failed to see that more than friendship held them together. Maybe taking their relationship out of the friend zone wasn't the treacherous step she'd imagined all this time.

And even if it was a risk, hadn't she vowed not to play it safe anymore?

She couldn't imagine Niall ever letting her down. Deceiving her. Misrepresenting himself. When he'd said he wanted her, he'd meant it. Not her company, not her friendship. Her. And she should have believed him, answered and not retreated.

She scrambled to her feet, ready to run all the way to Bed-Stuy, to Niall, if she had to. He deserved his answer, and she was ready to give it to him. Needed to take this leap of faith with her heart. "I've got to go. You were all so kind to listen, but really, there's nothing anyone can do."

"Hold on there, little lady." Mr. Tanner held up a hand, forestalling her. "How much money does she need, Pete?"

"About two hundred and fifty thousand to start and that much again in six months."

Her helpless gaze wandered to Gramps. What must he think of her colossal failure? He'd told her that the only way to win was not to give up when success was around the corner. But she'd made every turn and come up with nothing.

"Sounds reasonable," Annette Larson murmured. "Doable." And, to Kayleigh's surprise, all heads nodded.

"Agreed. Not a problem at all." Mrs. Perry looked up from knitting. "What do you think, fellas?"

Mr. Tanner and Mr. Jennson looked at one another then nodded, turning to Kayleigh with confident smiles.

"I don't have that in my bank account." She met her grandfather's gaze and mouthed, "What?" to him. He shrugged, looking as puzzled as she at his friends' strange reaction.

"But we do, honey," Mrs. Perry said, her needles clacking together. "Or at least, we've each got a fifth of it. Am I right?"

Mr. Jennson nodded again, along with Mr. Tanner and Mrs. Larson. A faintness stole over her, and she sank back down on the futon. "Are you saying what I think you're saying?"

Mrs. Perry waved a needle. "No fink is going to get one over on our girl. That's why I want to invest in your up-start." She glanced around the table. "I mean, start-up. What did I say?"

"You got it right, Grace." Mr. Tanner smiled at Kayleigh. "You remind me of my daughter. I'm in, too."

"You're a winner, and you come from good genes," Annette Larson said, her warm eyes twinkling at a dumbfounded-looking Gramps. "And I've always been a gambler. A smart gal like you, someone who could rope a programmer in for free like that, is a sure bet. I'm putting my money on you," piped up Mr. Jennson.

"I'm sorry. I can't accept," she protested, floored at this generous offer. They lived in an assisted-living facility, and that didn't come cheap. She knew her grandfather existed on monthly payments subsidized by his social security and his military pension. He didn't have that much in the bank, and if she took their money, she'd leave them just as broke.

"We're not asking you on a date. This is a bona fide business proposition. Are you going to let this chance slip through your fingers?" Mr. Jennson took off his glasses and peered at her, his sharp brown eyes making her squirm. He was right. She needed to think through this logically.

"We'd need to draw up a business agreement..." she began.

Annette nodded, her short curls bobbing beneath her ear lobes. "My son's a business lawyer. He can do the paperwork."

"We'll need to form a Limited Liability Corporation," Mr. Jennson put in, jotting notes on his paper pad.

"Who knows, we might want to fund other projects if this makes us a profit," crowed Mr.

Tanner. He brushed back the comb-over of gray hair that had flopped in his eyes. "When it makes us a profit, I mean. Just because we're retired doesn't mean we're out of the game."

Mr. Jennson rubbed his hands together. "Back in the game, baby!"

"That's what we should call ourselves." Mrs. Perry looked excitedly around the room. "Back in the Game."

Annette clapped her hands. "I adore it. What do you say, Frank?"

Kayleigh's heart squeezed when she saw her grandfather's embarrassed flush. "I'm not sure—" she began.

"I'll do it!" he interrupted, his voice firm. She glanced at him sharply, wondering where on earth he would ever find that kind of money. She needed to get him alone and ask, make sure he wasn't just trying to save face in front of his friends.

"Thank you so much!" She gave everyone a hug and helped her grandfather to his feet. "Gramps and I have a bit more to discuss. I'll be by tomorrow to iron out the details. Sound good?"

"You got it, toots." Mr. Jennson took off his visor and slid into her grandfather's vacated spot on the futon, cozying up to Annette.

"Maybe Annette and I can get started on some market testing."

Annette pushed him away and gave Gramps a wink. "I think we'll save that for the dance. Will we still be on for that in a couple of weeks?"

Kayleigh paused at the door with her grandfather and surveyed the amazing people who had come to her aid.

"If we get the patent in ahead of GSI. That's still up in the air. But with the financing secure, we won't quit. Not when we're this close." She eyed her grandfather, and he gave her a weak smile. Sitting here with these wonderful people offering her the financing she needed seemed like a crazy dream.

How on earth would her grandfather come up with his share?

"I'm so grateful to all of you." She kept her voice confident, despite her doubts. "I can't tell you how much your help means to me."

"Help?" scoffed Mr. Jennson, waving his hand as if to dismiss her. "We're going to turn a pretty profit on this. Mark my words. I've always had a nose for money, and it smells like it's about to rain."

Their excited laughter followed her out the door as she and Gramps made their way to his room. She waved to MaryAnne, gave her a reassuring smile but didn't stop. With so much up in the air, she needed to get to the bottom of Gramps's outrageous offer to kick in fifty thousand dollars he clearly didn't have. He was silent until he took his seat by his window.

"Gramps, I know you don't want to let me down, but you don't have to—"

Her grandfather held up his hand, and she quieted.

He stared out at a man riding a lawn mower on the back lawn. "Irene and I liked to collect a lot of things."

"I know, Gramps." She put a hand on his shoulder, feeling the broad bones shift beneath her fingertips. "And I still have the trunks in my closet. I've kept them, just like you asked me."

Gramps seemed to relax at her proclamation. "We actually met at a coin show. Did I ever tell you that?"

She smiled, remembering the story Gram had shared. "You both wanted the same Roman coin, but you scored a date with her instead, right?"

"When we married, I got the girl and the coin." His eyes looked far away, his smile as fleeting as a wisp of cloud. "But she was worth far more," he added gruffly, and blinked a few times.

Kayleigh sat on his bed and waited for him to continue. Her grandparents had lived the greatest love story she'd ever known. To this day, she took Gramps to the cemetery on their wedding anniversary, her grandmother's birthday and Valentine's Day, when he delivered her favorite flowers—fire-and-ice roses. She'd watched his lips move silently as he spoke to the air beside her grandmother's grave, conversing with an invisible presence that felt real to him.

Now that she recalled those cemetery visits, she wondered if love was like talking to the wind the way Gramps had. You sent your feelings out into the universe and hoped they came back to you. Sometimes they didn't, like with Brett, but sometimes, they did, possibly with Niall. Her stomach tightened. She hoped she was right about this. About them. After losing Chris, she couldn't bear to lose Niall, too.

"Your gram and I never sold any of our coins," Gramps continued after clearing his throat. "Even that first Roman one. We couldn't part with them for sentimental reasons. But you can."

Kayleigh shot to her feet. "What? No. Those are yours. I'd never sell them."

"Yes, my dear. You can." Gramps smiled kindly at her, the expression in his blue eyes reassuring. “And your gram would be the first one to encourage you. Would you grab me a pen and my pad from the nightstand, love?”

She retrieved the items and handed them over, heart heavy. Selling these items felt like losing her past. How many times had she pored over the shining, encased circles in their albums, hearing Gram’s tales about each one?

Gramps scribbled something on the paper and passed it to her. She scanned his writing and read a name and phone number.

“That man’s a coin expert who once assessed our collection for insurance reasons.” A bent finger pointed at the paper. “Fifteen years ago, he offered to buy them himself for forty thousand dollars. If you sell it, and our stamp and rare toys collections, I’m guessing I’ll have the capital to join Back in the Game. Will you do that for me?”

She marveled. He’d been so intent on having her keep the collection safe for him when he’d sold his house. Now he was willing to let it all go.

“Are you sure?”

“Honey. If there’s one thing I’ve learned, it’s to put the past behind you.” Gramps reached for her hand and she put her fingers through his. “Maybe I thought holding on to those things would keep me and your gram close, but now I know that there's a reason I don't hear her laughing at my jokes anymore. She wants me to let go. If I don't, it will keep me from being happy now."

She followed his glance to a pair of costume-jewelry earrings on the coffee table. Annette Larson's? Possibly. If selling his collection freed him to start a new relationship, then she'd do it.

And Gramps was right. You couldn't have the future you wanted if you weren't willing to let go of the past. She had to stop holding on to Niall as a friend if they ever wanted a chance at more. Time to be brave and trust that he wouldn't let her down.

"Okay, Gramps. Thank you. I know that you say you're not doing this just for me, but it helps so much. I love you."

They hugged each other, hard, and she could feel dampness on their pressed cheeks, though she wasn't sure who was crying. Probably both of them.

"Your gram would have wanted this."

"Yes, she would." Kayleigh's eyes burned as she thought about the amazing role models they'd both been in her life.

He pulled back and regarded her, his eyes shining. "Now, get on with your future. I expect a return on my investment."

She smiled and thought of Niall. “You’re right. I don’t have a minute to lose.”

And with that, she kissed her grandfather and hurried toward a future full of the bright unknown.

A COUPLE OF HOURS later, Kayleigh trudged up her stoop and let herself into her apartment building. Despite rushing to Niall’s home, he hadn’t answered his door. He was either gone or avoiding her. She suspected the latter. Why had she left him at the park that way? Sure, it’d been an emotional day, the rejection from ForwardTech a huge letdown. But still. He’d confessed that he wanted her, and she’d told him to leave her alone. To never say it again. How she wished she could take back those words. She’d blown it with Niall. And while her start-up was back on track, she cared the most about losing him.

Voices sounded behind her apartment door and her shoulders slumped. She wasn’t in the mood for company and definitely not another of Gianna’s eccentric dates.

“Kayleigh!” Gianna’s lithe form flew across the room and held her tight when she entered. “I’m so sorry about ForwardTech. I know we’re running out of money, but we’ll think of something. I'm close to finishing the program, and Niall—"

"Niall doesn't want anything to do with us anymore," she said glumly, her chin resting on Gianna's shoulders, her eyes closed to hold in her tears.

"Are you sure, because—"

"We didn't part on the best terms after the presentation. I've been trying to reach him to tell him some good news, except he wouldn't let me in his apartment or return my calls."

"Battery's out," spoke a deep voice from her living room. She pulled back and turned, her heart leaping into her throat and holding on for dear life.

"Niall! What are you doing here?"

He stood and stretched, sauntering close as Gianna backed away, her eyes wide.

"I told you I wasn't going anywhere." He smiled easily, showing the perfect whiteness of his teeth, a light growing in his brown eyes.

Happiness burst inside her. "I'm glad."

He stepped closer and ducked his head. "Me, too."

"Ahem. Still here." Gianna made a point of clanging some dishes together in the sink, and Kayleigh stepped back from Niall with a laugh.

"Good, because I have some business news." She beckoned, and Gianna returned. When she curled up in their floral seat, Pringles leaped onto her lap.

Niall waited for Kayleigh to sit on the couch then joined her, sitting so close she felt his hip against hers, the heat of his body through his white T-shirt.

"We have financing!" The words burst out of her in an excited rush.

Gianna's mouth dropped open, and Niall turned to her, stunned.

"What? How? Did you have another meeting?" Gianna's head swiveled from Kayleigh to Niall. "Because Niall's been here for hours waiting for you and—"

Kayleigh slanted her eyes his way and saw him flush. "Hours?"

"It felt like days," he said, unapologetically with a twist of his lips. "Now tell us what happened," he growled, mock serious.

"The people at my gramps's assisted-living facility heard about what happened and decided to form an LLC to fund us. They're calling themselves Back in the Game."

Gianna lifted a protesting Pringles high into the air and kissed his black nose. "I love it! This is incredible. I'd better get back to programming. We can't let GSI beat us." And with that she disappeared into her room, carrying the cat, rock music blasting from her open door.

Strong hands slid into hers, and Kayleigh shivered with pleasure. "I wondered where you went."

She forced herself to meet his kind eyes. "I'm sorry about that, Niall. Sorry for what I said. Sorry for lots of things. You've always been such a good friend to me, and I treated you badly."

"A friend?" His eyes searched hers, and she felt her heart open up to him like a flower touched by dawn. He wanted more than friendship. She couldn't predict how this would go, but after years of knowing each other, they had a good start.

"No. Not just as a friend," she admitted, and felt herself melt at the passionate flare in his eyes. She angled her head and leaned closer, aching for his kiss.

"We have to get out of here," he said suddenly and stood, pulling her with him.

"Huh? Why?" His words broke through her romantic fog, and she flushed, embarrassed. Had she misread the situation? Either way, she wouldn't regret it. But another look into his soulful eyes reassured her. She was right about him. She knew it down deep.

"Because I can't kiss you here." His eyes slid

to Gianna's open door then back to her, and heat raced up her neck and flooded her cheeks.

"Oh."

He lifted her fingers to his lips, then pulled her out the door.

CHAPTER SIXTEEN

AFTER A SUBWAY ride filled with meaningful glances and secret smiles, Niall led her to a bench beside the East River. They sat in the deepening twilight, and the summer night air felt like a soft caress, the glow of blue lights strung along the Brooklyn Bridge's wires reflecting on the rippling water. Other than a man jogging with his Labrador, and ducks gathering on the water's edge, they were completely alone. Headlights were a neon stream that flowed over the bridge, the traffic sounds muted from this distant spot. She inhaled the briny smell of the water and the spicy musk of the man she'd fallen for.

"We used to come here a lot when we were kids," she murmured. "It's so beautiful."

"I've always thought so." Niall reached down and ran his hand along the skin of her throat, sliding his fingertips under her long hair so they brushed the back of her neck. Her body trembled in awareness, sensitive to his gentle touch.

"I can't believe we're doing this." She leaned into his hand, her heart galloping.

"I can't believe we waited this long." His profile was outlined by the electric glow behind him, his face more relaxed than she'd seen it since he'd come back from the war.

She pressed her cheek against his palm. "You were the one who avoided me these past few years. I never gave up on us."

The cords in his neck stood out. "That was a tough time," he murmured through his teeth.

She thought of his tour in Afghanistan. "You never talk about the war."

He pulled her closer, and she curled against him on the bench, her face resting on his chest.

"No," he said simply, and something in his quiet tone told her not to push it. Not in this perfect moment that felt full of possibilities.

"I'm sorry I ignored you when I got back. Pushed you away" came his deep voice, the sound of it reminding her of a foghorn rolling out across the flowing river. "It wasn't because I didn't care. I always have."

"I know that now. I just wasn't sure if you only saw me as a friend, business partner or—"

She felt him stroke the crown of her head, his palm brushing over her hair. "You mean much more to me than that."

Her body felt weightless, as if, without his

arm around her, she could have slid off the bench and floated away. "I feel the same way. I was afraid to admit it because I didn't want to risk scaring you away. Especially after losing Chris."

Niall tensed, and she felt his heart pick up speed. She gave herself a mental kick for bringing up her brother and the army. He'd been affected when he'd seen Chris's picture, and he'd just cut her off when she'd mentioned the war. She needed to stop bringing up bad memories. Back at the apartment, he'd said he wanted to kiss her, but she was making that possibility less likely by the minute. And, oh, how she wanted that kiss.

"You still miss him," he said quietly, surprising her.

Since Beth avoided mentioning Chris, had even requested that the letters about his declassification be mailed to Kayleigh for fear that the boys would see them, Kayleigh had few people to talk to. Her mother became too upset anytime she brought Chris up, and her father's calls were always interrupted by his new wife or their children. She knew she should let go, but she still hadn't found it in her heart to say goodbye to Chris.

"Every day," she answered honestly. "Sometimes I feel like I can never get over his death until I find out what happened. Never have peace. I hope Senator Gillibrand is able to do something about declassifying his mission."

His arms tightened around her, and she glanced up at his harsh intake of breath. In the dim light, his eyes looked anguished, and she stroked his tight jaw, running her fingers over it until his clenched mouth relaxed.

"I shouldn't have brought that up. You've experienced enough loss, too."

"There could be more," he said in a choked voice. "Much more." She stared at him wonderingly. Yes, there was a chance they might not get their program submitted ahead of GSI, but she sensed he wasn't talking business. What, then?

"There always is. But that's life, I'm learning. I used to be afraid to take risks, to make a move without testing the waters. It's why I came up with the Must Traits list. After my parents divorced, I promised myself that I'd follow my list and never get hurt. That someday, it would help me, too. But now..."

He cupped both sides of her face and gazed down at her, his tender expression a wordless music that moved through the secret places in her heart.

"Now?" he prompted.

"You're all that I want. I don't know what's

on your list. You never showed me the one from camp, and you've never made one now, and I don't care. My heart is overruling my head, and that's the way it should be. I have to believe in that and trust in you."

A pained look crossed his face, then vanished so quickly she was sure she'd imagined it. His hands slid around the back of her head, cradling it as he lowered his face until their lips were only a breath apart.

"I trust you, too," he said unevenly, his voice grim despite the sweet moment. Was he worried about her? Them?

But before her thoughts traveled further, her heart stepped sideways in her chest when he leaned forward and kissed her full on the mouth. His lips were plush and warm, and his tongue brushed hers before he captured the swell of her lower lip.

She trembled against him, the feel of his mouth on hers like a candle flame. It made her glow warm despite the evening air and the faint mist that turned the air opaque. When he pulled his mouth away, it left her breathless with a racing heart. He looked at her, his dark eyes full of tender sweetness. When he laid his hand along her face, he brushed her cheek as gently as a flower.

"You're beautiful."

"So are you," she whispered back, although they were alone, surrounded in the fog rolling off the river. Her head felt as light as a windblown leaf. She laid her hand against the firm plane of his stomach, feeling the muscles jump against her touch.

She followed his gaze to his prosthetic leg, and her eyes met his for a breathless moment. "You're perfect."

"Hardly that." His laugh was unconvincing.

She traced his jaw, then lowered her hand to his false limb. "To me, this makes you even more perfect. While it shows that you've suffered, it also means that you survived, for which I am eternally grateful."

He seemed to stop breathing, his eyes holding a desperate hope she shared. At last, he captured her hand and pressed a fierce kiss to its palm. "Then, that's all that matters."

"Good."

"Good."

They grinned at each other like idiots and then, unable to help herself, she reached up and pressed her lips to his, loving his groan as she kissed him with all of the passion she'd denied herself. If this was what going with her gut and not playing it safe was like, then she'd give up her lists forever. They couldn't keep her warm this way.

When she trailed her mouth down his neck, she felt his rapid pulse at its base, tasted the slightest trace of salt on his skin. His hands roamed across her back and settled firmly on her waist. White air billowed around them, enveloping them in a world that included no one and nothing else.

At last, Niall pulled back and gazed down at her, his expression both playful and tender. "I'm glad I'm a partner. I wouldn't want you to think I did this for a raise."

She gave him a gentle kiss, then pushed at his shoulders, encouraging him to lean back on the bench. He did, and she nestled into the crook of his arm again, resting her head on his biceps. "Whatever you're making, double it." She gave a contented sigh and snuggled firmly into the circle of his arms before she looked up. He smelled warm and rich, like sunshine and cider.

The corners of his mouth lifted, amusement in his eyes. "Two times zero is still zero."

"We'll make this work, Niall," she said fiercely, not sure if she meant their start-up or their relationship. She was taking a huge risk with both. Was it too much for her to ask that both succeed?

He pulled her close again when the wind turned chill and gusty, with fits and starts of rain that spattered down lightly, then with growing intensity.

"Yes. We will."

She smoothed back the damp hair that stuck to his cheek. "Promise?"

He looked at her with heavy-lidded eyes and lowered his face to hers again, both of them heedless of the steady downpour.

"Promise."

"SHH! YOU'LL WAKE Gianna," Kayleigh said, giggling as Niall backed her through her open apartment door and kissed her hard again. He couldn't keep his mouth or his hands off her. She'd always been beautiful to him, but never more so than now, with her cheeks pink with happiness, her tangle of wet hair tumbling down her back, her lips swollen, her silver eyes glimmering up at him.

He used the back of his foot to close the door and embraced her again, the air too empty without her close. He breathed in the fresh smell of her, not wanting this moment to end. His lips found hers, and pleasure filled him when she moaned in the back of her throat. He sampled the berry taste of her, his hands running up and down her heaving sides, loving her soft silhouette.

The table by the door tilted when she placed

a hand on it to steady herself, spilling its contents to the floor. She half sat on the furniture piece as he moved his mouth against hers. Passion seized him, and he marveled that the moment he'd longed for had finally come true.

Someday, when Kayleigh found out about Chris, she might hate him. But he hoped she might eventually forgive him. Why deny himself this happiness by staying in his dark past? Living in fear. Master Jung was right. He needed to move past that bleak time. And Kayleigh was the light to guide him. She made him the luckiest man in the world.

"What you do to me," he groaned, pulling back to catch his breath.

Kayleigh put a hand on her heaving chest. "I could say the same thing," she gasped, her teeth showing in a wide smile.

He held her face between his palms and looked deeply into her eyes. He didn't know how much time they had together, but he wouldn't waste it by holding back his feelings anymore.

"I see you when I close my eyes," he murmured, touching his forehead to hers. "I can't stop thinking about you, wondering where you are and what you're doing. Things in my past made me closed off. You were right about that.

But I'm not anymore. My heart is open, and it belongs to you."

Her eyes squeezed shut, and when they opened, they looked like the most precious metal in the world. "I think I've always belonged to you. Even at camp. Growing up. We've been friends, but there was always something more. Now we have the rest of our lives to be together."

"You won't regret it," he whispered in her ear, holding her close and hoping that it could be true.

"Not for a minute. But for now, I'd better go to bed. We have some long workdays ahead of us if we're going to get that program in ahead of GSI, mister."

Her teasing words brought him back to reality. She was right. Their first priority was to get the patent and move ahead with the app. They needed to help provide for Chris's family, and it felt good knowing that they'd be doing it, and everything else, together.

"I need my beauty rest," she said, dimples flashing at him, and he knew that he'd never think anyone lovelier than her.

"Until tomorrow, then," he said, imagining the incredible days ahead full of her.

"Hang on," she said. "I'll get you something to take home with you."

Since she was already moving to the kitchen, he let her go.

While he waited, Niall leaned down to grab the gym bag he'd left by the door earlier and noticed unopened letters scattered on the floor. He bundled them together to place on top of the table.

"Do you want two cupcakes or three?" Kayleigh called softly as he heard a kitchen drawer open then shut.

"Two," he answered and his hands stiffened when he noticed the letter at the top of the stack. It was from the Department of Defense and was stamped *Priority.* His heart drummed. Had Senator Gillibrand come through and gotten Kayleigh the declassification? News about his role in Chris's death?

"I'd better make it three so you'll have one for breakfast and think of me." Kayleigh's voice came to him from a distance, as if he were underwater, already drowning. Without thinking, he slipped the letter into his pocket and turned as she appeared in the kitchen's archway.

"Actually, I'll take a rain check on the cupcakes."

"Oh." She seemed as if she wanted to say more, and suddenly he needed to get out.

"See you tomorrow?" Her impish grin was

a blow to his chest. He knew once she read the letter, she might never look at him that way again. Worse, he'd be kicked off the project when they needed him most, and he could lose the woman he desperately cared for.

While his heart splintered, his head told him to keep this letter from her until they sent in the program and he was certain of her success. Once that happened, he'd give it back and leave her forever if that was what she wanted, as impossible and painful as it seemed. He'd planned to tell her the truth when they'd finished the program regardless, but now she'd only believe he'd been forced to confess because of the letter. That he hadn't done it voluntarily. Not because he loved her more than anything.

He'd reached for the light, but already felt himself falling back into the dark.

Where he belonged.

Why had he let himself imagine otherwise?

"Sounds good," he said, and shut the door behind him, the envelope crinkling in his pocket. He paused on the landing and gripped the marked-up wooden banister. If the letter contained what he believed it held, his parting words had been a lie.

Things were not good.

In fact, they couldn't be worse.

CHAPTER SEVENTEEN

"KIHAP!" NIALL HEARD Josh holler as he watched the boy execute a series of punches, turns and kicks on the cracked sidewalk leading to Beth's apartment. In the humid, hot air, Niall's skin glistened, and his breath felt labored. The sky was no longer bluffing rain, and the gray clouds that had scurried across it had settled, water heavy, overhead.

Despite his troubled heart, Niall smiled at the kid's excitement. He'd earned a yellow belt today. Quite an accomplishment given the short time frame. He'd thrown himself into the twice-a-week tae kwon do lessons and had practiced for hours every day in front of his mirror, according to Beth. Better yet, he'd kept to his end of the deal by attending anger-management therapy followed by martial arts tutoring with Niall.

The boy was gaining skills, but even more important, he seemed in better control of his temper. Apparently, he and Samuel hadn't fought in a week. Things were looking up for the Renshaw family.

As for Niall—not so much.

After wrestling with the dilemma for days, he'd finally opened the letter from Senator Gillibrand's office a week and a half ago. His stomach had filled with lead as he'd read her notice that Chris's death was declassified, an appointment to give his family the details set. He winced as he recalled that the meeting was at three o'clock today. Two hours from now. And Kayleigh and Beth knew nothing about it. Guilt over keeping this from them tunneled through him. It was a lie on top of an even bigger deception, and Kayleigh might not understand his reasons or forgive him.

His fingers tightened around the letter. Now that he'd sent the Mesh app program to the patent office this morning—ahead, according to Gianna's sources, of Brett's team—he had no reason to keep the letter. High Dive Enterprises would be fine without him.

But he wouldn't be fine. Not by a long shot.

He should be satisfied with all that they'd accomplished. Happy that the Renshaws were off to the strong start they needed. Should be glad that he'd done what he'd set out to do—help Chris's family. Hadn't that always been the plan?

A squirrel scampered down a tree and leaped across his path, stopping him. He gazed after it, wondering if he could pinpoint when, exactly, his goals had blurred. Day by day, he'd fallen harder for Kayleigh. She'd opened him up to the world again. Opened his heart. After the war, he'd wanted the solitary life he'd thought he deserved. But Kayleigh had convinced him otherwise. Working with her, Josh and Master Jung's students had made him believe that there might be an expiration date on the time you paid for your sins. He'd stopped living in his past and started thinking of his future. And every moment he'd glimpsed ahead included Kayleigh.

Would she feel the same way after she learned the truth? Hear him out and forgive him? There was a chance, now that they'd started their relationship. He needed her to understand that he'd never meant for anything bad to happen to Chris. To see why he couldn't share the secret and had kept the declassification letter.

Until now.

"Look at Josh. He's wearing pajamas!" a boy's voice called, snapping Niall out of his thoughts. He looked up to see four boys Josh's age circling him. His white dobok seemed the brightest spot in the darkening day, the still, muggy air as motionless as Josh.

"Did Mommy forget to dress you?" sneered another guy.

Niall realized he'd let Josh get too far ahead and made to close the distance until he caught the boy's head shake. Pride filled Niall. Josh wanted to handle it on his own. Whether that was the right decision or not, Niall needed to give him a chance. It was time to see if he'd learned enough self-control in therapy and through tae kwon do to help.

He paused by a tree and leaned against it, his muscles tight and ready to respond if needed.

Josh's mouth set in a grim line, and Niall noticed that he set one foot ahead and angled the other behind him, a warrior stance. The muscles on his thin forearms stood out, as tight as twisted ropes.

"I dress myself," Josh snapped, his face flushing.

"Yeah, in pajamas!" hooted another kid, and Niall felt his fingers dig into the bark as he held himself in check. It was important to Josh to handle this on his own, and he needed to give him that chance.

"They're from my dojang. I'm taking tae kwon do." He sank into a crouch and brought his hands up.

"Oh, look at the Karate Kid over here!" one of the gang hooted, but impressively, Josh didn't react. Instead, he maintained his strong-looking pose.

"What? So you're a tough guy now?" A boy with orange hair and freckles jerked his chin at Josh.

Josh's face remained impassive, his eyes clear and calm. "No. I have a strong and gentle heart."

Niall smiled at the words Master Jung instilled in all of his pupils about the best qualities in a warrior.

"Sounds like a pansy. Let's see how tough he really is." And with that, the biggest and loudest in the group lunged at Josh. Niall leaped forward, but faster than he could blink, Josh had swept the other kid's legs out from under him, and the bully landed on his back with a thud. He blinked up at the sky, the breath knocked out of him. Josh extended a hand, but made no move to kick the kid when he was already down.

"I don't want to fight with you," he said firmly. "Words can't hurt me. But if you come at me, I'll defend myself."

Niall's mouth dropped open. It was the perfect response. Josh wasn't starting fights, but he wasn't a pushover either. Suddenly, he realized that this wasn't the first time Josh had met up with these kids. But by the looks on their faces, they'd expected a different outcome. At last, he understood Josh's mysterious comments about people messing with him.

The leader grabbed hold of Josh's hand and was hauled to his feet, looking pale and shaken.

"How'd you do that?" asked one of the smallest boys in the group, his tongue showing between a gap in his front teeth.

"Come to Master Jung's studio and learn. I just earned my yellow belt today." Josh pointed at the bright color strip around his waist. He'd been so proud of the belt that he'd insisted on wearing it home to surprise his mother.

"Cool." The freckle-faced kid stepped forward and touched it while another shoved him out of the way for a better look.

"Lame." The group's leader rolled his eyes, but the other kids were too busy looking at Josh to notice.

"So they teach kids how to fight dirty like that?" The gap-toothed boy rubbed the back of his dark crew cut, his large eyes bulging.

Josh shook his head, his light brown hair short after Master Jung had insisted on a haircut. "I thought that at first, too. But it's really about learning to control and defend yourself. Big difference."

"Let's get out of here." The leader backed away and twisted his baseball cap so that the brim faced backward. "This is boring."

"Yeah. Let's hang out at the park," said a boy with short dark curls. "Bet those stupid twins are there. We'll get them."

"Uh-uh." The smaller boy shook his head and pushed back his thin shoulders. "I'm going with Josh. I want to hear more about the dojang."

The boys scrunched their noses and eyed him skeptically before waving their hands. "Whatever," one of them shouted before sauntering away, though the redhead who'd touched Josh's belt swerved back and raced to rejoin their little group.

"I want to hear, too," he said, holding his sides and casting a fearful glance over his shoulder.

Niall stepped forward. "I take Josh there twice a week. If your parents agree, I'll bring all of you if you want to sign up." He scribbled his and Master Jung's numbers down on two pieces of paper and handed them to the boys. They might still come and possibly bring Josh. He'd miss the boy if the Renshaws kicked him out of their lives, and this could be his only way to see him again.

"Your parents can get a reference about me

from the owner of the center. Once they've signed you up, have them call me so we can confirm. Sound good?"

The boys' eyes were wide as they glanced at the prosthetic leg appearing below the hem of his long shorts.

"Are you a teacher?" The smaller kid took off his glasses and wiped his damp nose.

Josh smiled wide. "The best. Everyone says so. He's, like, part cyborg."

The other boys lost their anxious expressions and grinned at the familiar term. "Cool," said the redhead. "My grandpa lost his arm in Vietnam, and he's still tough. Hey, want to shoot some hoops with us before it rains, Josh?" He cast a glance up at the overcast sky.

Josh shook his head. "Tomorrow, maybe?"

"Cool." The kid nodded and grabbed the basketball his friend carried.

"See you, boys." Niall put a hand on top of Josh's warm head and guided him farther up the street.

"Later, Josh," they called, and that, Niall thought, settled that.

"Well done, kid." Niall ruffled Josh's hair and the once-defiant boy grinned up at him.

"I didn't hurt that kid too bad, did I?"

Niall looked over his shoulder and watched

the two animated boys chattering as they walked away.

"No. But you taught him a valuable lesson."

"What?"

"That you're no pushover. They've bullied you before, haven't they?" Niall unlatched the gate before Josh's apartment building and gestured for the boy to precede him. The smell of flowers filled the air as they passed urns bursting with yellow, white and lavender blooms and climbed the stoop. At the landing, Josh stopped and hung his head.

"Yes. I fought back, but they were always stronger, and they never quit. I didn't want Mom to worry, so I tried to handle it and be strong. Like my dad."

"And you did."

Josh peered up at him. "I was scared today. Would Master Jung be disappointed?"

Niall put a hand on Josh's narrow shoulder. "He'd be as proud as I am. You controlled your feelings and defended yourself while causing the least harm. It's all we can ask."

Josh threw his arms around Niall's waist, making him stagger backward.

"You're going to stick around, Niall, aren't you?" His muffled words moved against Niall's T-shirt, tears thickening his voice and dampening Niall's shirt.

His chest constricted. Beth might not welcome Niall when she learned the truth. Despair filled him. Josh needed him, and Niall needed Josh, too. Before now, he'd felt like a negative contribution to life. But seeing Josh grow made him realize that he could make a difference. That his life mattered. Only, his past had caught up to him, and now it might be too late.

"I hope so, buddy," he replied when he could keep the wave of emotions from washing into his voice. His arms tightened around Josh, and he wondered if this would be the last time he'd hug the kid. "I won't leave unless someone makes me." He glanced up at the gray-violet sky, the low clouds looking too heavy to move.

"Daddy had to go." Suddenly Josh's shoulders shook, and he sobbed. Pain, as sharp as a new blade, slashed through Niall. He was the reason Chris had left Josh's life, and now there was a real possibility that he wouldn't be able to make it up to him.

"I was mad at him before," Josh continued, "but Bob—that's what my counselor said to call him—said Dad loved me and wanted to come back home." Josh pulled back and stared up at Niall with a streaked face. "Before he died, he sent me a puzzle and a note that we'd put it together when he came back. Only the puzzle is still in its box."

Niall smoothed back Josh's wet hair and looked the boy square in the eye. "If I can, we'll put it together. You and me."

Josh snuffled, but his tears slowed. "Really? You'd do that?"

"I couldn't think of anything I'd like to do more. Although I bet your mom and Samuel would like to help, too." If they didn't allow him to be a part of Josh's life, then he'd at least plant the seeds for the family to do something together, in honor of Chris.

"But Mom is always busy, and Samuel is too little. The puzzle has a thousand pieces." Josh shooed away a bee that flew by them on its way to the flowers.

"A thousand pieces?" Niall whistled. "We'll need all the help we can get. Samuel can find the corner and edge pieces, and I know your mom will make time to work on it if you let her."

Josh's eyes brightened. "She always offers to help me clean my room."

"Maybe you could make a deal. After cleaning your room, you get some puzzle time together. I know she wants to play with you." She hadn't said so in as many words, but he'd seen her wistful expression when he'd come to pick up Josh for class.

A smile broke out on Josh's face, and Niall

hardly recognized the defiant boy he'd met back on the Fourth of July. "That's what Bob said. I can't wait to tell him about what happened today." And with that, Josh scrambled to the door, punched in a number and pulled it open, ushering them both inside as thunder growled deep in the city's throat.

Niall inhaled deeply, feeling the edge of the abyss at his toes, and followed Josh up the stairs. Once he'd dropped off Josh, he'd head to Kayleigh's apartment.

Hopefully, it'd be a clean start, his guilt revealed and forgiven. He pictured his future again. Would Kayleigh be there to share it with him?

CHAPTER EIGHTEEN

A FUMBLING AT the door had Beth brushing away her happy tears and Kayleigh on her feet. Josh was home. And Niall. Her heart raced as she imagined his handsome face. She'd missed it so much these past few weeks. Since he'd been busy finishing the program for the patent, they'd barely seen each other. But now that they'd sent it in, and she had this incredible news to share with him, they could finally pick up where they'd left off the night they'd kissed near the Brooklyn Bridge.

"Mom!"

At the shout, they rushed to the entranceway and pulled up short at a beaming Josh and a grim-faced Niall. Wasn't he happy to see her? Her quickening heartbeat skidded and tumbled to a halt.

"Hi, sweetie!" Beth hugged Josh tight, and Niall avoided her eyes and outstretched arms, making her more uneasy. Had his retreat into work been personal rather than business? It seemed impossible after their unforgettable night by the river. His sincerity and open-hearted confessions had made her realize how much they both cared. How right they were for each other, as more than friends. Had she been wrong?

Sam slid down the hall on stocking feet and skidded to a halt in front of Josh. "It's going to rain, Josh! Oh. Where'd you get that?" He yanked at his older brother's yellow belt, unraveling it.

Kayleigh tensed, waiting for the inevitable sibling row, but instead of shoving or yelling, Josh beamed. "I passed my test. You should have seen it. Not everybody made it, but I did, and it's all thanks to Niall."

Was it her imagination, or did Niall wince? He should look happy. Proud. He'd brought such positive changes to this family and to her. Josh had gained control of his temper, and she'd learned to trust her heart.

Maybe she needed to remind him of all that he'd done, that she still needed him now that the patent was in. In fact, after these past two weeks, she'd realized that he was the one thing she couldn't live without.

Kayleigh bent down to kiss Josh, letting her hair fall across her face to hide her worry. "I'm so proud of you."

"Thanks, Aunt Kay. I want to tell you everything."

"And I want to hear it." She smiled down at her nephew, thrilled that his anger had been replaced by pride. "But first I need to speak to Niall, okay?"

After sharing the news with Beth that Chris's death was declassified, she'd wanted desperately to tell Niall. He was sensitive about the war, but hopefully he'd be happy that she'd get the answers she needed at last.

She and Beth exchanged a significant look, and Beth led the chattering boys into the living room while Kayleigh joined Niall near the kitchen.

"It's nice to see you, stranger." She reached up to kiss his mouth, but he turned so that she caught his cheek instead. Something inside her wilted a bit. Did he not want to kiss her, or was he just self-conscious with kids nearby? She hoped it was the latter. *Please let it be that.*

She dropped down to flat feet and peered up at him. "Is something wrong? We've hardly seen each other lately. I know you've been busy finishing the program, but now you don't seem happy to see me."

"It's not that," he said, his mouth tight and his posture rigid. A proceed-with-caution sign couldn't have been any clearer.

She twisted her pinky ring. “Are you having second thoughts about us?” If he was, it would be her worst insecurities realized. She’d thrown away her list to follow her instincts. Had trusted that he had put her first in his life. “You don’t want to go back to being just business partners, do you?” she half joked, trying to sound light.

He shifted uneasily, and gave a sort of half shrug that made her heart sink to her toes. With his lids lowered, she couldn’t read whatever emotions his eyes held. Why wouldn’t he look at her? She hugged herself against the cold doubt seizing her insides.

“You said you were all in. Is that still true?” She turned away and slumped against the counter. “Did you mean it?”

“Yes. All of it.” His insistent voice soothed her frayed nerves. “But there’s something else.”

She whirled, hope making her light-headed. Caution had always ruled her, fear its trusty adviser. She shouldn’t have jumped to conclusions. Something else was bothering Niall, and it had nothing to do with his feelings for her.

“There’s something I have to tell you, too,” she blurted, weak with relief and excited to share her news. Niall probably wanted to tell her about a programming glitch that was bothering him or something business related. Whatever it was, it couldn't be as important as what she had to say.

Niall nodded solemnly, his face sadder than she'd ever seen it. Perhaps when he heard her out, his mood would lift. He'd be happy for her. She was sure of that.

"The Department of Defense called me. They hadn't heard back about a declassification appointment to discuss the details of Chris's death and wanted to confirm it." Her words tumbled over one another, a spring-fed brook that bubbled from the happiest part of her.

Finally, closure and peace about what had happened to Chris. Though she knew it would hurt to hear the grim details, she needed to know, to erase the horrors her imagination fed her nightmares.

She checked her watch. "It's in an hour, and I wondered if you would go with me. Beth doesn't want to hear it from strangers, and I don't want to go alone. I know it's hard for you to hear about the war and Chris, so I understand if the answer is no."

"You might prefer Gianna," he said, his tone off, and she saw that he'd turned pale.

She gave herself a swift mental kick for pushing him. "You're right. I should have asked her and not put you on the spot. I know you'd go if you could."

He shook his head and handed her a creased letter. "You won't want me there."

"Of course I would, but not if being there would bring back war memories." Why would he think she wouldn't want him? She'd leaned on him when her parents had split all those years ago and depended on him when she'd taken the risk on a start-up company. It was impossible to imagine ever not wanting him close.

"Look at the letter," he urged, and the defeat in his eyes made her throat tighten.

She stared down at the Department of Defense's logo. Was this the missing appointment notice? She peered inside and confirmed that it was.

Her eyes flew to his, her heart beating so hard it rattled her ribs. "How did you get this?"

He swallowed hard and seemed to push the words from his throat. "I took it from your apartment the night that we…uh…went to see the Brooklyn Bridge."

Her lungs went on strike and refused to pull in air. Her blood followed suit and froze in place. Her brain went along with the rest because she couldn't make sense of anything. "Why would you do that? You know how much this letter means to me." Although her words were a soft, jagged whisper, he flinched as if she'd struck him. Hard.

He swiped a hand across his eyes. “I do.”

Confusion and hurt mixed in her gut and rose to her throat. “Then why? Is it because you don’t like to hear about the war? Did it trigger a flashback?”

“Yes, but not in the way you think.” He crossed his arms against his chest and held himself tightly, looking as if he’d fall apart if he didn’t. Pain and sympathy battled each other inside. If only he’d open up and tell her what had happened in Afghanistan, she could understand this high-handed act that had shoved her needs aside for his own. How could he do that to her? It made no sense.

“Then please explain. I need to understand.” She pressed her fingers to her temples, feeling a dull throb that would turn into a migraine within minutes.

“Can we talk in the stairwell?” He shot a glance down the hall, and suddenly she was grateful that Josh’s excited retelling of his belt story had drowned out their hushed conversation. Caught up in the moment, she’d forgotten they might have had an audience.

“Okay.” Thank goodness he’d remembered the kids. Niall was always thoughtful like that. So why, then, had he behaved so insensitively with her letter? She held it to her beating heart, wishing like anything that she'd had it two weeks ago.

Once they'd seated themselves on the third-floor landing, Niall angled his body to face her.

"I was with Chris when he died." His quiet confession seemed to linger in the hallway, her brain refusing to absorb it as she stared at him dumbly.

"S-say that again," she breathed when she could, her mind pushing back against what he'd said, not wanting to trust her ears.

"We were together when I lost my leg."

Her hand rose to her heart, as if that futile gesture would keep it from shattering. Her brother and Niall? The two men who meant everything to her...together? Impossible. Yet it was true. Must be true. He'd just admitted it, and there was no reason to lie.

All this time, Niall had known about Chris, had listened to her talk about needing closure, yet he'd said nothing. *Nothing.* Her stomach tightened. It was a classified mission, but couldn't he have revealed something to ease her pain? Worse yet, he'd kept her from learning the truth by hiding the letter.

She sensed there was more to his story the way she might sense an oncoming thunderstorm, the hairs on the back of her neck prickling at the thunder's first growl.

"I couldn't speak before, but now—" His voice trailed away, and he looked around the dark, narrow space as if lost.

"I—I don't understand. You knew, all this time, how Chris died?" Her words were pinched off with pauses punctuated by breathy intakes of air. The answer was obvious, but she needed to hear it again. Might need to hear it several times to believe that it could be true.

"Yes," he said in the quiet gloom.

"And you kept the letter from me so that I wouldn't find out?" She covered her shaking mouth and stared at him as a desperate helplessness overtook her. She could see the blow coming that would crush her, and was powerless to avoid it. She'd trusted Niall. Believed in him. How could he have done this?

"Yes."

"Tell me what happened." Her fingers clutched his arm, as if needing to feel something, know that this was real.

"You'd rather hear it from anyone else." His eyes burned into hers, his face a splintered mask of pain. Underneath, Niall's expression was haunted, eyes half in this world, half elsewhere, remembering.

"No." She drew in a breath and winced at a tearing pain in her chest. "You were my friend, my business partner and my..." Her voice trailed off, and she let go of his arm, suddenly unsure about touching him. Her emotions were swerving all over this road she'd traveled too many times before. "You owe me the truth. If you care about me, then tell me everything."

Her gut twisted into an undoable knot as he began, his voice dragging her into that moment two years ago.

"I'd been sent to an outpost to fix their computer network, but when I woke, we were under insurgent attack. Bullets and grenades pounded us. We were outnumbered." When he began, it was as if he was speaking from the bottom of a deep well, his voice floating to her from some faraway place. "Another soldier and I crouched behind a sandbag wall, pinned down. I wasn't making it out of there. Not alive."

"But things didn't happen that way," she said in the quiet gloom that descended between them. She shuddered, thinking how close he'd come to getting killed. How many times had she imagined him and Chris in that kind of situation? Prayed that they were safe? But they'd ended up in danger anyway—incredibly, together.

Niall looked at her sideways, then back down to his clenched hands. "No. I was thinking about my mom. Wondering how long before she'd notice I hadn't come home. If she'd miss me. Then the commander ordered us to evacuate. The Special Forces had arrived to cover us."

"Special Forces?" A cold sweat swept over Kayleigh, and she felt nausea in the pit of her stomach. "That was Chris."

Niall looked at her gravely. "I grabbed my gun and ran down the tower steps. At the bottom, a Green Beret slapped me hard on the back and ordered me to move out."

"Was it Chris?" Kayleigh choked out.

"I didn't know at first, but found out later that it was."

She could picture her confident big brother in those last minutes of his life. How sure he must have been that this was just another day on the job. Only it wasn't. It was his last day on earth, and Niall had been there.

Niall reached for her, then dropped his hand when she scrambled backward on the step. She ached to be in his arms, but needed to hear this, to deal with it on her own.

He dropped his hand and continued in a wooden voice, "All hell was breaking loose. Humvees were in the distance. I had to make it there. Then I remembered that I'd left without the company's hard drive. If the enemy got it, local operatives' identities would be revealed.

I had to go back. As a signal combat officer, protecting information was my job."

She nodded, then started as lightning flickered outside the small window in the landing.

"I ducked out from behind a barrel and made it back," Niall continued in a voice so low she strained to hear it. "At the outpost again, I passed the tall man overseeing the evacuation."

"Chris," she whispered, her voice waterlogged. Oh, God. Was there ever a time when you were ready to hear how a loved one died? No matter how much she needed to know, the truth would stomp her heart flat.

"He said I was going the wrong way. I yelled that I had to get the hard drive, and he waved me through. In the command station, I tossed everything out of my pack to make it fit, all except one thing that I couldn't part with."

He looked at her, and the expression in his eyes was so full of sorrow that she leaned toward him until she caught herself. This memory had to be hurting Niall, too. He'd nearly died. Had lost his leg. She squeezed her eyes shut against the thought that she could have lost both of them that day.

"Is that when Chris died?" she forced herself to ask, tears now streaking down her face.

He shook his head and seemed to struggle to get out the words. It must be hard for him to tell this story. Maybe it was the first time he'd spoken it out loud. But right now, she couldn't comfort him. He was alive at the end of this tale. Not her brother. Yet a part of her ached to think how she'd feel if it were Chris sitting beside her, telling her how Niall had died.

"With the information secured," Niall continued, "I ran back and nearly knocked into Chris. He was the last guy I could see on the field. I'd wondered why he'd waited."

She swiped the moisture from her eyes, nearly blind from it. "Because he wanted to protect you. He would never leave until he knew he'd gotten everyone to safety. That's the kind of man my brother was."

Overwhelmed, she shuddered and rocked against the waves of pain crashing through her. *Oh, Chris.* Why? Why had he always been the good guy? The selfless one? Couldn't he have, just that one time, left others to fend for themselves? But that would have meant abandoning Niall, and another part of her shook when she thought of what would have happened if Chris hadn't been there to look out for him. Why wasn't there a version of this story where both of them could have made it?

Niall nodded as a thunderclap sounded nearby. "Yes. He was. When I came out, he asked if I got what I needed."

"What happened next?" she forced herself to ask, feeling as though the roller-coaster car she rode had reached the pinnacle, and she teetered on the brink of a terrifying fall.

"We ducked behind the door when a grenade exploded. When I told him I had the hard drive, we sprinted across the field. There was this loud noise, and I was tossed off my feet, something ripping through my leg. When I hit the ground, my head felt like it had split apart. I couldn't lift it and check out the damage. But I knew it was bad. The rebels would get the computer. And more lives than just mine would be lost. I'd failed."

Niall dropped his head into his hands, and a deep shudder passed over him. Kayleigh reached for him, then pulled back, conflicted. She wanted to comfort, but she hurt, too. She felt herself falling, heard herself screaming in her head.

"Someone yanked me up and carried me," Niall said after a long moment, his voice so full of tension, she felt he might break.

"It was Chris," Kayleigh said, the image laying like a hot knife in her mind. "He wouldn't leave you on that field."

He nodded slowly, his Adam's apple dipping as he seemed to swallow hard. The rain murmured on the roof above and ran in rivulets down the window behind them. At last, he blew out a long breath and began again. "I told him to leave me. That he'd get killed, but he just shook his head and started running with me."

Kayleigh imagined her brother, how incredibly courageous he'd been. He'd known the odds were against him, but he'd rolled the dice, unwilling to abandon the bad hand he'd been dealt. She swiped at her running nose with her sleeve, wishing with all her might that she could have been there. For Chris. For Niall. Oh, God. It was suddenly too much, and she buried her head in her arm and sobbed hard, her pulse surging beneath her skin.

Niall's hand fell on her shoulder and she jumped. "Do you want me to stop?"

She shook her head, beyond words. No. If Chris could see this through to the end, then so could she. "Keep going," she whispered when she could.

"He jogged us across the field. When an explosion hit, he'd swerve one way, then another. My pain cranked, and my vision dimmed. I told him I wasn't going to make it. To save himself. But I think he said we were almost there—not sure—but he kept going. Suddenly, he jerked, as if someone shoved him, as we hit the metal rivets of the Humvee. I thought we'd made it."

Behind her, a gust of wind rattled the landing's windowpanes. Kayleigh's eyes scrunched closed as she pictured it. Saw it all. The desperate dash to the waiting vehicles, Chris carrying a limp Niall through what must have looked like hell on earth. What had he been thinking in those moments? She would have bet he hadn't been scared. Not Chris. He would have been sure, right up until the end, that he'd come out on top. Win. Make it. Only he hadn't, and lay in the bottom of a grave in Arlington Cemetery instead.

The thought scorched her insides as she remembered the funeral and all the unanswered questions that had run through her mind. She'd never wonder again. Would this bring her the peace she'd hoped for? Right now she felt as though she were a storm-tossed vessel wrecked on a rocky shore. There was no safe harbor. Not for her.

"But you both didn't make it," she burst out. Sudden certainty tightened in her chest like a cold fist. Everything became a blur around her as she pulled the damp, stagnant air into her lungs.

Niall shook his head, his eyes wild around the edges, like a skittish horse. "Chris had been hit in the back with shrapnel. I lived because he shielded me."

Yes. That was exactly how Chris would have died in combat. Saving another. Someday, that thought might comfort her, but for now, it only ripped open the wound of his loss and she bled, inside, as her mind replayed that moment. She wished she could climb into the tree house in her head, escaping the horror below, pulling up the ladder behind her. Maybe she'd find Chris there.

"He didn't suffer, Kayleigh." Niall's voice turned fierce. "He was gone before they pulled him off me."

Kayleigh spoke from behind the hand covering her face. "How do you know if he suffered? How much he hurt? He could have been mortally wounded and still carried you because that's the man Chris was. He cared about others. Put them first."

He recoiled at her pained words, but met her eye when she lowered her fingers. "I'm sorry, Kayleigh. If I could go back, I would never have put your brother in danger. Would have taken that hit for him."

She imagined it. Saw her life with Chris inside the apartment behind her, proud of Josh for his yellow belt. And her missing her dearest friend, Niall, who'd died in combat. Neither was an option she could bear.

"But you didn't think of him, did you? You put what you needed ahead of others." She clutched the letter, the edge cutting into her palm. "And you did it with me, too. You hid my letter these past two weeks. Or would it have been longer if I hadn't gotten the phone call?" Her chest shuddered as air rushed in and out of her.

"I was planning to tell you today after I dropped off Josh. That's why it was in my pocket. I waited until we sent in the program because I wanted to make sure we had it done in case you kicked me out."

She nodded, despair smashing her insides to pieces. "I would have told you to leave the company. But that was my call to make. Not yours. I thought you were different. That you considered other people's feelings, but I was wrong."

"That's not true." He made an inarticulate gesture. "I was trying to help."

"Like when you turned me down in the restaurant at our first meeting? Ignored my phone calls the following week? That was you trying to help." Her voice was flat and filled with defeat.

"But I changed my mind when I met Chris's family."

His words cut her. "So it wasn't because I convinced you? Because you believed in me? It was all because you wanted to feel better about what you'd done. Repay a debt."

Niall studied her for a long moment then nodded slowly. "But I did believe—"

She put up her hand to stop him. She couldn't listen to another word. Not from Niall.

"Chris kept you alive, and what did you do with that gift? How did you honor it? You hid in your apartment and disappeared from the world. Disregarded the second chance you'd been given." Words bubbled up inside and spilled out of her. "And even when you decided to help, said you were all in, you weren't, because you had this secret. How could we ever have been a team, partners, a—a couple, with that between us? You kept that, and this letter, from me."

"You're right," he said, his voice hoarse. *Guilty*—there was no other word to describe Niall as he leaned against the wall, bowed over as if a great weight had settled on him. "But believe that I planned to tell you, whether it was declassified or not, once we sent in the patent."

She pointed down the steps. "I'm sorry, but I can't trust you. Not anymore. Please go. You lied to me. Deceived me. You manipulated me—and you stole that letter. I promised myself after Brett that I'd never fall for someone like that again."

He staggered back, his face full of anguish. "I don't want to leave you this way." His eyes searching hers. "I should get Beth."

"No. If you care the way you claim to, you'd know…to just…stay away from me and my family. Far away," she croaked out.

Niall blinked up at the ceiling, his jaw so tight it looked as if it would shatter. At last his shoulders slumped, and he nodded.

"Goodbye, Kayleigh," she heard him whisper as he clumped heavily down the stairs.

She watched until the top of his dark head disappeared from view, the sight leaving her feeling hollow, her conviction slowly draining away, thick, dark sorrow taking its place.

"Goodbye, Niall," she whispered before getting to her feet and holding on to the banister, her knees shaking.

She couldn't bear the feeling that something vital had been plucked out, uprooted from her chest when he walked away. Incomprehensibly, she'd wanted to cling to him, though she'd ordered him to leave.

But she had to let go. The happily-ever-after dream she'd imagined with Niall was like a Chinese lantern. Lovely to look at, but as flimsy as the winds that carried it far, far away…if it'd ever been within reach at all.

CHAPTER NINETEEN

A SHARP BUZZING startled Chairman Meow from Niall's chest. He scampered under the couch, only the swishing tip of his tail appearing from beneath the upholstery's edge.

Niall lumbered to his feet and trudged to the intercom.

"Yes?" he asked, a small part of him, a very small part, wondering if it might be Kayleigh—though after a week of not hearing from her, he knew it wasn't. Would never be, and the thought tore him apart again.

"Pizza."

Niall pressed the button to admit the deliveryman and headed to the kitchen for his wallet. He searched for it through the debris covering his counters and found it beneath an empty cereal box, a used bowl and spoon beside it. When had he eaten breakfast? His stomach rumbled. Not today.

The past week had rolled by like a fog, and he couldn't hold on to its events any easier than he could have grasped a fistful of cloud.

He'd spent hours on the couch, clenched in a knot, unable to sleep, unable to turn his mind to other things, unable to stop himself from remembering. Again. And again. And again.

At the knock on his door, Chairman Meow's pink, twitching nose poked from beneath the furniture. Was he smelling the cheese? At least one of them would enjoy the solitary meal.

A teenager with features too large for his narrow face and rounded, boyish shoulders grinned when Niall opened the door. "Pepperoni and sausage with a side of anchovies?"

He handed the kid the money, then added a tip. "Thanks."

"Haven't seen you in a while," the boy said as he passed over the box and pocketed the cash. "Used to come here at least twice a week but you haven't ordered in, what, almost a couple of months. Where've you been?"

"Nowhere," Niall muttered, then nodded goodbye and shut the door.

Only that wasn't true, he thought as he swept newspapers from his coffee table and dropped the box on it. *Nowhere* was where he'd been *before* the past eight weeks. Because of Kayleigh, the cogs of his life had spun again, a forward momentum that had propelled him into the world and out of this claustrophobic space.

The gray cat leaped onto the coffee table and

sidestepped empty soda cans and protein bar wrappers to reach the box, the briny smell of anchovies drawing him.

Niall opened the Styrofoam container of fish and put it on the floor. "Dinner is served," he muttered, but made no move to pick up a slice for himself. Nothing could fill up the emptiness in him. The pizza had been a mistake. Since leaving Kayleigh, a dark space inside had opened, and it yawned wider and deeper each day. Eventually, it'd swallow him whole.

His fingers pinched the bridge of his nose, and his eyes squeezed shut, the persistent ache that'd settled in his bones throbbing. He missed her. Once in a while, he imagined he heard her when footsteps passed his apartment. In that one moment, he'd feel perfectly happy until the truth clubbed him back to reality.

She was never coming over again, wouldn't see him or even think about him. As she said, she wanted him to stay away. Ironic that he'd wanted to disappear from life when he'd returned from the war. Yet now he wished for nothing more than to be with the woman he loved. He ached to think that she'd forget him. As for him, he'd never stop recalling their time together, not growing up, and especially not these past few weeks.

By lifting his blinds and opening his windows, she'd let in a pet he now cherished. After he'd met Chris's family, she'd shown him a path to the redemption he needed. And while he'd achieved that by helping Josh overcome his anger issues and Kayleigh succeed with her app, he wanted more.

How had he thought that his own suffering would repay the debt he owed Chris?

The more he thought about it, the more he realized that his thinking had been completely wrong. The only way to repay someone for saving your life was to make it worthy of the sacrifice. Something sharp scraped his bare foot, and he reached down to pick up one of MaryAnne's hair clips. Even she'd heeded his sharp warnings this week and had stayed away.

But hiding from the world, his family and friends, was not making a difference, he realized as he studied his sister's clip. Shame slammed into him at the realization. Kayleigh was right. He was a coward, only thinking of himself. His sister worried about him, and he should ease her mind, not push her away.

Chairmen Meow jumped back onto his lap and began licking a front paw and washing his face. Niall stroked the cat's back, no longer able to feel its vertebrae now that he gave him regular meals. Here, at least, he was making a difference. If the apartment building owner ever found out about the cat, he'd move. He knew that Chairman Meow had saved him as surely as he'd rescued the stray. Just like Kayleigh and Josh had freed him from the suspended animation of his old life. Could he return to the void again?

His hand froze on Chairman's Meow's back as his eye caught a picture he'd printed, framed and placed beside his computer. It was the shot the elderly man had taken of him and Kayleigh at the Japanese Hill-and-Pond Garden. He'd told them to look as if they were in love, and from the soft smiles they'd exchanged, he knew that, on his part, it'd been no act.

He limped on his old prosthetic to cross the room and grab the picture. Kayleigh's gray eyes glowed, her naturally pink mouth curved in a way that made him wish, fiercely, that he could kiss her again. Hold her. But that would never happen if he retreated from life again.

A week of stifling loneliness proved that he couldn't go back to his old ways. Speaking about what had happened in Kunar had released the pressure that had made it hard to push through each day. It had nudged his burden into a corner of his mind where he could safely view it from a distance.

With his secret gone, his heart no longer full of regret, he was open and ready to commit to

Kayleigh. Only, it was too late. He was now the last person she'd ever love.

A hard, fishy-smelling tongue scraped against his jaw as Chairman Meow stood on his back paws and gave him a cat kiss.

A smile ghosted across Niall's face. Here was the love he craved, and he'd done nothing more than let it into his life. Could it ever be that simple with Kayleigh? She was the only woman he'd ever love. If he couldn't work things out with her, he would sink and never surface again. There was simply no one else for him.

He grabbed the pizza box and headed for the kitchen. It was pointless to stare at it. Chairman Meow wove in and out of his legs, nearly tripping him until he stopped and gave the tall cat a behind-the-ear scratch.

Kayleigh had said that he put his needs first, had called him a deceiver, and he couldn't deny it. He shouldn't have taken the letter. It'd been wrong to keep it from her until the app was finished. It had been her call to make whether he completed the product. Not his. He'd done what he'd thought was best without considering her feelings, and she'd been right to call him out on it. To send him away. He'd behaved as selfishly as Brett, her parents or others who'd taken control of her life.

He stuffed the pizza slices into plastic bags, then opened his empty refrigerator. He'd told Kayleigh he wasn't anyone's hero, and it was true. Heroes rushed toward danger, like Chris. They didn't hide in dark apartments or give up. Both of which he was doing now.

After putting the food away, he closed the fridge and studied a brightly colored flyer beneath a magnet on its door. The High Dive Enterprises promotional-event announcement. He ran his fingers over Kayleigh's name at the bottom of the sheet. It was tonight. She was there, and he should be, too.

He wasn't a fairy-tale prince—perfect, charming and brave in every way. He glanced down at his prosthetic. Beast was the closest he'd come to a hero—transformed by fate, bitter about his situation but wanting to be a better man because of the woman of his dreams. Kayleigh.

Heroes could come in all shapes and styles, and he needed to act like one. He glanced at his watch. Six o'clock. If he hurried, he'd make it to the event and show Kayleigh that he was man enough to face his mistakes. To fight to make things right.

He strode to his room and pulled a dress shirt and tie from the hangers, along with matching slacks. When she saw him again, she wouldn't see the old Niall. He didn't exist anymore. This one confronted his worst fears. Even if it was Kayleigh's rejection. He'd faced it once, and he'd survive it again. Courage wasn't acting when you already knew the outcome. Bravery happened when you took action without knowing the results.

He loved her too much not to give it another try.

KAYLEIGH SAT AT a round white cloth-covered table, a pink, yellow and white floral centerpiece perfuming the early-evening air. Though she barely smelled it. In fact, since hearing Niall's stunning confession, and having it all confirmed by a sympathetic military official, a numbness had seized her, dulling all of her senses. And she welcomed it. The pain of Niall's betrayal was a blow to her heart. Anytime she thought about it, she struggled to breathe.

Josh, on the other hand, texted her every day, wanting to get Niall's phone number. He wasn't mad at Niall, Beth said, and neither was she. They were worried about how he was doing.

But did Niall care about them? About her?

She glanced at the arrival of an ice sculpture of two intermeshed hearts, her start-up's logo, and drew a line through an item on her to-do list. Everything was ready for the promotional event with her gramps's assisted-living home.

Everything but her.

She wished she could sneak away and hole up in her apartment as she had for most of this past week. Nurse her wounds in bed rather than force a smile at all of the hopeful singles looking for love. But she owed it to them to be here. To see that it all went smoothly. After everything the members of Back in the Game had done to help finance this party and her other costs, they, and the rest of the residents, deserved the night of their lives.

She added two more items on her to-do list:

1. Get my life together.
2. Stop making lists.

Today was filled with triumph and defeat, and she needed a moment to make sense of it all. And lists weren't working.

"Kayleigh Renshaw?" asked a smartly dressed young woman accompanied by a cameraman.

"Yes?" She stood and smoothed down the soft folds of the pink organza dress Gianna had insisted she wear.

"We're here with SBN, Senior Broadcast News, and wondered if we might get a quick interview before you start with the rest." She gestured to a small line of similarly dressed professionals behind her, some with accompanying crew members.

"Oh. Of course." Realization dawned, quickly followed by a spurt of happiness. In the misery of the past week, she'd forgotten that Gianna had contacted an uncle who ran a PR business. He'd sent press releases to various media outlets about this unusual human-interest story of senior singles using modern technology to find love. And by the look of the line, the PR team had succeeded beyond her wildest dreams. If only that had been her only dream.

When she'd taken this risk and begun the start-up, she'd simply wanted to prove Brett wrong and help provide for Chris's family. But after falling for Niall, the depth of those feelings only becoming clear after he'd left her forever, she realized that she'd wanted love, too. Had hoped to find it with him. But too much had happened to make that a reality. How could she ever trust him after he'd kept such a terrible secret and hidden the letter from her? It was a chasm too wide for her to leap across, the fall too long if she missed.

Kayleigh stood and forced a smile.

The reporter turned to the camera. "We're

here with Kayleigh Renshaw, co-owner of start-up company High Dive Enterprises, who has made an interesting app that targets seniors as well as the younger crowd. Ms. Renshaw, would you explain your product?"

A light breeze stirred the crisp early-evening air and blew back the interviewer's blond bob. Jazz music flowed from a live band in a corner by a garden pool lit with underwater lights and a flowing, lavender-tinted fountain. A laden buffet table stretched along a chain-link fence was manned by servers wearing tall white chef's hats. Beneath softly glowing paper lanterns, senior couples swayed. It was as though life had handed her the perfect night for romance, a consolation prize, she supposed.

She straightened her spine and began, "Mesh is a way for singles to define the qualities they want in a potential partner. Once they've inputted their Must Traits in the app, they can sync their list with others'. The software will provide a compatibility score so that, before committing time and feelings, it's possible to predict if the relationship will work out in the long-term."

Despite her mood, she felt proud of the concept. If only she'd followed it herself instead of opening her heart to a man who'd deceived her. Again. Her eyes pricked and her nose burned, but she kept her expression neutral. She owed it to too many people not to ruin this shot at exposure on a syndicated channel.

"And why choose seniors as one of your target markets? This dynamic age group is often overlooked in the business world except by medical and pharmaceutical companies."

Was it Kayleigh's imagination, or had a hint of bitterness crept into the reporter's voice? She understood the woman's frustration.

"There's no age limit on love," Kayleigh began firmly. "To overlook people because of their age is shortsighted and not the progressive approach High Dive Enterprises takes. Seniors are looking for a second chance at love and are all the more anxious to get it right and not waste time. Mesh will give them that opportunity."

The journalist smiled broadly and gestured at the animated assisted-living residents who'd formed small groups and exchanged phones. The cameraman panned around the crowd, capturing their excitement. "They certainly seem to agree. And I heard Mesh is nominated for a Shorty Award. How excited are you about that?"

After everything that had happened, Kayleigh realized with a shock, winning mattered so little to her now. "I'm honored, but win or lose, I've already gained so much." She thought about her wonderful friends at the assisted-living home, Gianna's help and…even Niall. "The best part of creating the start-up is the journey I've taken to get here, the people I've met along the way. People who've changed my life in wonderful, unexpected ways."

"Can you tell me a bit about how you began the business?"

Kayleigh opened her mouth, but no easy answer came to mind. In fact, all she could think of was the truth, so she spoke it.

"I'd recently left my position with another software company. After connecting with an old friend, a programmer, I came up with the concept that he and I developed."

And it was true, she marveled. She and Niall had done it together. Sure, it'd been her vision, but he'd helped to make it come true, had encouraged her to become the doer she'd wanted to be.

"He sounds like a good friend," prompted the woman when Kayleigh's pause extended a beat too long.

"Yes." The word rushed from Kayleigh, unbidden, before she could corral it. Why had she said that? Niall had been a friend, but not anymore. Yet a part of her protested that thought. Hadn't he put the business first to the extent of holding on to an awful secret rather than risking telling her and being tossed from the company before he'd finished writing the app? Mustn't that have been painful for him, as well?

Could that have been why he'd avoided her after he'd taken the letter? He'd said it before, but she believed it now. He'd been putting her needs first all along.

The woman smiled gently. "Is he here?"

Kayleigh's heart leaped until she mentally grabbed it and pulled it back in place. She wouldn't want Niall here…would she? "I'm afraid he wasn't able to attend."

"Sorry to hear that, and it looks like we might need a quick break, if you don't mind," the woman said. She gestured to the cameraman, who fiddled with his tripod.

"Not a problem." Kayleigh's eyes roamed around the party, watching as couples danced before the poolside band, the lantern lights glowing like fireflies in the purpling sky. When her phone buzzed with a text, she read an ad price estimate, then peered at her cell screen. Her gaze lingered on the picture Niall had sent her weeks ago, the two of them posing at the Japanese Hill-and-Pond Garden.

Funny that she hadn't removed it, but they'd looked so happy. So right together. The man who'd taken it had said they were in love, and now she knew he'd been right—about her, at least. Whether or not Niall had returned those feelings, she'd never know. She watched her grandfather dip a laughing Annette Larson and smiled wistfully. Niall should be here to see that.

He'd worked hard and deserved to savor this moment, too. She recalled her tirade, ordering him to stay away, and regretted it. A lot of her shock and pain over Chris's death had spilled into her terrible accusations. While Niall had acted badly by withholding the letter, he hadn't deserved the bitter words she now wished back. After a week apart, she missed him.

Her chest constricted. Even if he did show up, what would she say? Learning how her brother died had been torture to hear, but after she'd had time to process it all, she'd found the peace she'd wanted. Chris had died a hero, not taken by surprise by a hidden explosive or a malfunctioning weapon. Niall's revelations had given her pride in how her brother had passed, replacing the confusion and frustration she'd felt for two years.

Yet her mind had remained unsettled as she'd contemplated Niall's role in her brother's passing. How could she care about a man whose actions had caused her sibling's death?

Had he not gone back for the hard drive, not forgotten it in the first place…

Then again, perhaps he would have died as he'd run on his own rather than shielded by Chris. Fate had intended to take one of the men she loved that day. And if she could choose only one to save, then whom? Niall's smiling face came to mind, the way he made her feel when he looked at her, as if she was the only person in the room. But Chris had made her feel special, too; he'd been her rock in her unstable family.

At last, the cameraman gave a thumbs-up and the interviewer turned to her again.

"And is there any significance behind the name High Dive Enterprises? It's unusual." The woman gestured to the cameraman to come in closer and held the microphone in Kayleigh's face.

She thought back to that day when the name had come to her, when she'd imagined leaving the shallow end of the pool to test deeper waters. She'd taken the gamble, as Chris had, and for her, it'd paid off. Would Chris be disappointed or proud that Niall had been part of that process?

"It's about taking a leap of faith, a gamble. Without great risk, there can't be great gain."

Or pain, she silently added, thinking of Niall and Chris.

"But isn't that the opposite of what your app seeks to do?" the reporter asked shrewdly, "eliminate the second-guessing and make finding a relationship a guarantee?"

"I—I—" She fumbled for an answer, struck by the question. Sure, compatibility reduced risk, but it wasn't a guarantee. Love was more complicated than that. Life had a way of testing it, just as it had with her and Niall.

She held up a finger to stop the interview and turned to take a sip of water, gathering her thoughts. She'd pushed him away as soon as they'd run into problems. She'd vowed to take more risks in her life, yet when things had gone wrong, she'd left instead of working them out. Her insecurities and old fears had taken hold. She'd accused Niall of being a coward when she'd acted like one. While all the wishes in the world couldn't bring Chris back, there was something she could do to have Niall in her life again.

A sudden need to see him seized her. But given the media line, she was helpless to leave. She gazed across the pool to the gate and watched as a tall, handsome man stepped inside. Her breath caught. Niall. Unbelievably, despite what'd passed between them, he'd come to support her. He was still her friend and business partner. Would he still be, after what she'd said, her partner in life?

She gestured to Gianna, who hurried over, a male nurse wearing ear spacers the size of quarters by her side. Kayleigh held in a sigh. They'd been here for barely two hours and already Gianna had met someone. Or something. She eyed the tattoos on his neck. Her friend really had the worst luck with men.

"I'm afraid I need to leave," she said to the reporter. "But my business associate, product manager Gianna Ambrose, will be happy to take the rest of your questions."

She stood and hugged her friend. "Is that okay? Niall's here," she whispered in her ear.

Gianna pulled back, her eyes dancing. "Yes! Go. Run. I'll hold down the fort."

Kayleigh paused and wrung her hands, nerves making her hesitate.

Gianna shoved her. "Stop overthinking everything."

"What if he's only here for the party? Doesn't want to talk to me after all of those awful things I said?"

"There's no way to know without taking a chance." Gianna arched an eyebrow, and the gesture made Kayleigh square her shoulders. Right. It was a risk, and without it the greatest payoffs weren't possible. She wanted Niall. Should never have hurt him the way she had, and if he'd give her a chance, she'd tell him so. Hopefully, he wouldn't avoid her. If he did, she'd persist until she told him how she felt. Whatever he said after that—she gulped—she'd deal with.

She waved to a dancing Gramps and Mrs. Larson and dashed to the man she loved. "Niall," she gasped. "What are you doing here?"

"I came to see you," he said quietly, his hands in his pockets.

"Oh." Not sure if he was real, her eyes ran over him, his handsome appearance in a tailored suit registering. The rising moon cast pale light along the gorgeous angles of his face, shadows pooling beneath his deep-set eyes. "I'm glad," she said, her voice thick with the emotions swirling in her stomach.

He stepped closer and slid his hands into hers, pulling her back through the gate and around the side of the building where the air was perfumed with the soft scent of the rose garden.

"You said to stay away. That I thought only

of myself. But you're wrong. I didn't care about anything before you came along, but you woke me up and brought me back to life. And for that, I owe you everything. If I could give you back Chris, I would, but—"

She placed a finger against his mouth. "Shh—I can't choose between the two of you. Fate did that. There's a reason you're still alive, that you exist, and I want to be part of that. I should never have said all of those hurtful things. If I could take them back…"

"I deserved to hear them."

She smoothed a trembling hand along the side of his face, marveling at the passionate eyes boring into hers. "You were a hero that day. Just like Chris. I didn't see it then, but I've had time to think. Going back for that hard drive was brave. As for Chris, he always made up his own mind. If he hadn't carried you off the field, he would have grabbed someone else, and I am—" Her throat clogged as she struggled to hold back her tears.

His hand tightened around hers, and then he pulled her close. "It's okay, you don't have to say it."

"Yes, I do," she whispered in his ear, feeling the warmth of him against her. She forced herself to go on. "I am so grateful that the man he saved that day was you, because you are everything to me."

"Kayleigh." He sighed, then cupped her face and lowered his mouth for a searing kiss that left her breathless. "You mean everything to me, too. I love you."

Her eyes widened in shock, her body suffused with happiness and pleasure as his lips traveled along her cheek, then lowered to her arched neck. The light pressure made her moan as waves of sensation rippled through her. She slid her hands along his lean waist, then upward to his back, the muscles shifting and tightening against her touch. He was solid. Real. And hers.

His kiss intensified, his hands running through her hair, tugging out her clip so that her curls tumbled down her back.

"I love you, too," she whispered, a thrill running through her when he pulled back and studied her for an intense moment.

"You're beautiful," he said, his voice reverent.

"My nose has a bump."

He kissed the tip. "I love your nose."

"My chin is too pointy."

His lips found their way to her chin. "I love it, too."

She opened her mouth again, but he kissed her swift and hard, leaving her breathless.

"In fact, I love every part of you. Including that big heart of yours. You saved me, Kayleigh."

She flung her arms around his neck and nuzzled his cheek.

"You rescued me, too. You might have been holed up in your apartment, but I was hiding out in the open, playing it safe at my desk job, never pushing the issue of being overlooked until Brett's wake-up call. We brought each other into the light. Made one another better, stronger people, and isn't that what this is all about?"

"Not lists?" he asked, his voice husky in her ear, his breath sending tingles through her as it rushed by her sensitive lobe.

"I'm done with lists," she exclaimed, and leaned back to look at him.

His lips turned down in a mocking pout, though his eyes danced. "That's too bad."

Her nose crinkled. "Why do you care all of a sudden? It's not as if you ever even made one."

"Of course I did." He grinned. "At camp."

She waved her hand. "Oh. I thought you meant now."

He shrugged. "Doesn't matter. It would have

been the same—that's why I didn't make a new one."

Her mouth dropped open. So that was the reason. "I didn't know."

"Would you like to see it?"

Her heart thudded as he pulled a worn piece of paper out of his pocket. "Is that—"

He nodded, his eyes glowing in a way that struck a match to her insides. "The original from camp. I've always carried it with me, even when I was in Kunar."

"That's what you kept in your backpack that day," she breathed, suddenly feeling anxious. Whatever he'd written must be important for him to have saved it all these years. Did he have Must Traits that she didn't match? What if they weren't compatible? But then she looked into his eyes and doubt fell away. It didn't matter. The heart wanted what it wanted, and she wanted him.

"Actually, I don't need to see it."

"Yes. You do," he said, his voice deep and insistent.

He handed her the paper and held her tight as she unfolded it.

There, in the center of the page, was a single word.

Kayleigh.

She threw her arms around him, joy flooding her. "You knew. Even then. You knew."

He nodded before he lowered his face to hers once more.

"I've always known and always will. I'm yours, Kayleigh. I'm all in."

* * * * *